Three Blissful Days

What Reviewers Say About Dena Blake's Work

It's All in the Details

"First thought: I love all romance, to me love is love! ...This was my first LGBTQIAP+ Romance and it didn't disappoint. ...This book was well written, the characters were engaging and you truly invested in their development. There was a little enemy to lover trope as well as angsty romance mixed it. I just wished the ends didn't wrap up so quickly as I wasn't ready to say goodbye yet."—*Jensbooknookclub*

"It was a real drama packed, beautiful romance. ...Lane and Helen have a complicated relationship working at weddings and trying to deceive themselves they don't have feelings for one another. ...There were so many fun moments when they really got planning the wedding but you just had this feeling that something was going to creep up and cause the drama. ...I really loved every second of this and by the end was so happy for Lane and Helen for taking their own chance at happiness despite the chaos they were managing. It was a real drama packed, beautiful romance, with everything you could want from weddings, to cute moments with cake!"—*Lesbireviewed*

A Spark In The Air

"I was so invested in all these people...this is a feel-good Christmas romance: HEAT guaranteed. ...It's warm and cozy, with just the right generous dash of spice and wee-bit amount of angst to keep things interesting."—*Book And Coffee Addict*

"This was so good! Filled with festive cheer but also truly heart-warming moments. ...Highly recommend, especially to get you in a festive and giving mood. Loved every second of it and couldn't put it down."—*Lesbireviewed*

The Probability of Love

"So much fun! …What a great emotional ride, with magical moments and purely amazing connection between two fantastic women. If you've read other books of Dena's there are a few lovely surprises throughout this great story too, which were an absolute treat and made me smile!"—*Lesbireviewed*

Love By Proxy

"Brilliantly funny and sweet! …This was such an amazing story! Gripping, exciting, full of twists and turns, unexpected events, and most importantly a little touch of comedy. It really was the perfect rom-com. Packed with drama and lots of conflict, nothing was more exhilarating then being on this rollercoaster of emotions with Tess and Sophie."—*Lesbireviewed*

Next Exit Home

"I enjoy Dena Blake's writing, and I enjoyed this book a lot. ... I especially liked this book because the two single mums who have become mums for very different reasons/experiences are strong women. Proving they are super capable to solo parent and raise rockstar kids. There is something very sexy about a single mum grabbing parenthood by the horns and making it work. I really enjoyed that aspect! …Great small-town romance that packs a punch in the enemies to lovers trope! I'll definitely be rereading this one again soon."—*Les Rêveur*

Kiss Me Every Day

"This book was SUCH a fun read!! …This was such a fun, interesting book to read and I thoroughly enjoyed it; the characters were super easy to like, the romance was super cute and I loved seeing each little thing that Wynn changed every day!"—Sasha & Amber Read

"Such a fun and exciting book filled with so much love! This book is just packed with fun and memorable moments I was thinking about for days after reading it. This is one hundred percent my new favourite Dena

Blake book. The pace of the book was excellent, and I felt I was along for the fantastic ride."—*Les Rêveur*

"The sweetest moment in the book is when the titular phrase is uttered. …This well written book is an interesting read because of the whole premise of getting repeated opportunities to right wrongs."—*Best Lesfic Reviews*

"Wynn's journey of self-discovery is wonderful to witness. She develops compassion, love and finds happiness. Her character development is phenomenal. …If you're looking for a stunning romance book with a female/female romance, then this is definitely the one for you. I highly recommend."—*Literatureaesthetic*

Perfect Timing

"The chemistry between Lynn and Maggie is fantastic…the writing is totally engrossing."—*Best Lesfic Reviews*

"This book is the kind of book you sit down to on a Sunday morning with a cup of tea and the sun shining in your bedroom only to realise at 5 p.m. you've not left your bed because it was too good to stop reading." —*Les Rêveur*

"The relationship between Lynn and Maggie developed at an organic pace. I loved all the flirting going on between Maggie and Lynn. I love a good flirty conversation! …I haven't read this author before but I look forward to trying more of her titles."—Marcia Hull, Librarian (Ponca City Library, Oklahoma)

Racing Hearts

"I particularly liked Drew with her sexy rough exterior and soft heart. …Sex scenes are definitely getting hotter and I think this might be the hottest by Dena Blake to date…"—*Les Rêveur*

Just One Moment

"One of the things I liked is that the story is set after the glorious days of falling in love, after the time when everything is exciting. It shows how sometimes, trying to make life better really makes it more complicated.

…It's also, and mainly, a reminder of how important communication is between partners, and that as solid as trust seems between two lovers, misunderstandings happen very easily."—*Jude in the Stars*

"Blake does angst particularly well and she's wrung every possible ounce out of this one. …I found myself getting sucked right into the story—I do love a good bit of angst and enjoy the copious amounts of drama on occasion."—*C-Spot Reviews*

Friends Without Benefits

"This is the book when the Friends to Lovers trope doesn't work out. When you tell your best friend you are in love with her and she doesn't return your feelings. This book is real life and I think I loved it more for that…"—*Les Rêveur*

A Country Girl's Heart

"Dena Blake just goes from strength to strength."—*Les Rêveur*

"Literally couldn't put this book down, and can't give enough praise for how good this was!!! One of my favourite reads, and I highly recommend to anyone who loves a fantastically clever, intriguing, and exciting romance."—*LESBIreviewed*

Unchained Memories

"There is a lot of angst and the book covers some difficult topics but it does that well. The writing is gripping and the plot flows."—Melina Bickard, Librarian, Waterloo Library (UK)

"This story had me cycling between lovely romantic scenes to white-knuckle gripping, on the edge of the seat (or in my case, the bed) scenarios. This story had me rooting for a sequel and I can certainly place my stamp of approval on this novel as a must read book."—*Lesbian Review*

"The pace and character development was perfect for such an involved story line, I couldn't help but turn each page. This book has so many wonderful plot twists that you will be in suspense with every chapter that follows. "—*Les Rêveur*

Where the Light Glows

"From first time author, Dena Blake, *Where the Light Glows* is a sure winner…"—*A Bookworm's Loft*

"[T]he vivid descriptions of the Pacific Northwest will make readers hungry for food and travel. The chemistry between Mel and Izzy is palpable…"—*RT Book Reviews*

"I'm still shocked this was Dena Blake's first novel. …It was fantastic. …It was written extremely well and more than once I wondered if this was a true account of someone close to the author because it was really raw and realistic. It seemed to flow very naturally and I am truly surprised that this is the author's first novel as it reads like a seasoned writer…" —*Les Rêveur*

By the Author

Where the Light Glows

Unchained Memories

A Country Girl's Heart

Racing Hearts

Friends Without Benefits

Just One Moment

Perfect Timing

Kiss Me Every Day

Next Exit Home

Love By Proxy

The Probability of Love

A Spark in the Air

It's All in the Details

Three Blissful Days

Three Blissful Days

by

Dena Blake

2025

THREE BLISSFUL DAYS

ISBN 13: 978-1-63679-707-6

This Trade Paperback Original Is Published By
Bold Strokes Books, Inc.
P.O. Box 249
Valley Falls, NY 12185

First Edition: December 2025

Credits
Editor: Shelley Thrasher
Production Design: Susan Ramundo
Cover Design By Tammy Seidick

Acknowledgments

My favorite season of all is fall. To experience nature in all its beautiful glory is a treasure. I take a yearly trip just to enjoy the beautiful color changes in the leaves. The journey through natural park forests allows me to find joy in ways I cannot during my usual routine at home. It's a wonderful way to disconnect and unwind. I hope this book will transport you to one of my favorite places and allow you to enjoy my favorite season as much as I do.

Shelley Thrasher—my fabulous editor—you are so patient with me when I run late with drafts and need to make additions to edits. Life, again this year, has been not only busy, but challenging as well. Thank you for being so understanding and making me a better writer.

Rad and Sandy—There is no one I trust with my work more than Bold Strokes Books and the production team behind the scenes. You're amazing and I appreciate all you do to make my dreams come true. You really do make me feel like a professional writer!

My beautiful family, I wouldn't be able to keep moving forward on this journey without your support. I love you more than I could ever put into words.

All my readers, thank you from the bottom of my heart for reading my books. I know you have so many choices out there and it means the world to me that you choose mine.

Dedication

To my family—you remain my biggest support system and inspiration.

CHAPTER ONE

Kendall had just left the office and was mid-song, improvising a solo vocal to the pop song playing in her car when her phone rang through the speakers. She could see on the screen it was Cassie and hit the answer button on her steering wheel. "Hi, Cass," she said, trying to keep her voice steady. Due to their recent breakup, their conversations over the past few weeks had been strained at best.

"Hey, Kendall." Cassie hesitated. "I know this is short notice, but considering how things have been between us, I'm moving out of the office."

"What? When?"

"I'm doing it now."

Cassie must have been waiting until she was gone. "But you said we were gonna discuss that further. You know this isn't the best for our customers." Or for Kendall. She would never be able to afford the rent on her own.

"I know that's what I said, but considering our history, I decided it would be better for me to cut ties with you altogether. Even if the business suffers. The customers will understand."

"What the hell, Cass. It's not like I have an alternative place to work." Cassie knew Kendall didn't have another office and couldn't afford one right now. Unexpectedly having to plan for shelling out the first and last month's rent to acquire a new apartment had left her with barely enough money for gas.

"You don't have to be out right away. The lease is paid until the end of the month."

The back of her neck burned. "It's October seventeenth, which only gives me two weeks." Kendall could hear Cassie moving things around.

She made a U-turn and headed back to the office. She'd already broken her heart, but she wasn't going to let her take all her drafting equipment too. When Kendall arrived at the office, Cassie's white BMW X3 was backed into the space right in front with the back hatch open. No way was she was letting Cassie take all their files. Kendall had put just as much work into cultivating their customer base as Cassie had—probably more.

Kendall pulled her Ford Bronco into the space next to Cassie's SUV and threw it into Park. The car lurched as she got out and slammed the door behind her.

"I'm taking only the files for the customers I brought in," Cassie said, anticipating her thoughts.

"I can't believe you're doing this on top of breaking up with me." Kendall couldn't stop the shake in her voice.

"Listen, Kendall. This isn't the first time we've discussed this issue over the past couple of months. I cannot continue to support your family." Cassie's deep blue eyes burned into Kendall's. "Don't look at me like that."

"You're not supporting them. I am." And that support had lessened during this past year.

"Is there a difference?" Cassie yanked open the filing cabinet, fingered through the files, and pulled out a stack. "You support them. I support you. It still comes out of my wallet."

"I have never asked you for any financial support." She'd done without things she wanted and needed many times instead of asking Cassie for help.

Cassie narrowed her eyes. "You might not have asked, but you always took."

"That's absolutely untrue." She had no idea what Cassie was talking about. She'd been very careful not to touch any of their commingled funds for anything other than business.

Cassie whirled around. "What about all the times I filled your tank with gas, or when I bought your lunch each day? Even paid for all their groceries. Do I need to write it all down—show you the figures?"

"What?" Kendall was stunned at Cassie's accusations.

Cassie held up a hand. "Don't even try to talk your way out of it. I know you bought groceries for your family when you shopped for us. I saw the receipts, remember? I paid for all of them."

Kendall hadn't realized Cassie was so angry about the food. "Those are things partners do for each other and their families."

"Not this partner. Not anymore. You're going to have to find someone else to support you and your family." Cassie pulled another file-cabinet drawer open. "I'm not even going to discuss whether filet mignon and shrimp are staples again. When you live off someone else's income, you need to be more agreeable about the food items you request." She took a few more files and slammed the drawer closed. "You'd think your family was rich, given the way they eat." Cassie picked up the last file sitting on Kendall's desk and opened it. "Which client is this?"

"That one's mine." Kendall snatched it from her hands, hoping she hadn't seen any of the documents inside.

Cassie studied her for a moment, then flattened her lips. "Whatever." She put the top on the box of files. "You need to be out of here by the end of the month. The lease is only paid until then." She glanced around the office. "Do me a favor and don't destroy it. I'd like to get my security deposit back."

"What about the furniture?" Kendall glanced at the large design printer she'd meticulously picked out. It had taken her weeks to find one at a reasonable cost and would be expensive to replace.

Cassie shook her head. "Don't even think about it. I'm taking that printer. The rest you can keep if you have a place for it. Sell it, for all I care. I don't want it." She walked out the door.

Kendall followed. "Please don't go." Even after all the shitty things Cassie had said to her, Kendall still loved her and was still attracted to her. Whether she was still *in love* with her or afraid of being alone wasn't clear. Many aspects of their relationship had become blurred over the past year.

"We're done, Kendall. Completely done." Cassie loaded the box into the back of her SUV. "I'm having the printer moved tomorrow," she said before she slid into the driver's seat and peeled out of the parking lot.

Kendall flopped into the chair behind the desk and scanned the office. She would take a few things, but she would, indeed, sell the majority of the office furniture. Anything she couldn't sell would either go to her parents' house or remain in the office. She wouldn't have room for it in her new one-bedroom apartment she planned to rent when she had the money.

She crossed the room and ran her hand across the smooth top of the tilted drafting table before she relaxed into her chair. This was the first table she'd purchased, and it was still her favorite. Her mom had helped her set it up in the corner of her room next to the window and dedicated it to nothing but drafting. Keeping her little brother away from it had been a challenge, but after a number of candy bribes, he'd finally stopped messing with her space.

She'd practiced her drafting even before she had the right tools. Luckily, the fundamentals of creating crisp lines and designs had come naturally to her. It had been a struggle to get to where she was today. Having chosen a different, more stable career path in college would have been much easier, but when she was able to move forward with the proper drafting equipment, it was pure bliss. And when she decided to pursue landscape design as a career, it became a daily passion. To improve her plant knowledge, she'd gone on to earn a master's degree in botany with a focus on landscape ecology—the perfect combination for this career path. Her mind worked in a weird sort of animated world, where every unperfected landscape was mentally enhanced automatically. She imagined shrubs growing in dead space and grass where there was only dirt. Trees sprouted from the weeds, with beautiful fall foliage coloring the area. Even Cassie had found it uncanny. She'd told Kendall so on more than one occasion.

She opened the file she'd swiped from Cassie's hand. She'd tried to prevent her from reading anything inside and had hopefully been successful. It was the recent bid they'd made on the state lodge landscape-redesign contract. Kendall had found the Request for Proposal and written the original proposal. It was the last project she'd worked on during their partnership. She wasn't going to just let Cassie steal it from her. She couldn't. It was all she had left now.

She opened her laptop and tried to connect to the internet. No signal. "Fuck." Cassie must have cancelled the service. She opened her cell phone and clicked on the setting enabling the hotspot, but the phone network didn't show up in her laptop Wi-Fi settings. No connection here at all. Could this day get any worse?

She leaned forward and dropped her head to the table, letting her tears flow. It had been a miserable few months for Kendall since she and Cassie had broken off their romantic relationship, and having their work partnership collapse was the icing on the cake. Everything she'd known to be true for most of the past four years was gone. Would her life ever be normal again?

CHAPTER TWO

The air was brisk as Ivy stepped outside, just the way she liked it. Fall was her favorite time of year. The glorious scent of wood smoke floating from chimneys enhanced the season in a way Ivy couldn't explain. Her mood instantly improved, and when the frequent fog lifted from the valley, the Ozark mountains put on a magnificent display of color. She zipped her coat up closer to her chin as she stepped off the porch of her one-bedroom cabin, walked to her state-issued truck, and climbed inside. After firing the engine, she took the short drive to the lodge, where she was stationed. Being a park ranger was her dream job.

It was mid-October, which meant that soon the Arkansas mountains would be blanketed with gorgeous hues of gold, red, and orange, and the park visitors would change from summer hikers, campers, and mountain bikers to fall leaf peepers. With mid-range temperatures amplified by gorgeous sunrises and sunsets, Diamond Mountain showcased autumn's finest colors while allowing visitors to explore the landscape and sometimes see wildlife.

She stopped at the campsite area on the lower part of the lodge grounds to make sure no campers were having issues. Currently only a few pads were rented out for the week—groups consisting of hikers and parents who homeschooled their kids. Autumn leaves formed a common part of their curriculum, and Ivy liked to help out with their learning whenever she could.

The smell of fresh coffee wafted into her nose when she approached the first campsite that included a large four-person tent. She spotted a Coleman Camping Coffeemaker sitting atop a traditional two-burner camp stove set up just outside the front door. One of the best camping inventions ever. It worked just like the ones plugged in at home, though only the steel base sat directly on the camping stove. Ten cups of coffee had never been so easy to brew in the wild.

Not wanting to startle anyone this early in the morning, Ivy stood outside the perimeter of the campsite clearing her throat. "Good morning," she said.

After a few minutes, a man poked his head out of the tent before emerging to greet her. "Good morning, Ranger Patterson." He pulled a sweatshirt over his head and rubbed his shoulders. "A bit colder than I expected this morning."

"It's the dampness. Once the fog burns off, the sun will warm you right up."

"If not, we'll come up to the lodge for a while. Any events planned there today?"

"Other than the Pioneer Cemetery tour this morning," she pointed down the hill, "I'm not sure yet. I haven't seen the rest of the schedule."

The man glanced around the area. "Don't think the kids will be up soon enough for that." He picked up an empty cup. "Coffee?"

Ivy shook her head. "No. Thank you." Ivy raised her hand and stretched her palm in a short wave. "I'll be at the lodge after the tour. Maybe I'll see you around." She turned and walked to her truck, then climbed into the cab and drove the short distance up the hill to the lodge. After parking, she grabbed her backpack and made her usual check of the surrounding area for trash or anything unusual before walking into the lobby restaurant for breakfast. She shucked her coat and hung it on the back of her chair before she sat at her regular table by the window, took out her EMT exam prep book that she'd been studying for the EMT certification exam, and set it on the table. During this past year she'd participated in a few emergencies involving lost and injured hikers, including one rescue that had left a hiker critically injured. She'd felt helpless in that experience, which had prompted her to get EMT training. She wanted to be equipped to help with injuries in the future. After glancing around the room, she picked up the menu, flipped up the attached buffet page, and glanced over the main food items listed. Even though she received a discount on all food, she never ordered the buffet. She liked her eggs cooked to order—over easy and hot.

June came from the kitchen with coffee in hand and set Ivy's third cup of the morning in front of her. She'd already had the first two at home, a sorely needed warm-up on a chilly fall morning. "The usual this morning?" June touched her shoulder.

Ivy nodded. She always ordered the same thing, but June always asked. She leaned forward to disengage June's lingering hand and glanced out the window around the wooden pillar supporting the porch. "Looks like the frost will be earlier than expected this year."

"Maybe if the colors don't fire, the crowd will be less this year," June said, touching her shoulder again, undeterred by Ivy's movement as usual.

"Don't count on it. The people come anyway, and I don't blame them." Whether everything was still green or a frozen brown, nature still had its hidden areas of beauty. You just had to look a little harder to find them.

"I'll have your breakfast right out." June spun and headed to the kitchen.

Pushing her EMT manual aside, Ivy read through the local paper she'd snagged from the rack by the entrance as she waited for her food, only glancing up occasionally to observe the guests as the restaurant filled. Then she returned to concentrating on the story she was reading about the upcoming fall festival in the town nearby.

June appeared. "Hot off the griddle," she said as she waited for Ivy to move the newspaper.

Ivy folded the paper neatly and set it to the side of her place. "Great. Thanks."

June slid Ivy's breakfast in front of her and refilled her coffee. "I added an extra slice of bacon for you. My treat."

"That wasn't necessary, but thanks."

June grinned. "Enjoy."

Ivy glanced at her watch. It was later than she'd thought. She plowed through her breakfast and waved June over to get her check.

"You all fueled up to go talk to the plants?" June slid the check onto the table.

Ivy nodded. June liked to kid her about her passion for nature.

"Maybe I'll see you for lunch?" June asked, a familiar lilt in her voice. It beckoned Ivy to show an interest in her.

"Probably not. I'm scheduled to give a cemetery tour about that time." She lied. The tour would be over by then. Ivy knew June was sweet on her, but she was barely twenty-two, much too young to get involved with. Not that Ivy had age limits, but everyone at the lodge heard about June's love life, and Ivy didn't want to become one of those stories.

Ivy turned over the check to find the appropriate total and June's phone number written below it, as usual. She calculated the tip in her head, taking ten percent and doubling it before adding it to her check. She hadn't been a whiz at elementary math in high school, but college math had somehow come together in her head and stuck. She stood and went to the front desk to check the sign-up sheet. Several families were listed for the tour today, and she looked forward to sharing her favorite season with them.

Chapter Three

Kendall arrived at her parents' house in south Oklahoma City, her temporary housing. She swore to herself that she would stay here only until she could save enough to rent an apartment. Otherwise, she'd be expected to substantially contribute to the household expenses, and she didn't want to be put in that position again. Her mother had finally finished enough courses to obtain a stable teaching position in the local school district, which included benefits. She'd been a constant substitute teacher while she was taking classes, which gave her the opportunity to get to know the school staff. Her father had been able to snag a job as the daytime custodian. Knowing people at the school had definitely improved their situation. They both seemed to like the work and managed to fund the household now with little help from Kendall, but they still had some debts to manage. She remembered what Cassie had said earlier. Maybe she had helped them more than she thought.

As expected, no one was home since it was the middle of the day, so Kendall sat down at the kitchen table and logged into her laptop to find the digital file for the state landscape project bid. She'd be damned if she'd let Cassie steal this project—take credit for a bid she'd created. She found the folder and pulled up the PDF document she'd created from the email she'd received with the subject of *Invitation to Bid State of Arkansas Lodge Landscape Project.* It was the original notification of a state landscaping project that was open for proposals. She remembered that when she received it, she'd been just about to send the email to the trash, thinking it was spam, when she read the subject line, though she rarely received anything except junk mail. Her usual routine of delete, delete, delete had almost lost her the opportunity altogether.

CITY OF DIAMOND MOUNTAIN

LANDSCAPE DESIGN SERVICES FOR THE STATE LODGE ON DIAMOND MOUNTAIN

The City of Diamond Mountain requests proposals for an Architectural Design or Landscape Design Firm to provide a plan for refreshing and improving the landscaping of the state lodge located at the top of Diamond Mountain. The lodge has historically served as the area's most frequented area for lodging, camping, events, and dining.

The scope of services for the project includes:

1. A plan for creating more resilient and sustainable landscaping surrounding the lodge.
2. In developing the plan, the selected consultant will be expected to meet with key stakeholders to solicit their input before creating the final plan.

Final proposals must be received by 11:30 PM, September 26, 2025, in the Diamond Mountain Administrative offices by USPS mail or email.

Proposal documents are available at the Diamond Mountain State Lodge Website, and all proposals must be provided in the same format as described. The proposers must be registered as landscape architects or landscape designers with the State of Arkansas. Proposals are limited to six pages, excluding resumes and notices of transmittal. Consultant selection will be based upon weighted criteria as cited in this Request for Proposal.

The State of Arkansas reserves the right to reject any and all proposals, to waive formalities, or to accept any proposal that appears to serve the best interest of the Diamond Mountain State Lodge.

She searched her email to locate the most recent email regarding the proposal. "You have been invited to tour the park the weekend of October 31, 2025. Please respond with your availability by 11:30 PM, October 24, 2025." A rush of heat coursed through Kendall when she read the date out loud. "*Today.*"

Next weekend. She quickly checked her calendar to make sure she didn't have any appointments that needed to be cancelled before she found the original submission form, copied it, and modified the contact information to her and her alone. She'd kept all the proposal information with all the templates she'd pulled information from as well as the company name of Ken Cass Landscaping, which she'd created to prevent being locked out of bids due to gender. Even though such discrimination was unethical, not to mention illegal, it still happened. That company name needed to change, so she added "Also Known as Horizon Design" next to the company name. She also checked her bank account balance online. She'd have to go to Kinkos and print some of her plans before she left.

Cassie hated paperwork, so it had become Kendall's responsibility to complete the bids, and it had been a constant process. Proposal requirements were usually strict, and the bid had to be competitive to receive a response. Sometimes they made money, and other times they barely broke even. Government projects could go either way.

After she'd responded to the email with her availability, she picked up her phone, scrolled through her favorites, and hit the button for her best friend, Noah.

"Hey, buddy. Whatcha doing?"

"Just sitting on the porch having a beer. To what do I owe the pleasure of this phone call?"

"Well, I'm going to be in the area soon and thought maybe you might have some time to spend with an old friend."

"I'll absolutely make time." His voice rose. "When are you gonna be here?"

"I don't have the exact dates of the reservation yet, but I should be at the lodge next weekend around Saturday, November first."

"Why are you staying at the lodge? There's always a place for you here."

"Thought it might be too short notice for Taylor." Considering she didn't get along very well with Noah's girlfriend. "Plus, it's business. Landscape bid. Did you know they're redoing the whole place?"

"I'd heard. The place really needs some love. So, you and Cassie are going to make the place look beautiful, huh?"

"Just me. Cassie and I are no longer tied together in any way."

"Oh. That sucks. I'm sorry to hear that."

"Yeah. Me too, but it is what it is."

This could turn into a sticky situation if Cassie remembered anything about it. Kendall had mentioned it to her when she'd discovered the Request for Proposal, but Cassie hadn't given her any indication that she wanted to help with it. Cassie always seemed to have other priorities.

Chapter Four

The fog was still somewhat dense on the mountain that morning, as usual during this time of year. Ivy wasn't a fan of the fog because it masked the beauty of the mountain and inevitably caused several accidents on the winding road leading to the park. She stopped along the edge of the scenic outlet and got out of her truck, waiting for the tourists to arrive. A few cars pulled up, and several people got out of each one. A larger crowd than she expected.

"Welcome to the Woods Cemetery." She headed to the gravel-and-railroad-tie staircase embedded in the pathway that led down to the burial ground. "If you'll follow me, I'll fill you in on some of the history surrounding the area." She turned momentarily. "Watch your step. The rocky path can be slippery in some spots."

Ivy led almost a dozen people down the staircase and along the natural rocky pathway to the area marked with only one visible headstone. Then she turned and waited for everyone to gather around her before she began her session. "A total of fifteen families are buried in the Woods Cemetery, which has a total of twenty-three graves, and although some have headstones, most have rock markers. So be careful where you step." She laughed to herself as the guests stopped immediately and checked the ground below them. That statement always made them think. "The name didn't come from any one family, but from where the cemetery is placed in the woods cloaked by all these tall trees." She wandered farther down the path. "You're probably thinking that it doesn't look well cared for, but the National Park Service didn't acquire the land until 1923. Originally two acres, the cemetery was created in the 1800s. Today, this is all that remains of the Diamond Mountain community. It was established at the time of the Civil War by families looking to escape the ravages of war." She walked toward the edge of the trees and held out her hand. "The residents of the community had a bird's-eye view of the valley below and, to a certain extent, could see when intruders were heading their way."

"Is it okay to look around? I mean off the pathway?" a woman asked.

"Sure. Go ahead. Again, be careful of the rocks." Ivy moved toward the only headstone in the cemetery. "I'll be right here if anyone has any questions." Noticing some trash that had gathered near a tree, she took an empty plastic bag from her coat pocket, scooped it up, and deposited it inside the bag. She didn't know why people couldn't pick up after themselves.

A man approached her. "Forgive me, but I'm fascinated by old cemeteries in general. Do any records exist that show who the people are that are buried here and when they died?"

"There isn't much documentation on them, but some historians believe a teenage girl from a local family was the first person buried here." That remark got everyone's attention, and several of them came closer to Ivy again. Some of the kids continued to investigate the area.

The man took a pad and pen from his pocket and jotted down a few notes. "Tell me more."

"It's kind of a tragic story. According to legend, during one extremely cold winter, the girl's entire family, except for her, became ill. The daughter who wasn't affected by the sickness went out into the cold to fetch either firewood or water. While she was foraging, she encountered a pack of wolves and took refuge in a hollowed-out tree to escape them. Sadly, she didn't make it through the night and was found frozen to death the next day."

"That's so sad." A young girl, who Ivy suspected was the man's daughter, spoke up. "She was probably just like me."

"And also brave." Ivy was all about empowering young girls. "Just think about all the everyday tools you have that she didn't."

The girl smiled widely.

"Some say she still roams the area."

"What about the wolves?" a woman asked urgently as she surveyed the area. "Are they still around?"

"No need to worry about them here." Ivy shook her head. "The red wolves were killed out in the 1920s."

"What about bears?" the woman's husband asked.

"Bears were killed out on the mountain before then." Ivy picked up an empty pint liquor bottle. "People leave many things here. One day, up at the camping area by the lodge, a camper told a couple of women that one of the cemetery residents had told him he could really use a cigarette. So, he left him a pack."

"Was it a ghost?" a young boy asked.

"Could be. You never know." Ivy gave the little boy a wink.

"Why do they call it Diamond Mountain?"

"The mountain got its name due to the various gems and minerals discovered in the soil. Pioneers also found the soil to be rich and fertile for growing lush vegetable crops. Wild berries were also abundant."

"Even around all these rocks?" the man taking notes asked.

Ivy nodded. "People planted around the rocks because the ground was so loose it didn't require much tilling."

A woman raised her hand. "Were there any Native American settlers on the mountain?"

"No. The Native American settlers stayed by the river. Water was essential for their survival, providing drinking water and irrigation to sustain their crops. The river also gave them easy access to fish for food. Water allowed them to thrive in their environment, while the settlers relied on rain and wells for drinking and irrigation." Ivy waited for a few more minutes until everyone finished wandering about. "Any more questions?" She headed up the pathway to the stairs.

The man shook his head and followed her. "I'm going to do some research and might have some later. Will you be at the lodge?"

"Yes," Ivy answered over her shoulder. "I'm there most days. If you can't find me, check with the desk, and they'll locate me." She stopped at the top of the stairs. "Feel free to stay as long as you like." She pointed to the information sign. "This will give you a little more background on the cemetery. Again, I'll be at the lodge if you want more details." She got into her truck, fired the engine, and headed back to the lodge.

Ivy parked the truck and scanned the grounds as she walked into the lodge to see if anything had been added to today's schedule.

"Hey, you want a ticket to the movies next Friday, on Halloween night? They'll be playing *Night of the Living Dead*," Susan said as Ivy entered the lobby area. Susan was a longtime friend who managed the lodge's front desk area.

"Oh, yeah? Why do you have an extra?" Ivy loved classic horror films but was skeptical of Susan's sudden invitation.

Susan nodded. "I knew it would be sold out and thought you'd probably like to go."

"Who else did you buy a ticket for?"

"Just me and Charlie."

Ivy furrowed her brow. "I'm not sure I believe that." She brushed by her as she rounded the counter.

"Can't get anything past you, can I?" Susan grinned. "June's going to be there."

"No. Absolutely not. I can't believe you bought her a ticket too."

"I didn't buy her ticket. She bought yours and asked me to invite you."

"Susan—" Ivy dropped the schedule. "You know my thoughts on her."

"Come on. It's just one night. Live a little. So what if she's young. Have some fun for once." Susan blocked her exit. "No one's asking you to marry her."

Ivy moved from side to side, attempting to get past Susan.

"I won't leave you alone with her. I promise." Susan grinned as she pleaded.

Ivy stopped moving and pinched the bridge of her nose before she let out a long sigh. "Fine. But if you leave my side for one minute, I'm out of there." She held up a finger. "I swear I will leave immediately."

"Yea." Susan clasped her hands together and bounced up and down. "We're going to have so much fun."

"Well, at least one of us will." Ivy moved past Susan and out the door.

Chapter Five

Ivy parked in the small lot of the local movie theater and strolled to the entrance where Susan and June were waiting. The theater had been there longer than she could remember. When she used to sit inside and watch a movie with her parents, the seats and the screen had seemed huge. The seats, lined up on a slanted floor, seemed a bit smaller now, but the screen was still larger than any nearby theater's. Everyone had a perfect view of the movie. They hadn't updated it with fancy recliner seats, and Ivy loved it just the way it was. The place was an architectural masterpiece.

"Charlie's parking the car," Susan said before Ivy could ask.

June stood next to Susan, looking as determined as if she were at the starting line of a track meet waiting for the gun to go off. Ivy had debated all week on whether to come, but this movie was a cult classic, and she watched it every year. Seeing it on the big screen was always a treat. She was glad Susan hadn't asked her to pick up June. She would've had to politely decline, which Susan probably knew.

As Ivy approached, June must've heard the starter gun go off in her head, because she rushed toward her and snaked her arm around Ivy's. *Now* this really felt like a date.

"I'm so glad you came. I was afraid you wouldn't." She gazed up at Ivy. "You haven't been to breakfast all week. I thought maybe you were sick."

Ivy had been steering clear of June purposely to avoid any misunderstandings surrounding the event. Which hadn't seemed to make a difference. "*Night of the Living Dead* is one of my favorite movies to watch around Halloween."

"Really? Mine is *Hocus Pocus*." June clenched Ivy's arm tighter.

"That's a good one too." Ivy shifted uncomfortably.

"They don't ever play it here. Maybe you can come over to my place, and we can watch it together." June's voice rose excitedly.

Ivy shook her head. "I'm afraid I watched it last week with Susan." She glanced at Susan. "Right?"

"Yeah. We did. It was last minute." Susan touched June's shoulder. "I think you were working that night."

June frowned as she gazed at Ivy. "Maybe we can find something else to watch. It doesn't have to be a Halloween movie."

Charlie joined them just then, which interrupted their conversation. Ivy would keep her negative answer to that question until it was asked again. No need to spoil the evening so early.

They went inside, giving the attendant their tickets as they entered.

"I need to go to the restroom." June smiled at her. "Don't go inside the theater without me."

"Uh, sure." Ivy raised her eyebrows at Susan as June walked away. "Thanks for this." Her tone was appropriately sarcastic. "Did you even tell her it's in black-and-white?"

"I told her it's a classic. That's implied." Susan got in line at the concession stand.

Ivy followed her. "We'll see if she picks up on that point. To twenty-somethings, classics were created in the eighties."

"They play it at this theater around Halloween every year. She's bound to have seen it, don't you think?"

Ivy shook her head. "I doubt it." She ordered a small popcorn and a soda.

"I'll have some Milk Duds," June said, appearing from out of nowhere and cozying up next to her. She clearly thought this was a date.

"And some Milk Duds." Ivy pinched her lips together and looked at Susan.

Once finished at the concession stand, they found seats in the middle of the theater. Thankfully, they'd arrived early enough to have their pick. Ivy hadn't expected the theater to be full, but it was Friday night, and there was probably a football game at the high school. That was the only other entertainment this time of year in a small town.

"You like scary movies?" June asked.

"Not in general, but this is one of my favorite movies of all time. It's the GOAT of low-budget horrors." Ivy looked across June to Susan.

"Here's a little tidbit of trivia that you might not know. When the zombies are eating the bodies in the burned-out truck, they were actually eating roast ham covered in chocolate sauce."

"Seriously?" June scrunched her nose. "Yuck."

Ivy nodded. "The filmmakers joked that the combination was so nauseating the zombie actors ended up looking pale and sick even without makeup."

Susan laughed. "I guess they could've saved themselves the makeup part of the budget."

After a few previews, the intro began to roll.

"Why isn't this in color?" June asked as she glanced behind her at the projector booth. "Are they doing that for effect?"

"This is the 1968 original. They didn't always use color back then, especially for horror movies."

"Oh. Seems kind of goofy."

"It was actually pretty scary for the time." Ivy leaned forward and stared over June at Susan. "I watched it with my mom on TV when I was a kid, and I couldn't sleep alone for weeks."

Susan laughed. "I've heard this story before, and your mom sure regretted that."

The lights dimmed and the film began. The first scene contained a radio-broadcast interruption hinting that a major disaster was in progress. That scene always gave Ivy tingles, knowing chaos would soon ensue as Barbara and Johnny encountered the first zombie on the road. After they boarded themselves up in a nearby farmhouse, the theater was almost completely silent in anticipation to what came next. Out of the corner of her eye, Ivy saw Susan's hand creep slowly above June's thigh, then quickly take hold of her leg and dig her fingernails into it.

June let out a blood-curdling scream and shot out of her seat.

"Damn it, Susan. You couldn't just leave things alone." Ivy narrowed her eyes.

"I was just having a little fun," Susan said with a grin.

June dug her nails into Ivy's shoulder. "I can't watch this. It's too scary," she pleaded as she stared at Ivy. "You have to take me home. When Ivy didn't move, she said, "*Now.*"

Susan grabbed June's hand to get her attention. "Charlie will take you home."

"No. Ivy—I want Ivy to take me. Charlie should stay with you to watch the rest of this…whatever this is."

"Sit down. We can't see," the people sitting behind them said.

"Just shut it back there," June said.

"You set this up?"

Susan shook her head. "I'm sorry. I had no idea she was going to flip out and want to leave."

"You owe me now," Ivy whispered into Susan's ear as June tugged at her arm.

"Or maybe you'll owe me." Susan winked.

She glanced over to see that June was still standing and staring at the screen, completely stunned.

The evening had stopped being delightfully scary about halfway through and had become unexpectedly terrifying in more ways than one. Now Ivy had been put in the position of taking June home, which she hadn't planned to do—ever. It was probably better that June hadn't seen the unhappy ending, or she'd be asking Ivy to spend the night, which she might ask anyway.

"You want to grab something to eat?" Ivy had eaten all of her popcorn during the previews, but she could still squeeze in a piece of pie at Sid's Diner or even an onion burger, which was the usual after-movie plan with Susan and Charlie.

"Sure. But not at the lodge, if that's okay." June's tone had become much more pleasant than it had been inside the theater.

"We usually hit Sid's after the show." Ivy motioned June in front of her as she opened the door. She groaned to herself. Now who was making this seem like a date?

They opted to walk the short distance to Sid's, which wasn't too far down the street. Ivy kept her hands in her jacket pockets to avoid any awkward handholding attempts by June. She opened the door for June, probably a mistake, but forgive her for having manners. The sign at the front said, *Seat Yourself.* Ivy went to the first available booth and chose the side facing the door. She wanted to make sure she could see Susan and Charlie when they arrived. To be clear she wasn't inviting June to sit with her, Ivy slid into the booth, stopping in the middle of the seat. That, of course, was a futile attempt, as June proceeded to plant herself in the sliver of space Ivy had left. In hopes of placing some space between them, Ivy slid as close to the wall as possible, another futile attempt as June slid closer to her.

Ivy fiddled with her fork as she tried to find some neutral topics to discuss. "So…do you like movies?"

"Yeah. I guess." June was making the conversation more difficult than it needed to be.

"What kinds do you like?" Ivy asked, trying to keep the conversation going.

"Oh, you know, just regular movies...with acting and stuff. How about you?" June wasn't making this easy.

Ivy continued to probe. "Do you have a favorite genre?"

"Well, my favorite movies are rom coms. I just love romance films. They make me cry every time, but in a good way. The emotional connection of two people falling in love always gets me. What about you? Do you like romance movies?"

"Oh, wow. Uh...romance isn't really my thing. I'm more into action films and sci-fi, you know, with cool special effects and fight sequences. I like things that keep my adrenaline pumping."

"That makes sense. Why else would you take me on a first date to a scary movie?"

First date? Who said anything about a date? Ivy needed to nip this in the bud right now. "I think maybe you might—"

"I don't think I'll ever really like scary movies. Don't even try to convince me to go to another one." June snaked her arm under Ivy's. "Maybe you can come over to my place sometime, and we can watch a romance movie together." She gazed at her for much too long. "I'm sure I can change your mind about them. I like streaming them at home cozied up on the couch."

"I'll stick to watching movies in the theater. Action movies are better on the big screen." This conversation wasn't nearly as neutral as Ivy had planned. She plucked the menus from the holder behind the salt and pepper shakers and handed one to June.

The waitress came to the table. "You all here for dinner or a late snack?"

"Pie." June spoke up. "We're here for pie."

"Alrighty. We've got apple, peach, and cherry. What's your pleasure?"

"I'll have a slice of cherry and a cup of coffee," Ivy said.

"Peach for me." June scooted closer to Ivy.

"Coffee for you as well?" the waitress asked.

"Just water." June slipped her hand onto Ivy's thigh.

Ivy jumped and immediately removed June's hand. "I don't mean to hurt your feelings, June. I'm just not interested in any type of relationship right now."

"Who said anything about a relationship?" June whispered in her ear. "A little special attention is all I need."

The waitress delivered their orders and went behind the counter before the diner door opened and a teenage couple walked through it. They slid into the booth in front of them and immediately began making out.

"To be that young again," June said, smiling widely.

That young *again*? Ivy didn't think June was that much older than the couple. She cleared her throat loudly. Ivy was okay with public displays of affection. In fact, she enjoyed seeing people holding hands, hugging, and kissing lightly. Love made people happy. But watching someone shoving his tongue down his girlfriend's throat was a different story altogether. The hormones were getting out of control. She tapped her fork to her plate, and the guy turned his head to look at her. "Take that somewhere else. I'm trying to eat my pie."

The girl's face immediately turned beet red, and she scooted away from her date. At least one of them had some sense.

Chapter Six

Kendall stretched her neck when she stopped at the first light after exiting the interstate. She hadn't slept well, and her shoulders were reminding her of all the tossing and turning she'd done last night. She'd been up and down answering the door for trick-or-treaters until after nine, and then she'd stayed up past midnight reviewing the proposal, wanting to make sure it was perfect and included all the appropriate information. She'd been thrilled to receive an invitation to present in person and thought herself lucky to make the cut, considering she'd almost missed the original submission deadline. It wasn't unusual for a requestor to receive up to fifty bids.

She grabbed the ibuprofen from her console, shook a couple from the bottle, popped them into her mouth, and washed them down with water from her reusable insulated bottle. She remembered as a child from her family's previous camping trips and from her visits as an adult to see Noah what seemed to be the never-ending journey yet was less than a 250-mile drive. But it had been a while, so she'd also read more about it to refresh herself before she left. Visiting state parks were the only affordable vacations her family had taken during her childhood. The drive featured twenty-two scenic vistas and pullout areas. She most likely wouldn't be able to hit most of them and would have to view them briefly from afar as she drove by.

Before heading up the mountain, she stopped at the busy Native American convenience store, refilled her gas tank, and picked up an ample supply of snacks. She imagined this was the last stop for provisions and had no idea what kind of food would be available at the lodge, since she hadn't been able to find a menu listing anywhere on the internet for the lodge restaurant. The reviews were middle-of-the-road, which meant the food could be good or bad, considering most people reviewed the service rather than good food. Most comments focused on the daily buffets, scheduled for breakfast, lunch, and dinner. Kendall was a pro at working buffets, had been since she was a child. She'd brought several small plastic containers with her to allow her to sneak food back to her room. As a child, she'd been an expert at filling her plate multiple times and pretending to eat while her parents filled the containers with the excess food to provide meals for the rest of the week at home. It had taken her a while to perfect the process. As she'd grown older, she hadn't had to do it as often, but it was still a useful skill when she was running low on money. The cost of one buffet dinner could provide her with protein for a week.

The drive was like being on a roller coaster whipping through the national forest. Only a handful of other cars were on the road, which enabled Kendall to take her time. The tiny hairs on her arm danced as the crisp autumn air flowed through the open car windows, carrying the rich scents of decaying leaves and morning dew. Hickory, ash, black walnut, red maples, and a variety of oaks lined the winding road, their branches adorned with a vibrant tapestry of crimson, amber, and golden hues. Fiery red bushes of poison sumac dotted the landscape as well.

Kendall breathed deeply, savoring each inhalation as if it could be bottled and kept forever. When she reached the top of the first hill, she drank in the breathtaking panorama unfolding around every zig-zagged bend—every inch of the area surrounding the road blanketed in the warm tones of fall. During these peaceful moments, on the road behind the wheel, she let the stresses of life back home melt away, leaving only the pristine natural beauty and an appreciation for nature's yearly renaissance. A changing of the guard, if you will, from vibrant greens to muted browns. Autumn, Kendall's favorite time of year, was fleeting, but that made each kaleidoscopic scene all the more precious. The drive was especially picturesque today with the surrounding mountains clad in the yellows, oranges, and reds of autumn foliage. The lodge director had picked the perfect time of year to schedule presentations. She was looking forward to three blissful days immersed in nature at the lodge.

As she approached the park, Kendall assessed the camping area that preceded the entrance. Not much in the way of landscaping, just flat sections of dirt bordered by large square timbers sectioning them into what looked like a variety of camp sites from eight-by-eight to fifteen-by-fifteen. Good choices for any campground that provided pad rentals for individual backpackers as well as full families. Except for the smaller sites, each area included a pole barbecue grill and what looked like a water supply. A nice picnic table and some trees would be a great addition, especially in the summer. Memories of fun, family, outdoor adventures filled her mind. This had been one of her favorite vacation spots as a child even though some nights could be frigid. Staying in the lodge as an adult would be a whole different experience.

As Kendall approached the lodge, she drove around the building and pulled into a parking space across from the check-in loop. There, she noticed a tall, beautiful park ranger standing by the entryway. She had deep red hair that flowed onto her shoulders and moved like kelp in the sea with each breeze. Her green uniform fit her nicely, her bomber jacket hanging loosely from her shoulders, allowing the collar of the khaki shirt to peek out from underneath. The cargo pants she wore hung straight on her legs but clung just enough to show each and every curve from her waist to her calves.

The woman seemed to be watching her as she exited her car. Kendall's heart raced as the ranger paced directly toward her in beautiful confidence. If she was part of the welcome committee, Kendall's luck had changed for the better. As the woman approached, Kendall was captivated by gorgeous green eyes shot with sun-flecked gold, but the woman wasn't smiling. "Excuse me. Did I just see you throw that candy wrapper on the ground?"

"Um, maybe." Kendall scanned the console of her SUV and then the passenger seat. "I was just eating an energy bar before I got here, and I can't seem to find the wrapper." She glanced around the area where she was standing. Didn't see anything.

"It's under your car." The woman's voice was firm, demanding even. "I'm afraid leaving trash on the ground is considered littering in the park. You'll have to pick that up and dispose of it properly."

"Oh, sorry. I didn't realize. I guess I wasn't thinking." She'd pick it up as soon as she could find it.

"No problem. I'll wait while you retrieve it." The woman relaxed and tucked her thumbs into the waistband of her pants.

"Uh… Okay." Kendall dropped to her knees, spotted it under her car, and stretched to reach it. "Got it." She held it up as she stood, started to put it in her pocket, but instead walked to the trash can near the lodge and dropped it into the can in an overly animated fashion. She probably shouldn't have done that, but she didn't like being treated like a child. Even if the ranger was hot.

"Thank you," the woman said through gritted teeth. "Trash cans are located around the lodge and at the exits. Please use them to throw away any garbage while you're here. We try to keep the park looking nice for all visitors." She seemed to have her speech memorized. Probably gave it often. Kendall would give her the benefit of the doubt…this time.

"I apologize. You're right. I should've noticed. I'll be more careful from now on." Kendall realized the woman was just doing her job and probably hadn't singled her out.

The woman nodded. "We appreciate visitors doing their part to keep the park clean. Did you have any other questions I can answer during your visit today?"

"No. I think that covers it." She hadn't asked any questions to begin with. "Thanks for letting me know without making a big deal about it." *Just a medium-sized deal.* "I'll remember next time. Enjoy the rest of your day."

The woman stared at her, perhaps realizing she was being sarcastic. "You too. Take care." Then she turned and walked down the driveway area toward the campgrounds.

Well, that wasn't blissful at all. This weekend certainly wasn't starting out the way she'd expected. She reached inside her SUV, grabbed her bag, and headed to the lodge entrance. Hopefully she wouldn't have any issues checking in.

Kendall was delightfully surprised at the charming modern yet rustic decor in the lobby area, including wood beams, a stone fireplace, and plenty of windows for natural sunlight. She spotted the check-in desk, and thankfully, there wasn't a line. She'd already had enough stress for the day.

"Good afternoon." The woman behind the counter looked up from her computer screen. "Checking in?"

"Yes. I have a room reserved under Kendall Jackson." She hoped her room was ready.

"Oh. I see a note here that says you're here for the renovation presentations." The woman smiled widely.

Kendall nodded. "Thought I'd get here a little early to scope out the place." She placed her ID and credit card on the counter.

"Good idea." The woman took the items, set them next to the keyboard, and clicked a few keys. "I saw you talking to Ivy, our park ranger. She'll be your guide." She reached behind her, took a manilla envelope from the desk, and slid it across the counter. "This has the schedule as well as some information on the park."

Just what I need—a hot, uptight ranger with a rule fetish. Kendall rubbed the kink in the back of her neck and took a deep breath. "Are any other rangers available for that?" She leaned in, reading the name tag pinned to the woman's chest, and whispered, "We didn't exactly hit it off, Susan." She glanced over her shoulder to make sure Ivy hadn't come inside. "She accused me of littering when something fell from my car as I got out." She shook her head. She'd had a long drive and wasn't in the mood to be insulted by the litter patrol.

Susan grinned. "Don't take it personally. Ivy just takes her job seriously."

"Oh." She waved her hand in front of her face. "I'm over it." She scrunched her cheeks. "I might have been a bit…sarcastic in response." *Definitely sarcastic.* "Not sure she'll want to show me around." Kendall had certainly started this weekend off on the wrong foot.

Susan handed Kendall her credit card and license back. "She sounds tough, but she's a big teddy bear inside. She's actually really nice once you get to know her."

"I don't know. When I met her, she was cold and bossy. She doesn't exactly scream 'friendly.'"

Susan slipped a card key into an envelope and set it on the counter. "Ivy is just reserved with strangers. But she's honestly just an introvert who takes a while to open up."

"I'd call her comments rude and off-putting. Kind of hard to look past that."

"Ivy's pretty direct without realizing how she comes across to others. But her heart is in the right place."

"Evidently." Kendall glanced at the door as she ran through their interaction again in her head. "Her behavior makes it hard for me to want her as my guide."

"She's the best guide you'll get. Just give her one more chance. Once you two break through that awkward first impression, you'll see what an amazing person she truly is."

The hard sell was getting suspicious. "You sound like you're trying to set her up." Kendall leaned closer. "Is she the sister you're trying to pair off so you can marry the perfect guy?"

Susan laughed. "No. Not related and already married. But finding Ivy someone to date is always on my radar."

"I'm here to work, not date." She tapped her key card on the counter. "I'll try to start fresh with her, but she'll have to meet me halfway."

"Great." Susan's smile widened. "Ivy's loyalty is incredible once you get into her inner circle."

"Not sure I'll ever make it to her friend circle, but thanks for the information." She was still unsure why Susan was giving her the hard sell.

"Keep an open mind next time. She's been an amazing friend to me over the years—supportive, caring, and always there when I need her."

Maybe she'd judged Ivy too quickly. "Okay. I'll try."

"Just get to know the real Ivy before writing her off. I'm confident you'll like her once you see how genuinely sweet she is."

"I'll do my best." *This feels like a trap.*

Chapter Seven

Ivy pushed thought the door into the lobby, still unable to shake her irritation with the beautiful, but careless, woman she'd confronted earlier. She'd walked all the way to the farthest campground and back to settle her annoyance.

She spotted Susan behind the check-in desk as she entered. "You're not going to believe what happened this morning. This real piece of work pulls into a parking space like she owns the place." Ivy's neck heated as her irritation flared again.

"Oh, boy, here we go. What did Miss Entitled do this time?" This wasn't an unusual comment—Susan knew how much littering irritated Ivy.

"I'm doing my rounds, and this woman…" She gritted her teeth and cleared the unwanted slow-motion image of her exiting her vehicle… "gets out of her SUV and drops a power-bar wrapper on the ground right in front of me. No regard whatsoever for the park or the rules."

"Unbelievable. After all the signs and trash bins, people still just litter like that?"

"I know. It's infuriating! So I go up and say, 'Excuse me, but you dropped something,' and she looks at me like I've got three heads."

"Did she pick it up?" Susan raised her eyebrows.

"Yeah. Dropped to her knees and swiped it from beneath her vehicle and then marched to the trash can." Ivy shook her head. "And then she said, 'Thanks for letting me know' and told me to enjoy the rest of my day." Ivy had a hard time believing she was genuinely sorry. Replaying the action in her head, she held in a chuckle. The woman was clearly mocking her.

"What? No way. She said that to you?" Susan let out an abrupt laugh. "Next time, write her a big, fat, littering ticket."

"Your sarcasm is almost as bad as hers was." Ivy grinned.

"Maybe she really *didn't* see it fall?" Susan's tone softened. "She picked it up, didn't she?"

"Yeah." She had immediately located it and put it in the trash. Maybe she had been too hard on the woman. But Ivy couldn't help it. Seeing litter on the ground always left her frustrated—this beautiful natural area was meant to be an escape from the trappings of modern life, a place to reconnect with nature. Carelessly tossing trash went against the entire ethos of respecting and preserving these lands for future generations to enjoy. At the same time, Ivy knew people sometimes acted thoughtlessly rather than maliciously. Maybe the visitor was simply unaware of the impact or had been distracted in the moment. This was an opportunity for education more than harsh judgement. She made a mental note to emphasize the importance of *Leave No Trace* principles during the next guided hike or campfire talk. She would explain how litter can harm wildlife and why removing all trash properly is so crucial. With any luck, imparting that deeper understanding would ensure that this visitor and others would make more mindful choices going forward. "I might have scared her. I doubt I'll catch her doing it again. In any case. I'll probably never see her again."

"Don't be so sure about that. She's presenting for the landscape redesign, and she's been assigned to you for a tour." Susan fingered through a couple of papers. "There's another one on your list as well. Maybe she'll be more to your liking."

"Ugh." Ivy shook her head. "Change it now. I have other things to do than chaperone women around the park."

"Can't. Already told her. She's excited to have you as a guide."

"Really?" Ivy eyed her suspiciously, seeing the matchmaking wheels spinning in Susan's head.

"I spoke to Kendall—that's her name—when she checked in. Found her to be incredibly sweet. Susan shrugged. Maybe you're just afraid to get to know her."

"Maybe." Kendall…now she had a name to go with that beautiful face. She'd still wait to receive an official order from up-top to assist.

"Did you enjoy the movie last night?" Susan asked.

"Nope. I didn't even get to see my favorite part."

"Which part?"

"When the front door breaks in and there's that pause before Johnny drags Barbara out."

"You've got to be kidding me." Susan said as she dropped her head back. "The way they fade into the zombie crowd as she screams is just devastating."

"Yeah, but then they're zombies together and can live happily ever after in zombie world."

"Feasting on live people together forever sounds delightful." Susan rolled her eyes. "You're a hopeless romantic."

Ivy shook her head. "Just optimistic."

"Ridiculously optimistic for someone who doesn't date."

"I've dated."

"It's been over a year, Ivy. Almost fifteen months." Susan straightened a few papers on the counter and dropped them into a tray on the desk behind her.

Ivy raised her eyebrows "Has it? I hadn't been counting."

"Yes. It's been too long. You should really give June a chance."

"She's too young. We don't have anything in common." Ivy had opted for breakfast at home this morning. Last night had been awkward at best.

"Trying new experiences might be good for you. You know, teaching each other?" Susan winked. "Even if it's just for a night or two."

"Nope. Too much teaching with that one." Ivy didn't enjoy casual sex with women she saw regularly. Eventually someone always lost interest and made the situation uncomfortable.

"Whatever." Susan let out a deep sigh. "I hear you got a show from the couple seated in front of you at the diner."

"Teenage hormones aren't a show. Be thankful you didn't have to witness that."

Susan chuckled. "I would've whispered that I really enjoy watching them."

"That would've sent that little girl running for sure. Thanks for showing up and having my back." Ivy raised an eyebrow.

"Sorry. I ate too much popcorn and wasn't up for pie."

"Uh-huh." She didn't believe that for a minute.

"So, what happened when you took June home?" Susan's voice rose in a light melody. "Did you kiss her?"

"Don't you already know? You've clearly talked to June." Word traveled fast around a remote mountain lodge.

"She's not talking. Spill," Susan said.

"No." Ivy scrunched her face. "Absolutely not." That had been the furthest thing from her mind when she'd taken June home. "She wanted me to come in and watch some erotic movie with her."

"Ooh." Susan bounced her eyebrows. "Clearly you two have very different tastes in films."

"Yeah, very different." Ivy wouldn't find herself in a movie theater or alone anywhere with June again. "I'll be out checking the grounds if you need me." She held up her walkie-talkie as she strolled to the door.

Taking June home had been a fiasco. June had mistaken her consideration for something more, and Ivy had set her straight once again. Ivy didn't dare get out of the truck to open her door and walk with her, which was her usual standard for any date. She wanted no mistakes this time. Her first thought had been to unlock the passenger door, take the curve quickly, and let her roll out. That would've been the perfect gnarly ending to the perfect gnarly movie night. She really had to stop thinking in cartoons.

CHAPTER EIGHT

Kendall's phone buzzed as a text came through. Noah's name flashed on the screen. She'd told him last week that she was coming but hadn't been in touch since.

When do you want to sync up?

Soon. I might have to grovel first.

Seriously? I'm calling now.

Steve Miller Band's *Space Cowboy* rang loudly from her phone. She immediately silenced the ring and hit the button to answer. "Hey."

"Who are you groveling to?"

"The park ranger, Ivy. I think that's her name." She knew damn well what her name was. She'd noticed her as soon as she'd gotten out of her car.

"Why?"

"Some crap fell out of my car when I got here, and she accused me of littering." She opened the envelope she'd received at check-in and filtered through the documents to find her schedule.

"Yeah. She's a real rule follower, that one." He laughed.

"I've already apologized once, but I don't think she believed me." *Shit.* Her park tour was scheduled for two p.m., and her chaperone was indeed none other than the beautiful rule-follower.

"Were you going to pick it up?"

"Of course. Why would you even think I wouldn't?" She floated the schedule across the bed and flopped back on the pillow.

"I grew up with you, remember? I cleaned up after you all the time."

"Yeah, but that's back before I got serious about nature, and, besides, I knew you'd pick it up for me. You took good care of me and kept me out of trouble." As a deputy sheriff, he was still keeping people out of trouble.

"You're right about that. Too bad you decided to dump me."

"That was out of my hands, and besides, I let you down easy. Didn't I?" Breaking up with Noah was one of the hardest things she'd ever had to do.

"You tried, but it still stung…a lot. You were, after all, my first love."

"Well, if it helps, I haven't been involved with any man since."

"Can't compete with a woman." He blew a breath into the phone. "You want me to come up to the lodge, or do you want to come here?"

"How about I head your way right now? I could use some distance from the ranger."

"The place is kind of a mess. Let's meet at the diner downtown."

"I'll buy you lunch. See you in about thirty minutes."

"Sounds good," he said. The call dropped before she had time to press the end button on her phone.

She'd been happy with Noah when they were teenagers. At least she'd thought she was, but that was before she realized how much more she was turned on by women. The object of her affection had been unplanned. She'd never felt it coming. The bounce in her stomach followed by the subsequent wetness in her pants had hit her like a bolt of lightning, heat spreading through her as she watched the new girl in school cross the room in front of her. She'd been rattled by the natural response and had gripped the chair she'd been sitting in for support. Noah had noticed her discomfort, the heat in her cheeks. He'd thought she was nauseous and asked her if she was all right. She'd nodded and explained it away as hunger pangs. The girl wasn't beautiful, even particularly sexy, or what she'd call uniquely attractive, but the way she'd carried herself had certainly lit something deep inside Kendall. She hadn't even known how to begin to understand it herself, let alone explain it to Noah.

Sex with Noah hadn't been bad. He knew how to please a woman. But she didn't want to please him. She'd tried to convince herself that she was bisexual, that she could love Noah and still admire the beauty of women around her. But once she'd realized her interest in them, she had no desire to do anything out of the ordinary with him. Even the normal boy/girl heavy kissing became a challenge.

Thinking back, she realized her feelings shouldn't have been a surprise, considering the giddiness she felt when another girl took interest in her as a friend. Those relationships were always platonic, she hadn't crushed on any of her friends, but dressing in front of them had always felt awkward. She'd really thought that was normal modesty.

Kendall spotted Noah's truck as she pulled into the lot and glanced at her watch. Exactly thirty minutes. He'd be happy with her. Noah was always on time or early for everything. She, on the other hand, was always late. She parked in the first open space and headed to the door. A couple was exiting at the same time, and the man stopped and held the door for her. She always admired manners in a man and thanked him as she entered the fifties-themed diner. All the stools at the counter were full—the food must be good.

Noah, always the gentleman, stood as soon as he saw her, met her halfway and pulled her into a tight hug before kissing her cheek as he released her. "Good to see you." He held her at arm's length. "Have you lost weight?"

"You know better than to ask a girl that." She shrugged out of his grip and moved to the table he'd come from.

"You're not a girl. You're my buddy." He pulled out her chair for her. "My very beautiful buddy." He grinned.

"Aw. You know how to make a girl feel good." She slipped out of her jacket and hung it on the back of the metal-framed, red vinyl, padded chair, immediately noting there weren't any condiments on the table.

"So, tell me what happened with Cassie." Noah didn't waste any time getting to the point.

"Nothing to tell. She dumped me for another woman. Apparently, I cost too much."

"Seriously? What a bitch."

"Yeah. I found that out about her way too late."

"You still working with her?"

She shook her head. "That partnership has dissolved as well."

"Is she helping you with the lodge bid?"

"No. I kept it under her radar, put it in a while back without her knowledge. She wasn't interested in any state bids, said there wasn't enough profit in them. I don't want or need her help with it." When she'd mentioned it to Cassie, she'd given her an immediate no, but since they'd already broken up personally, Kendall had put in the bid anyway. It was a good opportunity for exposure, and she didn't want Cassie claiming she didn't contribute to the business. She was sure that Cassie didn't know or care anything about it.

"Let's hope she doesn't show up." He flipped the menu open and stared at it.

"What's good here?" She stared at the menu as well.

"Philly cheesesteak sandwich, burger, or meatloaf are my go-tos. Taylor's partial to the chicken pot pie. Pretty much everything's good. Not sure about the spaghetti, though. Never ordered it. "I think I'll take the meat loaf."

"Pot pie for me." She slapped the menu closed. "Are you going to get some hot sauce for that?"

He lifted an eyebrow. "Why don't you settle in first before you start adding to your collection?"

"You never know when you're going to need an extra bottle of Cholula." She clasped her hands together to keep her compulsion at bay. "How are you and Taylor doing?"

The vinyl chair seat crackled as he shifted. "All right, I guess."

Kendall raised her eyebrows. "You guess?"

"I think she wants to get married, and I'm not sure about that." He opened the menu and stared into it.

"How long have you two been together?" She knew it was at least a couple of years but couldn't remember exactly.

"Almost four years."

"That's pretty long to not be sure." She plucked the menu out of his hand and slid it behind the salt and pepper shaker rack.

"I know."

"What's holding you back?"

He shrugged. "I always thought I'd marry someone I couldn't live without."

"And you think you'd be okay without her?"

"I don't know, but I've been thinking about that a lot lately."

"I get it. I believed Cassie was that person for me, but I found out the hard way that I can *absolutely* live without her." That was far from what Kendall had planned. "I need someone who can't live without me too."

"Plus, she's talking about having babies all of a sudden."

"You being careful about that?" She pulled her eyebrows together.

"Always. Don't want to end up in a spot I don't want to be in."

"Your thirties will do that to you." Kendall had started having baby pangs a few years ago but wasn't anywhere close to where she needed to be to start a family.

"She ain't close to thirty yet."

"How old is Taylor?"

"Twenty-five, twenty-six."

"You don't remember?" Definitely not the woman he was going to marry. What else didn't he know about her?

He pulled his phone from his pocket and scrolled through it. "Twenty-six. She has a birthday coming up in a couple of months."

"Have you told her you're not ready for kids?"

"Not outright."

"Well, you better start being honest with her, or you're going to get into a situation you might regret." She slipped the paper sleeve from her straw, wadded it up, and tossed it across the table at him. "Otherwise, you'll hurt her very badly."

He tossed the paper bullet back at her. "I know how that feels. I thought you were my perfect girl."

Kendall laughed. "That ship sailed long ago, honey." She'd wondered when that subject would come up again. Even though it had happened over fifteen years ago, the fact that she'd broken up with him never seemed to go away completely.

CHAPTER NINE

Ivy was going about her normal duties patrolling one of the hiking trails when she received a radio call from her supervisor, Bryant. "Ivy, I need you to lead a tour this afternoon for one of the landscape designers who is bidding on the redesign project."

Ivy frowned. Tour duties weren't her favorite part of the job. "I was actually scheduled for a nature hike with the junior rangers. Can someone else handle the tour?"

"I'm afraid not. Several companies are visiting, and everyone's assigned to do at least one. You're one of my most knowledgeable rangers about the area's native landscape."

"Does this person have a name?" *Please don't say Kendall.*

"I've assigned you to Kendall Jackson. From the look of her bid, she's one of the top contenders." There was a moment of silence. "I have another one for you, but I don't have the name in front of me right now."

When Ivy's radio crackled with Bryant's voice asking for a confirmation, she reluctantly responded. "Copy that. Giving private tours this afternoon per your instructions." From what Susan had told her, she'd known this was coming, but she'd hoped Susan had been mistaken. That rarely happened. Susan had eyes on all the paper that came across Bryant's desk, and her ears caught everything spoken in the area.

"Meet Kendall at the visitors' center at two p.m. Don't be late."

Ivy ended the radio call, annoyed at having her schedule changed at the last minute. She sighed in frustration. The junior ranger program was one of her favorite parts of the job, allowing her to inspire an appreciation for nature in young minds. Canceling on them for a landscape designer's tour felt like a dereliction of her core duties, even if it was for the benefit of the park. But she knew better than to openly defy her boss's orders. He'd been applying more pressure lately to seek out revenue-generating opportunities like weddings, film shoots, and weekend farmers' markets during the summers. Wealthy visitors rarely frequented state parks unless a spectacular natural treasure or a once-in-a-lifetime view was present. They generally had their own properties where they could enjoy nature in private.

Giving private tours meant putting on a cheery face for outsiders instead of being able to truly immerse herself in the peaceful wilderness she loved. But it was part of the job, even if not her favorite part. Ivy began mentally preparing her most engaging speaking voice and upbeat demeanor. She'd make the best of it, as she always did. But deep down, she worried that this client-first approach was eroding the park's fundamental mission of conservation and public education.

When Ivy got back to the lodge, Susan met her at the door.

"I have an idea. Why don't you loosen up a little and take June out dancing or something?"

"No, thanks." Ivy pushed by her and walked farther inside.

Susan followed her into the office behind the check-in counter. "You can't tell me you don't dance. I've seen you two-step. Hell, I've two-stepped with you, and it was fun."

"I don't take anyone dancing around here anymore." Not since she'd had an altercation with a testosterone-filled male. "I don't want to get my ass kicked." Ivy shucked her coat and hung it on a chair. "Some men seem to think it's some sort of competition to see who can please a girl the best on and off the dance floor."

"I wonder if that sweet little landscape designer likes to dance."

"Stop. I'm not going to mix business with pleasure."

"See. You do like to dance."

"Of course I like to. Just not going to risk my health to do it in public."

"The event area above the lobby has a really nice wood floor."

"I know."

"Maybe we should have a little get-together for the staff—or, better yet, for the designers. A welcome reception. I should mention that to Bryant."

"Don't you dare." A flash of sunlit blond hair flashed through her mind, and she shook it from her thoughts. "They'll be too busy working anyway."

"You're not still mad at her, are you?"

"She apologized. I'm over it."

"Doesn't seem like it."

"What *I am* over is the fact that you keep trying to set me up with every single woman that comes across your path."

"Someone's got to find you a wife."

"What makes you think I even want a wife?"

"All the future plans you're making." Susan picked up a few of the magazines on Ivy's desk. "Tropical vacations, buying a house, having kids." Susan dropped the magazines one by one in front of her.

"Don't need a wife for any of those." She swiped up the pile of magazines, opened the drawer, and slid them into a hanging folder.

Clearly she needed to keep her magazines at home and her thoughts to herself around Susan, or she'd never stop until Ivy found a woman to date. "Now if you'll excuse me, I have a tour to guide." She headed outside to wait for the landscape designer from out of town.

Ivy scowled as she looked at her watch for the third time in the last ten minutes. Kendall was late, of course. She paced back and forth on the dirt path, kicking up dust with the toes of her pristinely polished boots.

This blazing summer was supposed to be over, but the unseasonably hot sun was beating down on her flat-brimmed hat. Sweat trickled down the back of her neck as she grumbled under her breath. She'd dressed for the chill of the morning and hadn't considered the heat of the afternoon. She much preferred being out in the park's rugged backcountry, away from the manicured lawns and gardens of the more developed areas where she'd been assigned to give a tour today.

Chapter Ten

Kendall was late as she headed to meet her tour guide, Ivy, because her lunch with Noah had taken longer than she'd expected. Time and time again she'd told him that there was no possibility of them getting back together, but for some reason he still held a torch for her. She probably should let their friendship go, but, considering their history and her current situation, that would be hard. She needed an ally nearby in case this whole bid blew up in her face. Having a deputy sheriff in her pocket might come in handy if the beautiful park ranger gave her trouble.

After she parked and made her way to the front of the lodge, she saw Ivy standing in front of the check-in driveway area that was still packed with cars, checking her watch. The woman was insanely attractive in her khaki pants and long-sleeve ranger uniform shirt. Kendall was deep in lust when she glimpsed a car that looked exactly like Cassie's white, BMW X3 pass by. She couldn't see the driver, but it didn't stop, so she hoped it was someone leaving the lodge. As she walked farther down the path, she saw the car approaching again. *Shit. It is Cassie.* She ducked behind a large GMC truck and watched her pass and park in the grassy area at the end of the spaces. Hidden by the parked cars, she crept closer to where Cassie had parked.

She caught movement off to the side and saw Ivy heading toward Cassie with intent, then watching and waiting for Cassie to exit her car.

"Excuse me. You can't park your car on the grass here, ma'am. You'll need to move it to the parking lot."

Cassie whipped her head around when she heard Ivy's voice. "Why not? There's nowhere else. The lot is full."

"Parking on the grass causes damage, ma'am. It kills the grass and leaves mud and tire tracks that can be difficult to repair. We need to keep the park lodge area looking nice. You'll have to find a space in the lower lot." Ivy pointed down the hill.

"It's only a little bit of grass. And for your information, my name is Cassie, not *ma'am.* I'm just running in for a minute to pick up something."

"I understand, but rules are rules. Everyone needs to park in the designated areas. I'm going to have to ask you to move your car." Ivy was being much more polite than Kendall would be.

"This is ridiculous! What gives you the right to tell me where I can and can't park? I'm not hurting anything."

"I disagree, and as a park ranger, it's my job to enforce the park rules and make sure visitors are not causing harm. I politely asked you to move, and if you refuse, I *will* issue you a citation for illegal parking."

"Oh, come on. You can't be serious! This is so stupid. I'm just trying to do some quick business inside and suddenly you're giving me a ticket? What kind of public servant are you?"

By the change in Ivy's stance, Kendall could see that she didn't like being referred to as a public servant, even though she was one. It was clear Cassie's entitled tone bothered her the most. "I'm just doing my job to protect this park, ma'am." She walked to the back of the BMW, took out a small pad folio, and wrote a few lines before she ripped the page from the pad and handed it to Cassie. "The citation stands, and you'll still need to move your vehicle, or I'll have it towed for being illegally parked. If you'd like to contest the ticket, you can do so in court on the date listed in the summons you'll receive in the mail." Ivy waited as Cassie got into her car, fired up the engine, and tore out across the grass, leaving a bare spot in it.

Kendall chuckled to herself as Ivy stepped forward, assessed the damage, and knelt to replace some of the dislodged grass. Cassie would be lucky if Ivy didn't add the cost of the grass repair to the fine.

Kendall used her most remorseful look as she approached Ivy. "Excuse me. Are you the park ranger in charge here?"

Ivy tilted her head to look up. "Yes. I am. The name's Ivy. How can I help you?" she asked as she stood and rubbed the dirt from her hands.

"Well, I wanted to apologize for something that happened yesterday during my arrival here. I wasn't paying attention when I got out of my car, and I'm ashamed to admit I let some trash fall to the ground. You were right to draw my attention to it."

Ivy frowned. "Ah. I see. We do ask all visitors to pack out any garbage they produce to keep our parks pristine. Leaving litter can negatively impact the wildlife and ecosystem."

"You're absolutely correct. It was thoughtless of me." Kendall smiled lightly. "I feel just terrible about it. I've always appreciated the natural beauty of parks and public lands. When I realized what I'd done, I immediately regretted it."

Ivy took in a deep breath. "I appreciate you taking responsibility. May I ask what made you change your mind and apologize?"

"Well, I watched that woman destroy the grass, and after thinking it over, I realized I'd violated a principle I deeply believe in—leaving nature unspoiled for others to enjoy. Littering was disrespectful to this park I love so much. I couldn't let it sit right with my conscience." The apology was a bit over the top, but she hoped Ivy didn't think she was being insincere. In light of Cassie's arrival, Kendall needed to get back into Ivy's good graces.

Ivy hesitated, then glared suspiciously at her. "I understand. Making mistakes is part of human nature. What matters is that we try to make amends."

"Thank you for hearing me out. I won't let it happen again."

Ivy nodded. "Now do you want to tell me the real reason you're apologizing again?" She raised her eyebrows. "I appreciate the sincerity, but I believed you the first time."

Kendall closed her eyes and let out a slow breath. She never had been good at sucking up. "That woman, the one you just gave a ticket to…is my ex-partner." She brushed the hair out of her face. "She's here because of the lodge-beautification project as well. I put in the bid without her knowledge before we ended our relationship."

"Oh." Ivy shook her head. "Yet she parked on the grass and destroyed a patch when she peeled out of here."

"Yeah. That's what she does. Leaves a bit of destruction in her wake." Kendall's gut wrenched. "Did that to my heart as well."

"Oh." Ivy blinked several times as though she was an overloaded CPU processing the information.

Kendall paused, waiting to see if Ivy would say something or shut down.

"Thank you for the warning. I'll be sure to keep an eye out for her."

That's it? That's all she has to say after I told her my life was decimated and I'm gay? Not even a drop of empathy. This woman's made of stone. Insanely attractive but built of granite.

CHAPTER ELEVEN

When Kendall had finally arrived at their meeting point in front of the lodge, Ivy's irritation at her had been replaced by her annoyance at the ridiculously rude Cassie.

"We're running late." Ivy turned and started trudging across the grass down to the trail into the woods, not even checking to see if Kendall was following.

"I'm so sorry. I got hung up on a phone call from home. My mom needed help with a computer issue."

Ivy slowed and took a deep breath. She shouldn't be mad at Kendall for taking time for her family.

As they walked the trail, Kendall chattered away about her recent projects designing amenities for a couple of luxury hotels in various locales and a children's hospital back home. Ivy tuned out most of it.

They approached a pristine mountain stream, the water sparkling as it flowed over rocks. "Oh, isn't this just beautiful," Kendall said excitedly as she kneeled and dipped her hand in the water. "We could build a lovely little footbridge over this brook, with some decorative gardens on either side."

Ivy cut her off with a harsh look. "This entire area is undeveloped wilderness. No construction of any kind is allowed here. That's the whole point of a state park."

Kendall blinked in clear surprise at Ivy's sharp tone but then simply smiled. "Well, I'm just throwing out some ideas. No need to get upset."

Ivy sighed. This tour was going to test every last ounce of her patience. "I'm sorry. I didn't mean to snap."

"I get it." Kendall gave her a flat smile. "You don't want to babysit me." She walked ahead of her. "That's okay. I can find my way around. If I get lost, I'll just follow the sun back to the lodge."

"The sun sets in the west."

"Right." Kendall pointed west.

"The lodge is east." Ivy pointed in the opposite direction.

"Thanks for the tip." Kendall kept walking. "Don't worry. I'll be fine on my own."

"No. Absolutely not." Her boss would kill her if something happened to Kendall. "You're my responsibility. I'll guide you."

"I'm no one's responsibility but my own," Kendall shot back.

Ivy grabbed her arm gently. "Listen. I acted badly, and I really am sorry."

Kendall glanced at Ivy's hand on her arm, and Ivy released her.

"Honestly. Walking the trails is one of my favorite things. It's where I gather my thoughts. But you're right. I hadn't expected to be taken away from my regular duties to escort you." She took her hat off and blotted her forehead. "I had a tour scheduled with some kids today and had to pass it off to someone else."

"You like kids' tours?" Kendall raised her eyebrows.

"They're my favorite. So eager to soak up everything they learn about nature."

Kendall smiled softly. "With you being so strict about the rules, I didn't see that coming."

"Adults break the rules more often than kids."

"Yeah. I guess they probably do."

"No probably about it. They always think they're right about their actions and don't like admitting when they're wrong."

"I admitted it. Even though what I did was unintentional."

"You did. In all your mocking glory."

"I know." Kendall grinned. "But I apologized for that as well."

Ivy tilted her head. "Did you really apologize? It sounded more to me like you were throwing some shade on your ex."

"Everything I told you was true. I *did* bid the project alone, and she *did* break my heart."

"I'm sorry that happened to you." Ivy truly regretted doubting her. "Why'd you put the bid in without her?"

"Cassie avoids state contract bids because there isn't a whole lot of money to be made on them."

In addition to Cassie being full of herself, Ivy had just found another reason not to like her. "She's right. You don't see it that way?"

"No. Not at all. I see it as a way to give back to the community." Kendall shook her head. "This lodge is a gorgeous castle in the sky, originally built in the late 1800s as a Victorian resort named The Stella Peak Inn. Do you know Stella means star in Latin?"

"Yes. I'm aware of what it means." Ivy didn't know Latin but was well versed in the history of the lodge.

"After facing financial troubles, it fell into disrepair and finally closed in 1910. Not much of the original was left when a second lodge was built and opened in 1963, but sadly that one was destroyed by a kitchen fire in 1973."

"This place has overcome a lot of hardship, for sure," Ivy said.

"It's very resilient. The current lodge was built in 1975. And after that it underwent a major renovation and expansion from 2012 to 2015. And now here we are to do it again. I wonder why they changed the name to Diamond Mountain?"

"Because, in addition to the mountain being rich in diamonds, during the restoration it was considered a diamond in the rough." Ivy was excited to provide a bit of information Kendall didn't know. Sounds like you've done your research." She was impressed by Kendall's knowledge. "Are you sure you need a guide?"

"Yes, please. I want to hear all the inside secrets of the park," Kendall said. "Oh, and can we take the Reservoir Trail? I read that the old rock wall that served as part of the reservoir for the original 1898 inn can still be found there on the side of the mountain."

"Okay, then. Come on. Let's get moving. We have a lot of ground to cover." It seemed that she'd misjudged Kendall. Maybe she wasn't so bad after all.

CHAPTER TWELVE

Ivy sighed heavily as she saw the sporty SUV pull up to the ranger station. She recognized it as belonging to Cassie, the landscape designer from out of town that she'd had the confrontation with earlier that day. She'd finished showing Kendall around less than an hour ago. It seemed that the parks department had brought in several resources to bid on the revitalization of the lodge and some areas of the park. All the staff had been buzzing about it, but Ivy loved this park and didn't think it needed revitalizing at all. It might be aged and weathered a bit, but it was perfect as the natural wonderland it was.

Cassie bounded out of her vehicle, designer sunglasses on and colorful printed scarf trailing behind her. "Ranger, so good to see you again," she said in an overly cheery voice.

Forcing a tight smile, Ivy muttered a greeting. *Here we go again.* She was dreading having to lead this excessively energetic, narcissistic woman around and listen to her critique every inch of the landscape. She noted the flashy leather boots Cassie was wearing. This would probably be a shorter tour than planned.

"Shall we head out?" Cassie asked, indicating the start of one of the hiking trails with a sweep of her arm. Without waiting for a response, she started off down the path.

Ivy stuffed her hands into her pockets and trudged along behind her, her scowl deepening with every enthusiastic comment Cassie made about remaking this perfect park into her own artificial vision. This was going to be a miserably long tour—so much different than the one she'd given Kendall.

"Have you read through my bid?" Cassie asked over her shoulder.

"Not my department. I'm a state park ranger."

"What does a state park ranger do?" Cassie asked with a flirty lilt in her voice.

"I'm a wildlife professional. I protect the land by ensuring park visitors adhere to wildlife rules. I'm responsible for educating the public about the guidelines and regulations of national and local parks."

"Like park law enforcement?"

Ivy shook her head. "I don't arrest people. I educate them."

"You gave me a ticket, though. So, you must have some authority."

Ivy nodded. "The authority to ticket people like you, who don't respect the land. I participate in search-and-rescue missions when necessary, and apparently, I now give tours to landscapers as well."

Cassie stopped and sat on a nearby bench. "Educate me."

"What do you want to know?"

"Tell me about the lodge. When it was built and opened to the public."

All things that Kendall already knew. She'd been telling the truth about the bid and Cassie.

Ivy remained standing as she proceeded to give Cassie a brief overview of the history of the lodge. "It was originally built in the late 1800s as a Victorian resort." She recalled Kendall calling it a castle in the sky. Very appropriate description.

"So, it's really old, huh?" Cassie pulled Ivy from her thought. "Rather than redesign it, maybe they should just tear it down and build something more modern."

"*It's a landmark.*" More like a local treasure. Cassie would probably never understand its significance. "It's already been rebuilt several times, due to unfortunate circumstances. The lodge underwent a major renovation and expansion that ended in 2015. It's structurally sound now, and it's unlikely to be torn down for a rebuild in the near future."

"You know what they say about old bones."

"What's that?" Ivy waited for Cassie's response before giving her own opinion.

"They're brittle and break easily." Cassie shrugged.

"I disagree." Ivy shook her head. "I consider old bones to be a strong foundation."

"Guess that depends on the way you look at the half-empty glass." Cassie certainly wasn't an optimist. If she was awarded the contract, the lodge would suffer. Ivy walked farther down the trail. "You ready to see more of the park?"

Cassie shook her head. "No. I think I'll go back to the lodge. These boots won't work for the trails." She took one off and wiped the dust from the leather top. "I still need to check in."

"Okay. I've got a few things to check out here. Just let Susan at the desk know if you want to continue the tour at another time."

Ivy turned and headed farther down the trail. She probably should've offered to walk Cassie back to the lodge but didn't really want to waste any more time on someone who didn't appreciate the lodge or the surrounding nature. It would take her a few minutes to shake the negative vibes she was currently feeling. Each and every step of the tour for Cassie, even though it was short, had been painful.

She now understood a little more about Kendall and her comment about Cassie leaving a bit of destruction in her wake. The news that Kendall was gay was interesting, more interesting than it really should be, but she wondered if the information Kendall had provided about her broken heart was a deterrent or just exactly that, information. She'd been waiting for so long to connect with someone who respected nature the way she did. Why did it have to happen with someone who had a clearly displayed warning sign above her head?

But why was she even thinking about that at all? She was here to do her job, not romance a park contractor, which is exactly what Kendall would be if she got the bid.

As soon as Ivy entered the lodge, Susan rounded the counter and rushed toward her. Pulling her aside, she whispered in her ear, "It appears the lodge is overbooked."

"What?" Ivy glanced at Kendall, who was waiting patiently at one end of the counter, and then at Cassie, who was waiting at the other with her hand on her hip. "How did that happen?"

"Seems that cute little designer, Kendall, has a partner who showed up as well."

"I'm aware. I've already met her." An unfortunate experience at best. "She's a real piece of work."

"Only one room was reserved for them, and I've already given it to Kendall. So, her partner doesn't have one." Susan moved closer. "Are they romantic partners as well?"

"According to Kendall they aren't any type of partners anymore."

Susan smiled widely. "She told you that?"

Ivy nodded. "Don't get any ideas. She only told me because Cassie showed up, and she hadn't expected her to."

"Well, now we have an issue. Do you think that Kendall can stay with you?" Susan asked.

"What?" Ivy raised her eyebrows. "No. Absolutely not. Have her stay with you."

"I don't have room at my place."

"Neither do I. My place is a one-bedroom, remember? That would put one of us on the couch."

Susan crossed her arms and looked at the two women at the counter. "What are we gonna do?"

"They'll just have to share the room. Their company, their issue."

"You know that will be a very awkward position for them."

"Awkward for them? Just think how I'll feel if I have to put up a total stranger." Ivy let out a low grumble. "This whole situation is unbelievable. I don't even know Cassie, and I hate her already."

"That's a very strong word you're using there."

"I know." Ivy closed her eyes and let out a sigh. "I've only heard a little about her from Kendall, and now that I've actually met her, I can see that it could all be true."

She heard Cassie raise her voice and move aggressively toward Kendall, who didn't back away. *Shit.* This situation was about to explode. She rushed toward them.

CHAPTER THIRTEEN

I can't believe you tried to steal this bid from me." Cassie moved quickly into Kendall's space.

Kendall's adrenaline rushed as she stood her ground. "It's my bid. I wrote it and I sent it in. You didn't even want to bid this project." She knew Cassie would try to take this from her.

Cassie glanced at Susan and several others in the lobby, who were now watching them. "That's not true. I just let you take the lead on it."

"Oh, yeah? Why don't you tell me about your presentation—how you plan to revitalize the lodge?" No way was Cassie prepared for the magnitude of this project. Kendall wasn't sure she was either.

"I'm not telling you that. It's confidential. You'll steal my ideas." Cassie gave her a tight-lipped smile.

"Your ideas." Kendall scoffed. "If you have anything in that little bag of tricks, you got it from me." Kendall looked around her. "Did you bring your new girlfriend to help?"

"No. I'm here alone."

"Didn't want her to see the cutthroat side of you, eh?"

"She's busy with her own job."

"Really? My needs never outweighed yours when we were together." What was that about? Cassie had required twenty-four-seven attention from Kendall.

Kendall caught a glimpse of Ivy and Susan as they rushed by them and went behind the counter.

Susan tapped a few keys on the computer keyboard. "Ladies, I'm sorry to interrupt, but we have a slight problem."

"What?" Cassie snapped.

"There she is." Kendall gave her a tight smile. "The real Cassie."

Cassie cleared her throat. "I'm sorry. What's the problem?"

"Only one room was booked for your firm, and we don't have any others available. So, either you two will have to stay together, or one of you will have to find a room somewhere else in town."

"I was here first. I'm already checked in." Kendall wasn't going anywhere. This was her bid.

"Well, I paid for all your work, and I'm not leaving."

"I earned every penny we made. You couldn't even run the copier." Kendall had been the bones of the company and had created all the designs. Cassie was the wrapper and mostly handled sales.

Cassie flipped her gaze to Susan. "Does the room have two queen beds?"

Susan shook her head. "One king."

Ivy stepped forward and put her arm around Kendall. "You can stay with me like we originally planned."

They all fell silent and stared at Ivy until Susan grinned. "Great idea. Problem solved."

Cassie glanced from Kendall to Ivy and then back to Kendall. "You sure didn't waste any time, did you?"

Kendall bit her lip, letting Cassie think the worst of her. She didn't like giving in, but she couldn't stay in the same room with Cassie. Not after what she'd done to her. The way Cassie had broken up with her had been so heartless and callous. And she'd done the same with their professional partnership.

"Key." Cassie held out her hand.

Kendall narrowed her eyes as she took the key from her pocket. "I need to get my stuff first." Thankfully she hadn't had time to unpack.

"I'll help you." Ivy reached out her hand.

Kendall's hand tingled as Ivy took it and led her down the hallway to the room. Kendall handed Ivy the keycard, and she swiped it in the door and opened it.

"Thank you for that." Kendall shook with relief as she held back tears. She'd escaped Cassie's proximity with Ivy's help—*with Ivy's help*. How had that happened?

"I'm sorry. I shouldn't have done that, but I couldn't watch her attack you any longer." Ivy paced to the other side of the room, creating some distance between them. "She seems like a horrible person."

"She is." Kendall was relieved to be out of the situation. "And don't be sorry. I really appreciate you stepping in. It was getting ugly."

"I meant what I said. You can stay with me if you need to. It would get Susan, and my parents, off my back and keep Cassie off yours."

"Why are they on your back?"

Ivy rolled her eyes. "They're always trying to set me up with women they know."

The lightbulb went off in Kendall's head. Now the hard sell when she'd checked in made sense. "So, if we pretend to be together, Susan will leave you alone, and Cassie will get a taste of her own medicine."

Ivy nodded. "My thoughts, exactly."

"Do you think we can pull it off?" After their first meeting, experiencing fallout from Ivy's rigid rules, Kendall had been skeptical about getting to know Ivy at all. But after the time they'd been forced to spend together earlier today, she'd found Ivy to be a wonderful, caring person who was passionate about nature. She now understood the reasons behind the rules.

"I think we can. How hard can it be?" Ivy pulled up the handle on Kendall's bag and rolled it toward the door. "I don't have a whole lot of room at my place. It's only a one-bedroom cabin. One of us will have to take the couch." It was sweet that Ivy hadn't immediately relegated her to it.

"No worries on that. I have a friend who lives in the area that I can stay with." She'd have to take Noah up on his offer after all. Kendall plucked her phone from her back pocket and began to text him. *Cassie showed up. The lodge is overbooked. I need to stay with you after all.*

She waited for a minute for a response before typing more. *Is that okay?*

Bubbles appeared on the screen, and soon a message came through. *Absolutely. Come on.*

"He's fine with it." It might be uncomfortable at first, but she would steer clear of any romantic memories he brought up, and hopefully they would easily cruise back into the friendship comfort she adored. "We'll have to be discreet about it. We don't want everyone knowing I'm not staying with you. That would look suspicious."

"Right…and we'll have to spend time together after work hours and develop a story of how we met previously."

Kendall bit her lip. "Oh, yeah. I didn't think about that. We don't want people thinking this is just a quick hookup." Playing the part of

Ivy's girlfriend might be harder than actually making the contract bid. She'd have to work around it somehow.

"True. Everyone here knows that's not my style." Ivy's cheeks reddened.

That was good to hear. Kendall hadn't slept with anyone she hadn't gotten to know a bit first. She glanced at Ivy, taking in her silent strength paired with her pink cheeks. Actually, a good roll in the hay with Ivy would probably be fun.

Ivy opened the door and waved her forward. "After you, sweetheart."

"Thank you, honey." Maybe it wouldn't be much work after all. It was nice being treated with kindness and respect.

CHAPTER FOURTEEN

Ivy had tingled all over as she'd stepped forward and put her arm around Kendall. She didn't know what had come over her, but she hadn't been able to just stand there and watch Cassie cut her to shreds. She'd been in shitty positions before, not exactly like that one, but similar. Ex-girlfriends could be vicious.

She tried to shake her anxiety as she walked Kendall to her car. "Are you free for dinner?" Her cheeks burned as she continued on this unknown journey. She'd never been good at connecting with women.

"Yes. I am absolutely free." The excitement in Kendall's eyes made Ivy even more nervous. "Why, Ranger Patterson, are you asking me out to dinner?"

"I guess I am. In the name of research, that is. I mean, to get our stories straight." It was best to keep this as professional as possible, but there was nothing professional about how she was feeling.

"Right. Yes, of course." Kendall didn't sound quite so energetic. "We have a lot to talk about."

"Dinner seems to be the appropriate time. Unless you want to do it now." She really needed a little time to get her own feelings in check. This was a ruse. Kendall wasn't really her girlfriend. No matter how exciting it felt to have a smart gorgeous woman by her side, it was all a masquerade.

"No. Dinner is fine. I have to get my things over to my friend, Noah's, and settle in there."

"Noah Cramer?" Ivy was sure there wasn't another Noah in the area.

"Yeah. You know him?"

"He boards my horse. We hang out at the arena sometimes." How crazy was it that they actually knew someone in common.

"Oh. You ride?"

Ivy nodded. "It's easier to get around this terrain on horseback sometimes. Other than on foot, it's the best way when searching for lost hikers. The ability to cover more ground in less time is essential." However, trail access wasn't always easy with a thousand-pound equine. "You?"

"Not so much anymore, but Noah's family had horses and he and I rode a lot together when we were younger."

"We should go for a ride while you're here."

"We should." Kendall's voice rose in excitement. "I'm sure Noah has a gentle old mare I can take out for a bit." Kendall's eyes widened. "That can be our connection. We both know Noah. We can say I came to visit him."

"And maybe he had a party." Ivy finished Kendall's sentence.

"We clicked at the party and spent some time together while I was here. That's how you and I got to know each other." Kendall threw up her hand for a high five.

Ivy slapped Kendall's hand. "Great idea." Excitement bubbled inside. "Pick you up at six?"

"Sounds perfect." Kendall smiled widely.

Ivy grinned, tingling again. She was beginning to wish that she actually had met Kendall at a party a long time before now.

She could see Susan watching her from the lobby doors as she walked back to the lodge. She'd have to figure out something to tell Susan or just bring her in on the secret. She'd be ecstatic that Ivy was involved in some sort of relationship, even if it was fake. She couldn't lie to her. Inevitably, she'd screw up the story, and Susan would call her on it. Plus, Ivy needed Susan's help in keeping up appearances. Someone else had to have some knowledge of the relationship for it to look real.

The door opened, and Susan came speeding out. "I can't believe what I just saw. You and Kendall? Really? How did you keep that from me?"

"Not *really*. She needed help. Her ex is a nightmare, and I felt bad for her."

"But she's staying at your place, right?" Excitement bubbled in Susan's voice.

Ivy shook her head. "She's friends with Noah and is going to stay with him." She glanced around. "But don't tell anyone. She needs her ex to think we're involved."

Susan tugged her down the pathway. "I want to hear every morsal of this whole story."

"Kendall told me that her partner, Cassie, had ended their relationship abruptly a while back, before summer, I think."

"That's good."

"Yeah, but they were professional partners as well, and Cassie recently pulled the same crap with her on that." Ivy kicked a stray rock out of her path.

"But they're both here to present for the landscaping contract?"

Ivy nodded. "Kendall said she wrote up the bid and sent it in. Cassie wasn't interested in it."

"And now she is?"

"Apparently." Ivy shrugged. "I got a dose of Cassie this afternoon when I was showing her around. She's a real piece of work—knows nothing about the park at all and has some weird ideas for the renovations. Thinks they should just tear the lodge down and rebuild."

"Well, we don't need that." Susan stopped and put her hand on her hip. "I know you were a bit miffed at Kendall when she arrived. What's your impression of her now after showing her around?"

Ivy smiled. "She knew all the history of the lodge."

"Really?" Susan's voice rose.

"Yeah. I couldn't believe it." It had been refreshing to talk to someone who actually had done some research about the lodge and the nature surrounding it.

"Changed your opinion about her then, have you?"

Ivy nodded. "I made a snap judgement, and I was wrong about her. Kendall is really very nice."

"And cute." Susan grinned. "And now your pretend girlfriend." She danced around. "I absolutely love this situation."

Ivy laughed. "I knew you would. You have to keep all of this a secret." She drew her eyebrows together. "I mean no one else can know. Not even Charlie."

Susan put her thumb and forefinger to her lips and twisted, locking in the secret. "I promise I won't tell anyone. What are you going to say to your parents?"

Ivy felt the ball drop in her stomach. "I hadn't thought about that." She sighed. "Guess I'll have to tell them the same story as everyone else. You know my mom can't keep a secret to save her life." They'd have to stage a breakup at some point in time, or her mom would be hurt when this was all over and the truth came out.

"True. But if you like Kendall and she likes you, maybe it won't be a lie after all. Could be the beginning of something gloriously romantic. You never know." Susan was always optimistic.

"I wouldn't count on that. She doesn't even live here."

"Where does she live?"

"I have no idea." Ivy rubbed her forehead. "It hasn't come up yet."

"Well, you'd better get on those details, or this is going to blow up really quickly."

"I know. We're having dinner tonight."

"Like a date?" Susan's eyes widened.

Ivy shook her head. "Not a date. A fact-finding mission." Ivy questioned her own judgment in getting herself into this whole mess. Yet, oddly, she was looking forward to visiting with Kendall. She seemed to really love nature and was easy to talk to. If nothing else, it gave her something to do in the evenings.

CHAPTER FIFTEEN

Kendall pulled each thermal shirt and sweatshirt from her bag one by one and tossed them onto the bed. Next, she went through her bottoms. Athletic leggings that she'd brought for hiking, casual jeans, and joggers for relaxing. She unzipped her suit bag and took out the suit and blouse she'd included for the presentation. That wouldn't do either. Why hadn't she thought of packing a couple of nice sweaters or a dress to wear? She wouldn't wear athletic pants or a sweatshirt to dinner for the first time with anyone, let alone a date. At least she'd thrown in a pair of ankle boots that could dress an outfit up or down.

Taylor, her friend Noah's girlfriend, came into the room carrying several items of clothing on hangers. "My pants won't work for you." There was a definite height difference between them. Taylor was a petite five feet, three inches tall, and Kendall was five feet eight. "But I have some nice sweaters you can choose from. I tend to wear larger-sized tops to cover the girls better." She held one of the sweaters to her chest.

"That's so sweet of you." She took the sweaters from Taylor and looked at them one by one. Then she chose a burnt-orange tunic, held it up against herself, and looked in the full-length mirror in the corner of the room. "This one might work."

Taylor nodded. "The color brings out the brown in your eyes."

She glanced at her own eyes in the mirror. It definitely brought out the chestnut flecks in the brown. "This one it is." She handed the others back to Taylor. "Thank you so much for this. I should've planned better."

"Who knew you'd have an instant girlfriend?"

"Right." She'd already confided in Taylor about the ruse. Should she have done that? She wasn't sure, but keeping it from her would put Noah in a bad spot.

"I'll leave these in case you need something else over the weekend." Taylor hung the remaining sweaters in the closet. "Ivy's a nice girl. I like her."

"Do you know her well?"

"I wouldn't say that we're best friends, but we hang out some when she's here grooming her horse."

Kendall sank onto the bed. "Does she date much? I mean, does she have someone I should be aware of lurking in town?"

Taylor laughed and shook her head. "No. As far as I know, she doesn't date at all. Hasn't in quite a while."

"She mentioned something about a waitress at the lodge that Susan keeps setting her up with. What about her?"

"June?" Taylor's voice rose. "She's way too immature for Ivy. I doubt they have anything in common."

An odd sense of relief rushed through Kendall. "Great. Thanks. That's helpful. I didn't want to have any run-ins with jealous lovers." She had enough of that here already.

"She'll probably take you to her favorite Italian restaurant over on 3rd Street. It's been there a long time. You can use that as your first date spot."

"Great idea." She plucked her computer from her bag. "I'll look at their menu online to find some dishes we might have eaten." She glanced up at Taylor. "The more we prep, the more realistic it'll sound when we tell people the magical story of how we met." She grinned. It would have to be a story that even Kendall herself would believe and possibly even wish had actually happened. "What's the name of the restaurant?"

"Enzo's. They have pizza and pasta." Taylor sat on the bed next to her. "I've only been there a few times, but it was really good."

"That's easy." She pulled up the menu from the restaurant on her laptop and scrolled to the main courses. The menu had so many items listed Kendall had no idea what she or Ivy would order. She turned the screen for Taylor to see. "What do you usually have there?"

"My go-to is spaghetti and meatballs."

"What about Ivy?"

"Chicken piccata or linguine Bolognese. If you say she ordered anything else, they'll know you're lying."

Kendall raised her eyebrows. "Every time she eats there?"

Taylor shrugged. "She likes those dishes."

Kendall pulled her lips into a sideways grin. "Nothing wrong with being predictable. Makes it easier for me. I'm partial to shrimp scampi, along with a house salad and garlic bread." Her stomach growled as she set the laptop aside and stood. "Now I'm hungry for Italian food. I hope that's what she has planned."

Taylor stood, crossed the room and leaned against the door jamb. "Be careful with Ivy. She's really sweet and, from what I hear, doesn't play games."

"I don't plan to hurt her. This is all just for the weekend. Besides, she's the one who suggested it."

"Nevertheless, she might look tough on the outside, but she's very vulnerable."

"Oh. How do you know that?" How close were they? What was Taylor keeping from her?

"She was here a lot after her last breakup. Rode for hours on end. We talked quite a bit too. The woman took everything she had—squeezed every bit of compassion out of Ivy and then left her broken-hearted. It wasn't pretty."

"I'm sorry to hear that." A knot formed in her throat. "Does the woman still live in the area?"

Taylor shook her head. "Moved out of state, thankfully. Ivy didn't need to be reminded of her in any way."

"I would never do that to her or anyone else," Kendall said sincerely. It made her sad to find out that someone had taken advantage of Ivy and broken her heart.

Taylor gave her a wary look. "I'll take you at your word." She turned and left the room.

Why wouldn't she take her at her word? Kendall had never treated a woman badly and resented the fact that Taylor might even think she would. She had to face the fact that her tenuous relationship with Taylor would probably never change. She checked the time on her phone, already five thirty. She needed to finish getting ready. Ivy would be here soon.

Kendall's ankle boots clicked as she paced the rail-framed porch while waiting for Ivy to arrive. She hadn't expected to be so nervous tonight. The information Taylor had provided earlier had been unsettling and made her angry that anyone would treat Ivy badly. She pulled at the hem of the burnt-orange tunic sweater she'd chosen from Taylor's offering, hoping it covered her butt enough. Even though it was larger than the rest, it was still shorter than she preferred. The athletic leggings she'd brought were very form-fitting and outlined her shape more than she'd expected. It had taken her much longer than necessary to get ready. Thankfully Taylor had come to her rescue. There it was again…that feeling about Ivy. This wasn't a date, but she couldn't help thinking it was…hoping it was.

Noah whistled as he stepped out onto the porch, breaking through her thoughts. "That outfit oughta make anyone think you're dating."

"Thanks. You don't look so bad yourself." The deputy uniform fit him well.

"Women love a man in uniform." He winked. "You nervous?"

"A little." She nodded. "I just want to make sure we're believable as a couple." Kendall had filled Noah in on the whole room debacle when she got there this afternoon. He and Taylor had been super understanding, which was nice. She'd worried how Taylor would react to her staying with them. Taylor had always been a bit jealous of Kendall's friendship with Noah. Plus, old stories and inside jokes always made the situation worse, and Kendall didn't know how to avoid them or find a way to include Taylor in them. Sometimes she just didn't get their jokes. Most people didn't get them because they were based on their past experiences together. She would make a real effort to keep those to a minimum during this visit. No need to upset her hostess.

Kendall's stomach jumped when she heard the rocks on the driveway crunch and saw the dust trail forming in the distance. Ivy was just about here.

Chapter Sixteen

Ivy let her foot up off the gas, and the truck crawled down the tree-lined drive to Noah and Taylor's ranch house. It wasn't dark yet, but even if it were, she could make the drive with her eyes closed. She'd spent more than enough time here after her last breakup. The back of her neck burned at the memory of that miserable time in her life. She pushed the unwanted reaction aside and focused on her positive feelings for Kendall and the night ahead. Drinks, dinner, and whatever else Kendall might be interested in. She was looking forward to getting to know Kendall, even though she would be here for only a short time. Ivy had put herself in a precarious position and hoped to make the best of their time together.

She spotted Kendall as soon as she cleared the trees. As she drove closer, her stomach bounced at the sight of Kendall dressed in black leggings and an orange top that fell only halfway down her thighs. She took in a deep breath to settle the butterflies in her belly, glad she'd taken time to prepare appropriately for tonight. She'd pulled several shirts from her closet that would've worked for a meet-up with friends but had settled on a dark brown pearl snap that she reserved for special occasions. It went well with her dark blue jeans and ostrich cowboy boots, which she'd recently conditioned and polished.

She pulled up to the front of the house and got out.

Noah met her at the steps. "Good to see you, Ivy."

She nodded. "You too. How's my horse?"

"Good. Figured you'd be by tomorrow to give her a ride as usual."

"I will be." She glanced at Kendall, who was now standing next to him. She looked even prettier close up. Ivy slowly took her in. "You look great."

"Thank you." Kendall smiled widely. "You look pretty great yourself." Kendall stepped down off the porch onto the driveway and then turned back toward Noah. "I shouldn't be late, but don't wait up for me if I am." She glanced back to Ivy. "I think I'm in good hands."

Ivy nodded. "I'll get her home safely." She headed to the passenger side of the truck and opened the door. Kendall followed her and took the hand she offered to help her climb into the 4x4.

"I made a reservation at a nice little Italian place in town. I hope that's okay." It was a cozy place with sections and private rooms. Ivy thought it would be better to not have spectators while they worked out their stories.

"Sounds great. I love Italian."

Then silence filled the cab of the truck, the drive becoming increasingly uncomfortable. "Okay. Let's go over how we met again to make sure we have our story straight," Ivy said to get the conversation moving.

"So, we're telling people that we met through Noah, right?"

"Yes. That's the most believable story. We'll both say you were here for a visit, and we met at some kind of party he had over the weekend."

"What was the party for?"

"I don't know. No special occasion. Just a summer cookout. Maybe I was there riding, and they invited me to stay for dinner."

"Good call. One less detail we have to remember."

"And we started chatting while we were helping in the kitchen."

"I complimented your sweater or something."

"Blouse, not sweater. It was summer."

"Let's just leave that detail out." Ivy searched her mind for something they might have in common and landed on her large collection of books and DVDs at home. "Do you like reading or watching movies?"

"I do." Kendall's eyes widened.

"Then let's say we started talking about movies or books."

"Or both. Maybe about how well some books translate into movie adaptations."

"Exactly." Ivy felt they really did have a connection. "And then we really hit it off talking about our interests when we found we had a lot in common like horseback riding and hiking. It was so natural." *It is natural.*

"Right. Then, after chatting for a bit at the cookout, I asked if you'd like to continue the conversation over dinner later that week." Kendall seemed to know what she wanted, so that seemed plausible.

"Which I happily agreed to. And the rest was history." Kendall smiled, and Ivy's stomach bounced again. "We'll need to remember a few key details, like the day we met and when we had our first date, little things I was wearing or carrying. That will help our story seem authentic if anyone asks any questions later."

"True. Can we go with what we're wearing now, or will that be suspicious?"

"I think we can make it work. We've been out together several times, so we're bound to have repeated outfits. Although I did borrow this tunic from Taylor."

Ivy glanced at Kendall's shirt. It brought out the bourbon tones in her brown eyes. "Not that I know her whole wardrobe, but I don't think I've seen her wear it before." Even if she had, she didn't remember anything ever looking that good on Taylor. "It looks really great on you."

"Thank you," Kendall whispered, her cheeks reddening.

Ivy hadn't intended to embarrass her, but the words had just spilled out. Kendall was a beautiful woman, and Ivy found her very attractive.

"How about you tell me why you got into landscape design?" Ivy asked.

"Mostly to make a difference in my community. I liked the idea that I can have a tangible impact on beautifying my surroundings. Also, it gave me the opportunity to work for myself, which wasn't always great. If work has to be done, and there's no one else to do it, the work falls on me. I've spent a lot of long hours finishing projects."

"I'm sure you have. Otherwise, the state wouldn't have invited you to present." On their walk earlier today, Ivy had seen how passionate Kendall was about her work and about nature.

"The possibilities are endless. Most people can't even imagine how many combinations there are in visual design. Colors, shapes, and textures. Mix and match the elements, and you have a whole new experience."

"I admire your passion. I've always loved and respected nature, even as a kid."

"I never could shake it. Designing nature has always been my dream. I bought my first drafting table when I was in high school, but jobs were scarce for my parents, and I had to help our family survive, so

I took a different path. I went to college, paid for by grants and student loans, and worked part-time in the evenings to help pay the bills."

"That sounds like a whole lot of responsibility for a young woman." Ivy couldn't imagine being put in that position as a teenager.

"I managed. My family needed me." Kendall sighed. "After I graduated, I chose careers I thought would be more stable—first accounting, and then web design. The latter wasn't completely horrible, since I was actually creating something. But most jobs I held left me hating my day-to-day work so much that I struggled through my morning routine, which was filled with status reports and project meetings. I was miserable locked up inside day after day."

That would be miserable for Ivy as well. "What made you decide to change careers?"

"I just couldn't stand it anymore, so I enrolled in classes at night to pursue my passion. It's not nearly as difficult when you're learning about something you love."

Ivy pulled into a spot in front of the restaurant. "Can we continue this inside?"

"Of course. I'd like to hear a little more about you, though." Kendall clicked out of her seat belt.

Ivy rushed around the car and opened the truck door for Kendall. "Allow me." She held out her hand to help her from the truck.

Kendall grinned. "I feel like I'm getting the royal treatment."

"That's what any girlfriend of mine gets." And Kendall deserved it after the story she'd just told her. Ivy took her hand as they walked toward the entrance. "Wait until you taste this food. It's amazing."

CHAPTER SEVENTEEN

A twinge of nerves hit Kendall as Ivy rushed ahead of her to open the door. She could get used to this treatment. Cassie had always been first in their relationship and had never opened a single door. Kendall shook off the negative thoughts, deciding to stay in the moment with Ivy. Perhaps Ivy was a bit nervous as well. The ride to the restaurant had started quieter than Kendall had expected. Thankfully, once conversation began, it flowed easily. It was going to be fun getting to know this side of Ivy.

Kendall took in the cream-colored walls accented with deep burgundy borders. Pictures of the owners and their family members hung in random patterns throughout.

"This is such a cute little restaurant!"

"Yeah, and, like I said, the food is outstanding. They also have an extensive wine list if you're into that."

The hostess appeared quickly. "Hello, Ivy. Follow me. Your table is ready." She glanced between Kendall and Ivy.

"Thank you." Ivy ushered Kendall in front of her to follow the hostess into one of the rooms.

"This is nice and private." A good place to get to know Ivy without others overhearing their conversation.

"Peaceful," Ivy said as she pulled out the chair for Kendall to sit.

"I take it you dine here often?" An obvious question. The hostess knew her by name.

"As a matter of fact, I do. It's one of my favorite places." Ivy didn't touch the menu. "Shall we start with some bruschetta?"

"That sounds perfect. I didn't realize how hungry I was until we started talking about food."

"I'm going to order the chicken piccata. It's excellent here."

"I've never had it but have always wanted to try it," Kendall said.

"No time like the present."

"But I think I'll have the linguine Bolognese." Taylor had told her it was one of Ivy's favorites as well. "It's probably a better choice for a first date than scampi. They put so much garlic in that." She noticed Ivy chewing her lower lip. "I mean in case we have to get close for any reason."

Ivy glanced up momentarily and then quickly down at the table. "Probably so. I think you'll enjoy the Bolognese." She ran her finger across the red and white weave pattern of the tablecloth.

The waitress appeared at the table. "What can I get you two?"

"We're going to start off with the bruschetta." Ivy glanced at the menu. "For dinner, the lady will have the linguine Bolognese and a house salad."

"House Italian dressing?" The waitress asked.

Ivy glanced at Kendall, and she nodded. She kind of liked having someone take all the responsibility for ordering. She had no doubt that Ivy knew how to take care of a woman.

"Yes, and I'll have the chicken piccata with a bowl of the minestrone soup." Ivy handed the menus to the waitress. "We'd also like a bottle of the Chianti Classico."

"Good choice." The waitress turned and headed out of the room.

Kendall waited until the waitress was out of earshot. "Now for the hard part. We have to get to know a lot about each other really fast. Tell me about your mom and dad and how you ended up becoming a park ranger."

"That's a lot." Ivy fiddled with her knife, accidentally clinking it against her spoon.

"Okay. I'll continue." She'd already opened that can of worms. "As I told you, I've pretty much worked since I was sixteen years old. Been contributing to the household income since before that with the babysitting money I earned."

Ivy scrunched her eyebrows together. "What did your parents do for a living?"

"Before they started at the school district, my dad used to be in construction until he got injured, and my mom was a stay-at-home mom and didn't have many marketable skills."

"That's rough." Ivy dropped back into her chair.

"It wasn't easy, but she got a job as a substitute elementary school teacher, and they needed her quite often, so that helped. She went back to school in the evenings while also working days as a sub. Once my mom was working at the school fairly regularly, my dad's back finally healed enough for him to work some light duties, and she convinced him to apply for the daytime custodian position. She was able to have a couple of people she knew put in a good word for my dad, and he got the job."

"Sounds like your mom is pretty resourceful…just like you." Ivy was good at compliments.

The waitress delivered the bottle of wine, opened it, and poured a small amount into Ivy's glass. Ivy pushed it across the table to Kendall, and she took a sip and nodded at the waitress. She filled Ivy's glass and added more to Kendall's.

Kendall stared across the table at Ivy, more nervous than usual. She'd been surprised at her own reaction to the sight of Ivy when she'd gotten out of her truck. Her stomach jumped—still reacting. Kendall sipped her wine before she leaned in and clasped her hands together on the table. "Okay. Now you."

The waitress appeared with the bruschetta just in time to give Ivy a quick reprieve, but Kendall had spilled all the dysfunctionality surrounding her childhood and family, and she expected Ivy to do the same.

Ivy offered Kendall the first piece of bruschetta and then took one for herself. After thoroughly chewing a bite, she set the bread on her plate and wiped her mouth.

"My family is pretty vanilla, I suppose. My dad's retired now. He was a game warden. Also, a stickler for the rules of the parks and nature."

"So that's where it comes from."

Ivy nodded. "I used to ride shotgun with him on the weekends when I didn't have school. But my mom tried to steer me toward other less dangerous office careers."

"She lost that battle, huh?" Kendall chuckled.

"Partially. I'm a ranger, not a warden, so I don't carry a weapon or arrest poachers. But I still get to experience the beauty of nature and all the other perks, good and bad. I'm also studying for my EMT exam so I can be more useful in rescues."

"That sounds difficult."

"Like you said, it isn't hard when you're studying something you're passionate about."

The salad and soup arrived. Kendall's salad was huge, much larger than she could eat alone, if she was planning on eating the rest of her meal as well. She eyed Ivy's soup. "That smells delicious."

Ivy gripped her spoon tightly as she glanced up at Kendall. She bit her bottom lip as she relaxed her hand and set the spoon on the table. "Would you like some?"

"I was hoping you'd say that." Kendall glanced at her salad. "How about we switch halfway through?" She waited for Ivy's response, then added, "My mom and dad share, and I've always seen that as an act of love."

Ivy nodded. "Not to mention the cost savings."

Kendall laughed. "That too." It seemed that Ivy understood some of her childhood after all. "Now tell me more about your family." She reached for the bottle of wine and filled both their glasses. She was going to get more out of Ivy somehow, even if she had to ply her with alcohol to loosen her up and get her to share more.

CHAPTER EIGHTEEN

Ivy wasn't sure how much she should tell Kendall about her family. They really hadn't set any boundaries, but she decided she should probably stick to the mainstream information that anyone around the area might know.

"I've already told you about my dad. My mom used to work at the lodge."

"Oh yeah? What did she do there?"

"Ran the office mostly. Balanced the books and made sure everyone got paid." Ivy spooned a bite of minestrone soup into her mouth.

"You ready to switch?" Kendall pushed her salad to the middle of the table.

Ivy set the spoon beside her plate before she moved the bowl across the table. Sharing food was one thing, but she wasn't ready to share utensils. She pulled the salad plate closer, picked up her fork, jabbed a substantial portion of lettuce, and slid it into her mouth.

"Sounds like she's pretty smart."

She finished chewing. The bite was probably larger than it should have been. "She is. Always helped me with my homework when I was a kid." She set down her fork and picked up her glass of wine. "Dad taught me the outdoorsy stuff, and Mom made sure I could balance my checkbook and stay out of debt."

"Quite the opposite of my family." Kendall scooped some soup into her mouth. "Not that mine is bad, but I would've loved for my parents to be able to support us better."

The conversation stalled momentarily as they stared at each other. Then their food arrived, thankfully—one plate of linguine Bolognese and one of chicken piccata.

"Parmesan?" One of the servers held up a block of cheese and a grater.

They both nodded, and he began grating cheese over each plate. Kendall signaled for him to stop much sooner than Ivy did. She could never have enough cheese on her pasta.

Kendall spun a forkful of pasta, put it into her mouth, and softly moaned as she chewed, then quickly covered her mouth with her fingers. "Sorry, but this is delicious." She spun another forkful and ate it before washing it down with a sip of wine. "I can't believe Noah has never brought me here."

"Don't think he eats much outside of chicken-fried steak and hamburgers." Ivy had been to dinner with him and Taylor a few times, his choices strictly American.

Kendall laughed. "You're right about that. We've only been to the diner when I've visited before."

"They have great meatloaf there as well." Ivy cut a chunk of chicken piccata and put it into her mouth, holding back a similar sound of delight as she enjoyed one of her favorite dishes.

"Is that one of your go-to places as well?" Kendall asked.

Ivy nodded. The last time she'd been there after the movie with June hadn't been good, though, and it wasn't about the pie. "Everything I've ordered there has been good. Closer to homemade than I've had anywhere else."

"I went there for lunch with Noah today."

"Oh yeah? What'd you order?"

"Chicken pot pie, and it was delicious."

"It is. But you have to wait a few minutes to let it cool. If you're super hungry that can be an issue," Ivy said.

"Do you go there for lunch a lot?"

"No. I usually pack my lunch or eat at the lodge restaurant. Sometimes I'm in town and stop there before I get back to the lodge. If I forget to pack a morning snack, I'm usually starving by the time I break for lunch."

"So, you pack your lunch?" Kendall raised her eyebrows. "You're thrifty. That's good to know."

"I am. I don't like to spend money when I don't have to." She was having such a nice time, she'd almost forgotten why they were having dinner together.

"Growing up in my family, being money-conscious was a must. We rarely ate out, and when we did, it was an all-you-can-eat buffet." She looked down at her plate and rearranged some of the noodles. "There were rituals regarding leftovers."

"Rituals?" That was an interesting description. Ivy wondered what exactly she meant.

"My parents snuck containers in and sent us to the buffet to get food to fill them." Kendall glanced up warily. "Eventually we got caught and were banned from a few restaurants."

"I'm sorry you had to do that." Ivy's stomach tightened. She set down her fork and relaxed into her chair, contemplating her next words. "I'm sure your parents were only trying to make sure you had food to eat."

Kendall smiled softly. "I believe they were."

"Nevertheless, that seems like a lot of pressure for a kid."

"It taught me how to support myself—know that the only person I could rely on was me." Kendall kept eye contact. "It's not that hard once you get used to it."

Ivy reached across the table and took Kendall's hand. "That's not always the case, you know." She rubbed her finger across the tendons just below the surface of Kendall's hand. "I'm someone you can rely on."

Kendall slipped her hand loose and placed it in her lap. "For now, at least."

Ivy nodded. "Yeah." She wished she could relieve some of the responsibility that Kendall held inside and the guilt that seemed to go along with it. She pushed her plate forward. "Now, how about some dessert?"

"I hear they have really good tiramisu."

"I've heard that."

"You've never had it?" Kendall raised her eyebrows as if she'd just told her she saw a UFO.

"No. I usually stick with the raspberry jam bomboloni."

"Doughnut holes. They sound good. Do you want to share an order?"

"Sure." Ivy could pound the whole serving down herself, but refusing Kendall's request to share would be rude and might put her back a step in getting to know her." Ivy wasn't a fixer of souls, but something about Kendall made her want to help.

CHAPTER NINETEEN

Since they really had only scratched the surface in getting to know each other, after dinner Ivy drove them to her cabin. They both felt it was a good idea for Kendall to get to know how and where Ivy lived. Considering the size and complexity of the project, there would most likely be follow-up interviews after this weekend. They would need to keep up appearances if Kendall made it through the initial round.

"Welcome home, honey." Ivy pushed open the door and allowed Kendall to enter.

"You don't want to carry me inside?" Kendall asked with a laugh.

"Only when you're drunk." Ivy winked, which sent a rumble deep into Kendall's belly. It was good to see that Ivy could be playful and loosen up a bit.

Kendall was surprised at how minimalistic the cabin was. It contained a kitchen with the standard appliances—refrigerator, oven, stove, and microwave. All black finish, rather than stainless steel. The counters were clean except for a coffeemaker and a toaster. She also spotted an air fryer shoved back into a corner like it might not be used much. Kendall had the same one at home that she used practically every day.

Ivy's place wasn't too small, but it was definitely a limited space. Not a lot of furniture and not a lot of anything else. Kendall noticed the shelf loaded with books and DVDs and walked directly to it. There were many titles she loved and some she hadn't seen or read yet. This could be a good start to finding common interests, especially since they'd discussed that would be one of the intriguing points they would use in their story for when they met.

"Looks like you have a great collection here." She plucked a newish fantasy adventure movie from the shelf and read the blurb.

"When it's too hot or cold, I like to settle in on my days off and have movie marathons."

"Ooh." Kendall nodded. "I do that too." She put the DVD back and slid a book from the shelf. "What about reading?"

"I do that to settle my mind. It keeps me focused more than watching a movie does." Ivy took a poker from the set on the fireplace hearth.

"I've never thought about it, but I think it works that way for me too. I end up playing games or checking social media when I'm watching something." *Too much multitasking for sure.*

"Then you miss some of the movie." Ivy leaned into the fireplace and opened the damper.

"You're probably right. You'll fill me in though, right?"

"Maybe." Ivy grinned as she scrunched some old newspaper and placed it between the already stacked logs in the fireplace. She was getting to be a flirt.

Kendall slid the book back into its slot on the shelf and spun around. "So, what should I call you?" Kendall didn't know if she didn't like certain pet names or ones that had been used in a previous relationship.

"I usually go by Ivy." She pulled her eyebrows together.

Kendall let out a short laugh. "Right. I mean an intimate name like honey, dear, or baby."

"Oh. I hadn't thought about that." She tilted her head. "What feels natural to you?" She took a match from the hearth, swiped it against the surrounding stone, and lit several edges of the paper, then tossed it into the fire.

"Honey?" It was simple and sweet. Kendall took in a breath as the cabin began to smell of pine and wood smoke from the small fire now crackling in the stone fireplace.

Ivy nodded. "That's okay with me. What should I call you?"

"I'm good with any or all of the above." She didn't have a preference because Cassie had never used any of them. That should've been her first clue that their relationship wasn't going to work out.

"I'm good with 'honey' as well, but we shouldn't overdo it. That would look unrealistic."

"Agreed." Too much was a sure sign something was going on, especially since they'd just made their relationship public.

"No kissing or touching of any kind unless it's for show." Seemed Ivy had already been thinking about the ground rules.

"And then nothing unnecessarily showy. I've never been one to do much kissing in public when people are watching, and never during dinner or conversations with other people."

"Got it." That seemed reasonable. Kendall wasn't much for public displays either.

"Maybe we should create a contract." Ivy leaned forward and put her palms on her knees as if she might launch off the couch. Clearly, she'd been thinking about this subject a lot.

"Okay. We can do that, if that's what you want." It would be good to have something in writing in case some of the lines became blurred.

Ivy stood, walked to her bedroom, and came back out with a yellow pad and pen. "I kind of started writing one earlier before I picked you up." She handed it to Kendall. "I don't want to do anything that might make you feel uncomfortable."

"That's sweet of you. I don't want you to feel uncomfortable either." Kendall glanced at the list, which contained several items but wasn't too extensive. "I'd like to try to keep it fun. You know, we can lay out the groundwork and then make it kind of a game where we get to know each other more as we play our respective roles. That would be fun."

"We can quiz each other on what we learned each day at dinner."

"You want to go out to dinner with me every night while I'm here?"

"Wouldn't we do that if this were real?"

"Yeah. I guess you're right. When I'm in love, I can't get enough of my person."

"Same." Ivy smiled. "It hasn't happened all that often, but I know the feeling."

Kendall hadn't expected to hear that from Ivy. She seemed so cool and composed, even aloof. A chill ran up her spine. Now she had Kendall wondering what it would be like to have Ivy so into her that she couldn't stay away.

"Maybe not go out every night." Kendall shook off the tingle. "Sunday night I might have to work on reviewing my presentation."

"Right." Ivy nodded. "When is your last day here?"

"I present Monday afternoon and had planned to leave Tuesday morning."

"We're going to have to figure out a plan for you to arrive here in the evenings and then somehow get over to Noah and Taylor's place."

"We could go horseback riding after work. That would make sense."

"True. But if we end up here instead, there's a shortcut off the main road that will take you to Noah's. It's very steep and dark at night, though, so I might have to deliver you. I mean, just to make sure you make it home safely." Ivy's cheeks reddened. "You're welcome to stay here once in a while…and when you come back for the next round as well."

"You have a lot of faith in me. I might not make the cut."

"I've seen your passion for nature and have no doubt you will." Ivy's cheeks reddened even more.

Ivy's insecurities were making her cuter by the minute. Time to get back to business. "What about social media?"

"I don't have any."

"None?" Kendall widened her eyes. "Not even Facebook?"

"Nope," Ivy said matter-of-factly. "I'm a pretty private person."

"Well, that could be a bit of a problem because I have several accounts. I use Instagram mostly, but all my posts automatically appear on Facebook too." Kendall started writing notes on the pad. "I'll run anything by you before I post."

"I'd appreciate that. I really don't want my personal life plastered all over the internet, real or fake." Ivy chewed her bottom lip. "Especially since my folks aren't aware that you even exist yet."

"I understand. We'll ease into it." Kendall added a note. "We'll also need to text or call each other a lot. Just like if we were in a relationship. You know, keep each other updated on how our days are going. That will make it look and feel more authentic." Kendall noticed that Ivy had put a lot of things not to do on her list, but not many things they should do. Someone in Ivy's past had indeed hurt her badly. Kendall would need to know at least the high-level story to keep things real, but only time would tell whether Ivy would let her in on the deepest parts of her past.

She stood and wandered into the kitchen, which was spotless. "Do you like to cook?"

Ivy nodded as she followed her. "Yes. Just don't get to do it much anymore. Cooking for one isn't all that much fun."

"Maybe we can cook together?" Another thing they had in common. "Are you a recipe follower or a pinch-and-dash kind of girl?"

"Recipes are created to be followed." Ivy seemed to do everything by the book.

"Definitely for baking, but general food recipes can be modified for the better sometimes." She bumped Ivy's arm. "You know, adding a little onion and garlic or removing a little cumin and pepper flakes can make the same dish taste vastly different."

"I've never thought about it that way. You'll have to show me that trick sometime." Ivy leaned against the counter in a position that affected Kendall way more that it should've. Ivy's sexy, lean body paired with her sly, cockeyed smile made a tingle roll from Kendall's belly to the back of her neck. Ivy was cute, sure, but tonight she was looking so much sexier than Kendall had expected.

CHAPTER TWENTY

Ivy had just sat down at her usual table at the lodge restaurant, the one with the view of the huge beam on the deck—a horrible view, generally reserved for park staff rather than guests. She rubbed the back of her neck. Last night's *date* with Kendall had gone later than she'd expected. Dinner had been exceptional, as always, and the conversation had been interesting. She actually liked Kendall, which she had originally thought might be difficult, considering her actions when they'd first met. Before she realized, it was midnight, and she'd needed to get Kendall back to Noah and Taylor's place.

This morning, she'd walked her favorite point trail to catch the sunrise, which was her usual Sunday ritual. Ivy wasn't necessarily an overly spiritual person, but she did take time to enjoy nature and all its beauty on Sundays. It helped her relax and collect her thoughts.

Sunsets during the week and sunrises on the weekends. Since she was a child, she'd always felt a deep connection with nature. Recognizing that connection gave her a calmness deep within. She supposed that was why it upset her so much when park visitors disrespected the land. Even the wild forces of nature that, at times, ripped through the countryside during spring kept her in awe. Mother Nature could bring beauty and destruction with the same wave of her hand.

Ivy veered her gaze to the room and spotted Kendall entering the restaurant. She hadn't planned to see her this early, expecting her to sleep in this morning. She glanced around the room, plenty of tables available, but she wouldn't expect her to take one of them. She glanced back at Kendall, who was now looking straight at her. No avoiding it now, and she shouldn't, considering they were supposed to be a couple. She held up her hand and waved her over. Not the way she wanted to start her day…filled with lies.

Weaving in and out of tables, Kendall quickly crossed the room. "Good morning." She slipped into the adjacent chair. "I came by your place, thought it might look more realistic if we arrived at breakfast together." Kendall's nose crinkled, forming a line across the bridge.

"I didn't think about that. I thought maybe you wanted to sleep in after last night." Ivy slid her menu in front of Kendall as she spotted the waitress coming their way. Thankfully June didn't always work mornings. "You want coffee or tea?"

"Coffee with cream, please. I drink tea only when I'm sick."

"Gotcha." Ivy made a mental note.

"Well, look at you," the waitress said. "I heard you had company."

Ivy glanced at Kendall and rolled her eyes. Great. Now everyone was going to be in her business.

"Just didn't hear how pretty she is," the waitress said.

She couldn't argue with that. *Time to make it look real.* Ivy smiled and slipped her hand on top of Kendall's. "I guess I should've put out a bulletin."

Kendall's cheeks flushed, which made her chestnut eyes sparkle. "Thank you."

"What can I get you to drink?"

"She'll have coffee with cream and a water." She glanced at Kendall. "You want juice this morning too?"

"Sure."

"Orange juice as well."

The waitress stood there for a minute, waiting to take the rest of their order.

"Give us a minute to look at the menu."

The waitress nodded before she spun around and headed to the kitchen.

"Do you usually get the buffet?" Kendall glanced across the room at the food setup.

Ivy shook her head. "Eggs over easy, bacon, and toast. Otherwise hiking the trails would kill me."

"Sounds good to me. I'm not much of a fan of buffets anymore." She glanced down at her hands. "Considering what I told you about before, the food stealing. It kind of gives me a bad feeling in my gut whenever I think about it now."

"Well, then don't think about it. I promise not to take you to any buffets while you're here. This one is kind of unavoidable, though, and the food is fresher than most. A lot of motorcycle groups stop on the weekends because of the affordable price and variety of food."

The waitress appeared again with orange juice and coffee. "Ready to order?"

Ivy rattled off her usual order, and the waitress looked at Kendall for hers next.

"I'll have the same. Crispy bacon, though, and instead of toast, can I get one small pancake on the side?" She leaned near Ivy and whispered, "I like a little taste of sweet in the morning."

"I'm not enough sweet for you?" Ivy shot back with a grin. She was getting good at this flirting thing.

"Oh, no. You're plenty sweet for me." Kendall quickly kissed her cheek.

Heat rolled through Ivy. She hadn't anticipated the contact and definitely hadn't expected the way it affected her.

"You two are so cute," the waitress said before she spun and headed to the kitchen.

"So, tell me how you got to where you are today in your career," Kendall requested as she leaned forward. "I mean, I know how passionate you are about your job, but not how you got that way."

"I really wasn't all that interested in nature when I was a kid. I loved being outside and all when it wasn't too hot. Running free from morning till night was a thing around here." She frowned. "Kids can't do that nowadays without their parents worrying something might happen to them."

"True. It's a dangerous world out there for such innocence," Kendall said. "So, what changed?"

"It was either go to work with my mom in the office or ride along with my dad in the woods."

"The choice is obvious." Kendall grinned. "I can't see you cooped up in an office all day."

"Right. I would've driven my mom crazy."

"What's your mom like?" Kendall was getting good at rapid-fire questions.

"She's the best mom ever. Always in my corner no matter what. I couldn't wish for anything more in a mom." Ivy smiled widely as warmth filled her. "I'm sure I was a handful when I was a kid. She has lots of stories that prove that, but she never made me feel inadequate or unloved."

"I can't wait to hear some of those stories." Kendall seemed genuinely excited.

"What about your mom? What's she like?"

"She's very loving and supportive too. I only wish we hadn't struggled so much when I was younger. She never let on, but the pressure to provide for us was enormous." Kendall smiled softly. "Especially after my dad injured his back and couldn't work for a while."

"But you said he's working now, right?"

Kendall nodded. "Yes. And thankfully they both have health insurance."

"Glad to hear that. I'm sure it takes a huge weight off your shoulders."

"It does. I didn't realize how much until they finally found permanent jobs."

Ivy's stomach clenched, and she set her napkin on the table. "Will you excuse me for a minute. I need to check on something." Without waiting for an answer, she stood, crossed the room, and exited the restaurant. Needing a minute to settle herself, she stood in front of one of the plate-glass windows in the common room of the lodge and stared out at the valley below. Kendall's childhood story had upset her—left her feeling sad and anxious. She didn't know where she would be today if she'd been in the same situation growing up. She could've ended up living off the grid in the woods fending for herself along with the wildlife. Ivy didn't think of herself as entitled or even spoiled. Getting an education had been a lot of work, but she'd had that opportunity and was thankful for it. Her biology degree had been useful in her job, mostly because she'd emphasized botany so she could become a park ranger. She'd also minored in chemistry to help her understand photosynthesis and respiration in plants in more detail. Nature was fascinating and she loved it, wanted to know all about the plants growing around her. If her parents hadn't afforded her the opportunity to go to college, life could have been very difficult, as it had been for Kendall.

CHAPTER TWENTY-ONE

Kendall waited patiently for Ivy to return as she glanced across the room at the food spread on the main table. She'd lied to Ivy about the buffet. The aromas of bacon, eggs, pancakes, and freshly brewed coffee had drawn her into the lodge's restaurant breakfast room like the melodious tune from mythical sirens. She'd experienced these lavish morning spreads before and was always instantly overwhelmed by the vast array of food options.

She gazed around the space, struggling to take it all in. Some stations were dedicated to eggs, and bowls piled high with fruit glistened under the lights. She spotted strawberries, melon, pineapple, and other tropical treats. And the pastries—oh, the pastries. Trays showcased croissants, Danishes, muffins, scones, and tiny cakes.

If she'd been here with her family, she would've wandered around the entrance until no one was watching, then grabbed a plate to check out the selections. She would've sampled a little bit of everything, piling her plate high with fluffy scrambled eggs, crispy bacon, hash browns, and a freshly baked cinnamon roll, the icing still warm and gooey.

When she had gotten here earlier, she'd searched the room looking for an inconspicuous place to sit and spotted Ivy sitting at a table by the window. She'd immediately wanted to retreat. Ivy wouldn't understand her lust for a good buffet. Instead, she'd remained frozen, staring at the beautiful ranger. Once Ivy had waved her over, she'd purged the buffet from her mind and headed straight to her table.

Ivy's manners were impeccable. She'd stood and pulled out the adjacent chair for Kendall and had delayed ordering breakfast until Kendall had made her selection. But now they were having a simple conversation about their parents, and Ivy's attention seemed to wander.

Then Ivy had stood abruptly and excused herself before she'd rushed through the entrance of the restaurant and taken a turn toward the common room.

Kendall's stomach knotted. Had she made Ivy nervous? She glanced around the restaurant to see if she'd missed something else going on…or maybe she'd said too much.

Ivy appeared at the entrance and quickly crossed the room. "Sorry about that." She slipped into her chair. "I forgot to make sure my schedule was cleared this morning so I can help you find your way around."

The knot in Kendall's stomach loosened. "No worries. I appreciate you taking the time to show me the park."

Their conversation waned, and the bustle of the restaurant provided a gentle backdrop as Ivy and Kendall sat adjacent to each other at the small table. Kendall was pulled from her thoughts as the waitress appeared and delivered their plates, loaded with perfectly cooked eggs, crispy bacon, toast for Ivy, and one lightly browned pancake for Kendall.

Time to get out of your head, Kendall. "I can't believe we've both known Noah for years, and last night was the first time we've actually interacted," Kendall said as she carefully cut into her egg yolk and watched it spread across her plate. "Though I did know he was friendly with everyone around here, I just didn't realize he knew any single women."

"It's not like I wear an additional badge on my uniform that says single." Ivy laughed as she reached for the pepper. "Although that might be helpful."

"Yes. That news would've been helpful a few years ago." *Along with a set-up from Noah.*

Ivy smiled, scooping up a forkful of eggs. "Sorry I didn't text you this morning. I'm usually up and out before sunrise. Sometimes I hit the gym before work. This is actually the first day in ages that I've been this late."

"No apology necessary. That's my fault. I kept you up too late. I had fun last night, though." Kendall smiled as warmth spread through her.

"Me too." Ivy reached for the salt, adding a bit to her eggs.

"What machines do you use at the gym?" Kendall took a bite of bacon and savored it for a moment before chewing and swallowing.

"Pretty much all of them, although the rowing machine is my favorite." Ivy stretched her arms forward and pulled back in a rowing motion.

"Rowing? That explains your strong arms." Kendall gestured with her fork. "I was wondering if you were a rock climber or did something like scale the sides of mountains for fun." Her biceps were perfectly shaped, her form-fitting shirt accentuating them.

"Thanks, I think?" Ivy laughed, flexing playfully. "What about you? Do you work out?"

"I have…" Kendall let the word drag out. It wasn't that she didn't like working out. She just never seemed to find time to do it.

"I haven't made it there recently because I've been studying for my exam, but you're welcome to join me the next time I go," Ivy said as she scooped up another bite of eggs with her fork.

"Or I can just sleep in." She grinned.

A man appeared at the side of the table. "Well, good morning." The man gripped the back of the vacant chair as he spoke. "Do you have a minute this morning to let me pick your brain about the area?"

"Absolutely. Feel free to grab a cup of coffee and have a seat. We're just finishing up some breakfast before heading out." Ivy gestured to the empty chair at the table.

"Does that happen often? People interrupting your breakfast?" Kendall asked as she watched the man walk to the coffee station at the end of the buffet.

"All the time. Can't be shy in this job." Ivy took a bite of toast and washed it down with a sip of coffee. "I enjoy chatting with visitors and answering any questions they might have about the park."

The man returned with his coffee, took a seat, and held out his hand. "Dale Arthur."

"Ivy Patterson." Ivy shook his hand and then motioned to Kendall. "This is Kendall Jackson."

He raised his eyebrows. "Like the wine?" A common revelation when being introduced to new acquaintances.

"No relation, but yes."

Ivy smiled softly at Kendall. "Hmm. I hadn't put that together." She returned her attention to Dale. "Where are you visiting from, Dale?"

"Rolla, Missouri," he said, his deep voice strong.

"Oh, I've been there before. Nice place to visit." Ivy pushed a forkful of eggs toward the toast she was holding in her other hand. "Don't they have a big carnival over the Fourth of July holiday?"

He smiled widely. "We do. The Lions Club puts it on. I help out with that a lot." He relaxed in his chair and crossed his legs. "You should come next year. We have the usual rides, games, and fireworks, but we added a drone show this past summer since it was our 90th annual carnival."

"Ooh, that sounds like fun. We should go," Kendall said, bouncing in her chair a bit.

"Putting it on the list." Ivy circled her finger in the air. She was getting good at playing along. "So, Dale. Planning to take in the sights or go for a hike today?" she asked.

"Yes. I'm looking for some beginner trails to take my grandkids walking."

"We've got maps in the discovery station in the lobby. I can mark some recommendations based on your interests. The waterfalls are really flowing strongly this time of year if you want some beautiful scenery. And bird and wildlife sightings have been excellent recently too."

"Perfect. That would be super." Dale tapped the table with his finger. "Let me ask you this. When we arrived, I saw that some of the landscape had been dug up. What's going on there?"

"We're having it redesigned. In fact," Ivy pointed her fork at Kendall, "Kendall is one of the people bidding the job."

"Oh, really?" His eyebrows flew up. "I've been wanting to plant some additional shrubs and flowers around my place back home. Can you give me some ideas of low-maintenance plants that grow well around here?"

"Missouri has similar temperatures but is a bit more humid during the summer. Do you get heavy snow there?" Kendall asked.

"Occasionally, but we don't really get harsh winters like they do up North."

"I think you can get by with some boxwood and holly bushes, along with some hosta plants. They handle mild winters well. If it gets too cold you can add some mulch or hay to insulate them."

"Great idea." Dale took a swig of coffee before he stood. "Well, I'll let you finish your breakfast. Will you be around the lobby later to show me those spots on the map?"

"I will. Give me about thirty minutes to finish my breakfast, and I'll meet you in the common room at the front of the lodge."

"Thanks." Dale dipped his chin. "Nice meeting you, Kendall."

"Nice to meet you as well," Kendall said with a smile. "I'm so impressed that you invite all these people into your life," she whispered as Dale walked away.

Ivy pushed the last of her eggs around on her plate. "Actually, everyone who visits the lodge invites me into their lives in one way or another. Some more than others." Ivy relaxed into her chair and scanned the room again.

Kendall noted as she watched her that they both had laughed, and the conversation flowed easily as the morning sun climbed higher outside the window. Their coffee cups were refilled, and the remains of their breakfast had grown cold on their plates as they'd enjoyed each other's company. This situation was becoming easier than she'd anticipated. Maybe too easy.

Ivy's family didn't seem much different from her own, except for the financial aspect. It was, however, much different than Cassie's family. She recalled that the similarities between them had been sparse, which had been an issue from the start. Kendall came from a family of four, whom she'd helped support since as far back as she could remember. Cassie had come from an upper-middle-class family, and although Kendall wouldn't describe them as wealthy, she hadn't had to work during high school, and her parents had paid for her college education. Kendall hadn't benefited from that luxury.

"How was it growing up with a park warden for a father?" Kendall honestly wanted to know about that experience, especially how it had shaped Ivy into the rigid rule follower she seemed to be.

Ivy pushed her chair back. "Let's get Dale his maps, and then we can talk as we walk some of the trails."

Kendall still hadn't found out as much about Ivy as she'd wanted to, but she supposed that would come with time…and she wanted more time with her.

Chapter Twenty-two

They got Dale situated with his trail maps and destinations for the day and headed out the front entrance of the lodge.

"Give me a sec. I need to get my backpack." Kendall sprinted to her car.

"We probably won't go that far from the lodge." Ivy had no idea what Kendall was bringing, but provisions wouldn't be necessary on the nearby area she planned to show her.

"These are for my assessment. I'll need to create some additional detailed design plans."

"Oh, yeah." Ivy had almost forgotten Kendall's initial reason for being here. "What do you have in there?"

Kendall unzipped the backpack and reached inside. "A tape measure, soil-sample containers, my phone for pictures, and a notebook and pencil," she said as she pulled out each item and then dropped them all back inside except for the notebook and pencil.

"Hm. I didn't realize it was so complicated." Each time she spoke to Kendall, she gained more respect for her knowledge.

"It really isn't. I just have to consider a lot of factors," she said matter-of-factly.

"Well, don't stop there. I'm intrigued." She knew a lot about nature but not how to manipulate it.

"Things like light patterns, along with existing features like drainage and utilities, can affect whatever tools and resources we decide to use." Kendall walked to the retaining wall lining the trail and strummed her fingers across it. "Like this. Have you ever seen any sign of water seeping out?"

Ivy thought for a minute but couldn't recall ever seeing any issues like that. "No. It seems to hold pretty well during all kinds of weather."

"Good." She jotted something down. "Then we don't need to do anything with it."

"That's good news. It's been here for a while."

"I can see that. It has character that we can build on." Kendall seemed to see the beauty in the structure.

"So, how do you actually do what you do?" Ivy was curious about Kendall's process.

"You mean, like how do I figure out what needs to be done here?"

Ivy nodded. "Yeah. I know a lot about nature, but I wouldn't have a clue where to start changing it."

"Well, first I do this." Kendall motioned between them with her hands. "Walk around with someone knowledgeable, take notes, and let my imagination work. You know, develop mental ideas of what improvements would make the lodge more attractive."

"You must have some wild imagination."

Kendall smiled. "Actually, I do. I can close my eyes and move structures around and change the landscaping by removing or adding trees and plants."

"Sounds like you have quite a gift."

Kendall nodded. "I've been able to do it since I was a kid."

"So, what do you do next?" Ivy moved farther down the pathway.

"Then I develop scaled drawings that show proposed layouts for plants, hardscaping, and other elements." Kendall followed her closely. "Next comes plant selection and placement, which require deep knowledge of local climate, plant characteristics, growth patterns, and maintenance needs."

"That's why you need me?"

"Partly." Kendall grinned. "You're also very good company."

Ivy's cheeks heated. "I enjoy your company too." Ivy glanced at the lodge and saw they had an audience. June, the woman who'd been chasing her, was watching them through the windows. She must have come in early to prepare for the lunch shift. "Do you mind if I hold your hand?" She tipped her head toward the lodge.

Warmth rushed through Ivy as Kendall slipped her hand into hers and laced their fingers together.

"Not at all." Kendall glanced that way. "Who's that?"

"Just someone who wants something I don't." Ivy needed to use this situation to her advantage. "So, what's next?"

"I don't know." Kendall raised her eyebrows as she turned to face her. "Should we kiss?"

"I meant what's next in your process." Ivy could see the disappointment in Kendall's eyes. "But maybe a short kiss would send a good message." She leaned forward, closed her eyes, and waited for Kendall's lips to meet hers. The anticipation was sending wild sensations to her belly, which she hadn't felt in a very long time. Her expectations were met with soft, slightly wet lips crushing lightly with hers. She snaked her arms around Kendall and drew her closer. When their bodies met the heat was unreal. Every single one of her nerve endings fired. She could feel every part of Kendall in the deepest, most sensual, way as they came together in the embrace. This light kiss was much more than she'd expected. This woman was much more than she'd expected. She broke away. "That should do it."

Kendall touched her lips with her fingertips. "Yeah. That was… uh…something." She cleared her throat. "That should do it." She turned and pulled Ivy farther down the pathway.

They walked for a few minutes in silence, Ivy a bit stunned and unsure what to say next. Should she comment on the kiss or just move forward with landscape questions?

Kendall made the choice for her. "So, next, I consider factors like blooming seasons, maturity sizes, water requirements, and how different species work together aesthetically and ecologically." Not making eye contact, she jotted down a couple more notes.

"What about the structure and concrete?" Their comfort level had changed, which was a relief. It was time to stick to business.

"Hardscape design, including paths, patios, and retaining walls." Kendall pointed her pen toward the concrete pathway below them and then at the lodge area. "In addition to water features, outdoor living spaces require understanding of construction materials and techniques, local building codes, and how to integrate built elements naturally into the landscape."

Ivy's respect for Kendall was rising rapidly. She truly hadn't realized all the education and creativity that went into what she did. Though skeptical when Kendall arrived, now she felt completely comfortable with her getting the bid award to make the lodge area more beautiful. That wasn't just about the amazing kiss they'd just shared.

CHAPTER TWENTY-THREE

As they walked farther down the trail, Ivy seemed to become quieter than usual. Was Ivy overthinking the kiss they shared? It was just for show, wasn't it? That mind-blowing, toe-curling kiss? Kendall's belly tingled. It wasn't a kiss she was going to forget anytime soon. "Whatcha thinkin' about?"

"What went wrong between you and Cassie?"

Not the subject Kendall was expecting. The tingle in her stomach quickly turned into a knot. "I'm not really sure. I keep trying to figure out where I messed up. I know that sounds clichéd, but I did everything I could to please her, and it was never the right thing." At least she thought she had. It was clear now that she'd been in some sort of delusional state during the whole relationship.

"Are you still trying to figure it out?" Ivy asked quietly.

Kendall shook her head. "No. I realize now that it wasn't me. It was all about her not caring about anyone but herself. Sometimes I think maybe her confidence attracted me in the first place, but she was a complete narcissist. I have no idea how I ever stayed involved with her. I'll never go back."

"Why is that?"

"Cassie was cheating on me. She'd moved on from the relationship long before I had any idea of what was going on. She broke up with me through text while I was on a weekend trip with my mom. By the time I got home she'd moved out of the apartment. And she ended our professional partnership just as abruptly. I caught her moving out of the office without my knowledge."

"I'm so sorry that happened to you," Ivy said sincerely.

"Thanks, but don't be. The delivery sucked, but it needed to happen. The spark between us had died long ago, and no matter how hard I tried, I couldn't figure out how to rekindle it."

"Still." Ivy shook her head. "She doesn't sound like a very nice person."

"She was blunt, to the point, and very callous. Still is." Cassie had perfected the art of the blindside in work and play. "She didn't always seem that way. She put up a very good front. Otherwise, I wouldn't have fallen in love with her." Kendall sighed. "She's just so beautiful and can be very charming when she wants to be." Kendall had always been awed by Cassie's beauty. That illusion had never faded for her.

"Pretty wrapping doesn't always make the best gift," Ivy said matter-of-factly.

"Yeah. I found that out. When I hear her talk now, I have to remind myself how horrible she can be."

"She can be very charming. I saw that when she tried to sweet-talk me after the parking incident. Didn't work, though."

Kendall nodded. "She can turn disingenuous quickly." Kendall hadn't admitted it to herself at the time, but she'd gradually been falling out of love with Cassie as well. When she'd first been attracted to her, it had been instant, surreal even, but Kendall held back. She'd been hurt before and couldn't fathom why someone so attractive would be interested in her. Cassie had romanced and pursued her without bounds, and Kendall was eventually swept up in the passion swirling between them. It was overwhelming, so much so that Kendall thought it would never fade, and she would be with Cassie forever.

The last time she'd made love with Cassie, it had just seemed so right. Kendall had cooked a wonderful dinner—vegetable pasta, one of Cassie's favorites. They'd eaten, drunk wine, laughed, and then tumbled into bed, making passionate love. She shook the vision from her head. Everything had been perfect. Then, a few days later, during that next weekend, she'd received a text from Cassie letting her know that she'd left, totally moved out, and that she didn't want to be with her anymore. She'd had it planned all along and had made love to her anyway. Who did something like that?

"Maybe we should get back to the lodge," Kendall said. "I need to look over my notes and start making adjustments to my plans."

"All right," Ivy said. "I'd love to see what you come up with over dinner."

"I'd love to have your input. You know much more about the lodge than I can gather in only a few hours." She needed Ivy's insights in order to gain any type of edge over her competitors.

"I'm happy to help." Ivy swept her arm in front of her. "After you."

Conversation was sparse as they walked, but Kendall didn't find the silence awkward any longer. It was just a lull between two friends enjoying each other's company.

Ivy left Kendall back in the lobby. They'd enjoyed a nice morning walk on several of the most common trails, and she could have honestly spent all day with her, but she had work to do. She smiled to herself. And dinner was going to be a regular thing with Ivy when Kendall was there. Not a bad way to end her day at all.

CHAPTER TWENTY-FOUR

Ivy's dad cleared his throat awkwardly. "So, who was that I saw you with earlier?"

Ivy looked up from her phone. "At breakfast? That was Kendall. She's bidding the lodge-renovation contract."

"Not at breakfast." He dug his hands into his pockets. "Outside in front of the lodge after that."

Ivy's cheeks warmed. "Oh. You saw that?" She hadn't expected him to be at the lodge this morning.

He nodded. "It was hard to miss through the plate-glass windows in the common area of the lodge. Everyone in the room was watching, including Susan and that little waitress who's been after you to take her out."

Ivy sighed. "That was Kendall as well." She rubbed the back of her neck. "We met a while back and have been kind of dating long distance. I was going to tell you and Mom about her soon. I just haven't had the chance."

"How soon is soon? Because from what I saw, things seem pretty serious. And if someone else tells your mom, she's going to be upset."

"She just got here yesterday, Dad. She was planning to stay at the lodge, but there was a mix-up with the booking, so now she's staying with me." She hated lying to her dad.

"How did you two meet?" He wouldn't stop with the questions until he was satisfied.

"She's friends with Noah and Taylor. You know them. They own the place where I board my horse." Thank God they had a mutual acquaintance, or the story would be hard to believe.

"Right. I remember them. Noah's a good deputy."

Ivy nodded. "Well, they had a cookout when she was here during the summer, and we just kind of hit it off." That was absolutely possible.

He pulled his bushy eyebrows together. "Have you run a background check? Asked about her credit score? Family medical history?"

Ivy rolled her eyes "Dad. I'm not going to do that."

He held his hands up in surrender "I'm kidding. Does she make you happy?"

Ivy reached over and squeezed his hand "Really happy. I think you'll like her." That was only a partial lie. She'd found over the past couple of days that spending time with Kendall did make her happy.

"If you like her, I'm sure I will as well." He smiled. "I hear you cancelled for Sunday dinner tonight. I thought it was because you were studying, but now I understand why." He winked as he squeezed her shoulder.

"Yeah. I didn't want to tell Mom over the phone." So she'd chickened out instead.

"Well, once I tell her, she'll expect you two for dinner. Maybe sometime this week?" Her parents didn't keep secrets.

"Absolutely." She gave him a hug. "Thanks, Dad. Just promise me that you won't pull out all my school pictures to show her."

"I won't, but your mom will for sure." He gave her a squeeze before releasing her. "I think I can safely say that your mother and I are looking forward to meeting this girl who makes you so happy."

She watched him walk away and raced to the desk to talk to Susan. "My dad saw me and Kendall outside earlier."

"I know. I was there." Susan raised her eyebrows. "You should've seen the surprise on his face. Never seen such a strong jaw drop so quickly."

Ivy shook her head. "That is not the way I wanted him to find out."

"June saw you too. She was kind of upset," Susan said, wincing.

She dropped her head back. "I have never given her any indication that I was interested in anything more than friendship." She hadn't wanted to hurt June, but she wasn't listening to what she'd been saying, and she'd been saying no for a long time.

"I know that, but a girl can dream, can't she?" Susan rubbed Ivy's back. "I don't think you'll be hearing from her again, though."

She wasn't sad about that at all. "Now my dad's going tell my mom about Kendall. She's probably going to be upset that I didn't let her know sooner."

"Just tell her you weren't sure how it was going to work out until now, being long distance and all."

"You think she'll understand that?"

"No. She's gonna be pissed." Susan grinned. "But it's worth a shot."

Ivy took out her phone and typed in a message to Kendall.

Need to plan dinner with my parents this week. She erased the last part, since Kendall was only here until Tuesday, and replaced it with *Monday. My dad saw us this morning.*

She watched the text bubbles appear on the screen before the message popped up.

I'm in. Just let me know what time.

She hesitated before responding and then typed, *Thank you.* After she hit send, she continued typing. *Want to take a quick horseback ride tonight after work?*

I'd love to. Kendall's response came back quickly. She stared at the message for a minute. It was amazing how those three little words made her feel so good.

Ivy adjusted her grip on the reins as Willow's hooves found their rhythm on the familiar trail. The afternoon sun filtered through the pine canopy, casting shifting patterns of light across the path ahead. Beside her, Kendall swayed naturally with her mount's gait, surprising for someone who'd mentioned just yesterday that she hadn't ridden since she was much younger.

"So you really grew up out here?" Kendall asked, gesturing toward the sprawling wilderness that stretched beyond the marked trail boundaries.

"Not literally in the park," Ivy said with a laugh, "but close enough that I knew every creek and ridge before I could drive." She guided Willow around a fallen branch, automatically scanning the forest floor for signs of recent wildlife activity—a habit that would never leave her. "My dad used to say I was part mountain goat."

Kendall's horse, a gentle bay named Rusty, nickered softly as they approached a small clearing. "I can see why you never left. This place has a way of getting into your bones." She paused, studying the meadow filled with vibrant goldenrod and sunflowers with the keen eye that Ivy was beginning to recognize—the way Kendall could look at a landscape and see not just what was, but what could be. "Speaking of which, I've been thinking about the erosion issues near the visitor center."

Ivy felt that familiar flutter in her chest, the one that appeared whenever Kendall shifted into her professional mode. Only one day into whatever this was between them, and she found herself captivated by the way Kendall's mind worked. "The drainage problems by the parking area?"

"Exactly. Instead of just reinforcing with more concrete, what if we created a series of bioswales? Native grasses and wildflowers that could handle the runoff naturally." Kendall's hands moved as she spoke, painting pictures in the air even while holding the reins. "It would be beautiful and functional. Visitors would hardly realize they're looking at infrastructure."

Ivy considered the idea, her ranger's mind already cataloging potential challenges and benefits. "The maintenance crews would need training on native plant care. And we'd have to ensure it doesn't create new habitat that might attract wildlife too close to the facilities."

"See, this is why I need you not only as my guide but as my reality check," Kendall said, turning in her saddle to meet Ivy's gaze. The movement caused her light hair to catch the dappled sunlight, and Ivy had to remind herself to keep watching the trail. "I get carried away with the vision sometimes and forget about the practical details."

"Your visions usually sound pretty good," Ivy said, thinking of the meditation garden Kendall had mentioned earlier today—an idea that had initially made Ivy skeptical but now could see as becoming one of the park's most beloved quiet spaces. "Besides, that's what partnerships are for, right? Balancing each other."

The word 'partnership' hung in the air between them, carrying weight that went beyond their fake relationship. They'd been dancing around defining their arrangement for only a couple of days, both of them cautious in their own way.

"Is that what we're calling this?" Kendall asked, her tone light but with an undercurrent of something more serious.

Ivy felt Willow respond to the slight tension in her body, the mare's ears flicking back attentively. She relaxed and took a breath, steadying herself. "I would call it a partnership of sorts. Wouldn't you?" She met Kendall's expectant gaze.

Kendall's smile was like sunrise breaking over the ridge. "Good. Because I'm all in on evening trail rides, and not just for site-assessment purposes."

They rode in comfortable silence for a while, the only sounds the rhythmic clip-clop of hooves and the distant call of a hawk circling overhead. Ivy found herself thinking about roots—how some grew shallow and wide, others deep and narrow, but the strongest systems did both. Maybe that was what they were beginning to build here, something that could weather the seasons, adapt to changes, and still reach toward the light.

CHAPTER TWENTY-FIVE

Thanks for meeting me today," Kendall said, extending her hand to the park director, Daniel. "I've been looking forward to discussing the visitor center redesign."

"We appreciate you bidding on this project," Daniel replied, gesturing toward a woman beside him. "This is Elena, our head of visitor services. She'll be one of the people making decisions regarding the project."

Elena smiled warmly. "The visitor center desperately needs an update. It hasn't changed since the 90s, and it doesn't showcase our park's natural features properly." She gestured to the landscape just outside the windows of the lodge common room.

Kendall nodded, pulling out her notebook. "I've been studying the site information for a few weeks now. I'm thinking we could create a more cohesive approach that blends with the surrounding forest while providing better traffic flow for visitors."

"That sounds promising," Daniel said. "Our biggest concern is maintaining access during construction. Considering that this project will most likely start by the beginning of next year and be in full swing in the spring, we expect it to stretch into summer, which is our busiest season."

"I've dealt with similar constraints before," Kendall assured him. "We can work in phases to keep essential areas accessible. What other priorities should I keep in mind?"

Elena leaned forward. "Sustainability is key. We want to use native plants, minimize water usage, and incorporate educational elements about local ecosystems."

"Perfect," Kendall replied, taking notes. That was exactly what she'd been counting on. "I'm thinking of a rain garden near the entrance that captures runoff and showcases native wetland species. We could include interpretive signage explaining how these ecosystems work."

"I love that idea," Elena said. "Our educational programs could incorporate it into their programs as well."

"What about maintenance?" asked a man dressed in a khaki uniform, who had been quietly listening behind them. "My team is stretched thin as it is."

Daniel turned around. "This is Ron, our facilities manager."

"I understand your concern, Ron." Kendall smiled reassuringly. "That's a crucial consideration. I design with low maintenance in mind. Once established, native plants require minimal care, and I can provide a maintenance schedule that works with your team's capacity."

"When could we see some initial concepts?" Daniel asked.

"I already have some preliminary sketches ready. Once you decide on exactly what you want, I can have something more robust ready in a few weeks," Kendall replied. "Then we can refine, based on your feedback, before developing a more detailed design."

"That timeline works for us," Elena said. "We're excited to see your vision for the space."

"I've been admiring Diamond Lodge for years. My family used to take camping vacations here when I was a child. The natural topography here is stunning. I'd love to hear what you're envisioning for the space."

Elena smiled, seeming to appreciate the fact that Kendall valued her opinion. "We want something that showcases our native ecosystem while also being practical. Our visitors often comment that the current entrance feels disconnected from the wilderness they came to experience."

"I see what you mean. The transition is kind of abrupt." Kendall flipped through her sketch book and turned it around for them to see one of her drawings. "What if we create a gradual immersion experience, starting with more manicured landscaping near the building that gradually transitions to wilder plantings that mirror what visitors will see on the trails?"

"That sounds promising. Budget is still a concern though. Maintenance especially." Daniel reiterated Ron's concerns.

"I completely understand. Native plants would actually reduce long-term maintenance costs. Once established, they require minimal irrigation and no fertilizer. I'm thinking of using meadow grasses, brown-eyed Susans, and downy serviceberry shrubs, which are all indigenous to this region."

"Would you incorporate any of our endangered butterfly-habitat plants?" Another woman's voice chimed in from behind her. "The monarch migration route passes right through here." Kendall glanced at the woman's name tag, which read *Emma, Park Ecologist.*

"Absolutely. We could dedicate the south-facing slope to milkweed and other pollinator plants like butterfly bush, goldenrod, and sunflowers. It would serve as both a habitat and an educational opportunity."

"I love that." Emma's voice rose. "Could we integrate some interpretive elements? Perhaps identification markers or a self-guided tour component?"

"You bet. What about a meandering path with stations that highlight different ecological zones?" Kendall flipped her pad to a blank page and sketched quickly. "We could use permeable materials that won't disrupt water flow and include seating areas made from local stone."

"That addresses another need," Daniel said. "Our visitors often look for places to rest and observe. How would this design handle our seasonal flooding issues?"

"I was noticing the drainage patterns earlier. We could implement a series of rain gardens and bioswales here and here." She pointed to a couple of areas on her drawing. "That would slow the water, capture runoff, and prevent erosion while also creating microhabitats."

Emma smiled. "This sounds like it could become a showcase for sustainable park design."

"That's my hope. Would it be possible for us to walk the site together now? I'd like to note any existing plant communities you know of and identify any special features we should preserve or highlight."

"Let's do it," Daniel said. "Emma, you should come along as well. Afterward, we can discuss timeline and phases. As I said before, we'll need to minimize disruption during the peak visitor season."

"Perfect. After I get an idea of what you're envisioning, I'll draft a new proposal that breaks the project into manageable sections with that point in mind. The fall would actually be ideal for initial planting to give roots time to establish before summer heat."

"I also have a site survey with GPS markers that might be helpful for your planning." Daniel opened the door for her, and they went outside. "I'll grab a copy of it when we return."

"That would be invaluable." Kendall glanced over to see Ivy standing not too far from them. "Daniel is going to take me on another tour. Do you want to come along?"

"Oh. Right." Daniel stopped. "You've already been interacting with Ivy."

"Yeah. She's been my main contact throughout the process so far." She smiled.

"Feel free to come along." Daniel waved Ivy toward them.

"No need." Ivy shook her head. "Sounds like she's getting what she needs from you. I've got my walkie-talkie if you need me." Ivy lowered her voice. "I know dinner with my parents isn't what you expected while you're here, but my mom's an excellent cook."

"Great. I'll absolutely look out for wild turkeys," Kendall said, trying to downplay Ivy's whispered tone. The short notice made her nervous, but if they didn't go, it might look suspicious, and she didn't want Ivy's parents to get wind of their arrangement.

"All right. Then, shall we?" Daniel headed out in front of them, leading the way.

As Kendall followed him, she felt a sad ping in her stomach as she gave Ivy a slight wave. She was sure that Daniel and Emma had lots of things to show her, but having Ivy with them would make the walk much more enjoyable. Even if she was just there for support.

CHAPTER TWENTY-SIX

Kendall sat across from Cassie at the picnic table, nervously tapping her pen against the wood plank. She'd avoided Cassie since the scene they'd made in the lodge lobby. She'd seen her when she was walking through the park with the director and the rest of the group. Cassie had caught her off guard, asked her to meet when she was finished. Agreeing was unavoidable, considering her audience. Kendall had contemplated ghosting her and still wasn't sure why she'd actually come. Something about closure, she'd told herself. As if she needed more of that.

"You look good," Cassie said, studying Kendall's face. "Still doing that thing where you pretend everything's perfect?"

Kendall stiffened. "I'm not pretending anything. Life's just better now."

"Right." Cassie nodded slowly. "You know what I was thinking about the other day? That time we drove past that Italian restaurant—Luigi's—and you completely freaked out. You never did tell me why."

Kendall's stomach tightened. "I don't remember that."

"Come on, Ken. You practically had a panic attack. I had to pull over."

"I just don't like Italian food." A total lie. Just the other night, she'd had a wonderful Italian dinner with Ivy.

Cassie leaned forward. "No. It wasn't about the food. It was about that place specifically. And then I remembered something you mentioned once, when you were half-asleep. About your parents ditching you at a restaurant without paying."

"Can we talk about something else?" Kendall's voice was tight.

"That was Luigi's, wasn't it?" Cassie pressed. "You were what—eight? Nine? Your parents told you they were going to the car to get something with your brother, but they never came back."

Kendall looked away, focusing on a spot on the table.

"The waitress found you sitting there alone, waiting. She yelled at you, didn't she? Made you tell her where your parents went, but you didn't know."

"Stop." The word came out sharper than Kendall intended.

"You always talk about your childhood like it was this idyllic time, but it wasn't. Your parents made you do things you didn't want to do all the time. They were awful, Ken."

"You don't know anything about my parents," Kendall said, her voice low. She'd gone to many hours of therapy, talked through her childhood issues with her parents. They'd actually come with her a few times to help resolve her feelings about the situation. Her parents had apologized a lot, and they'd been able to move forward with their lives, but thinking about the situation still made her anxious.

"I know they left you, *their kid*, to take the heat for their dine-and-dash. I know that same waitress ended up calling the police, and you sat in the back of a patrol car while they tried to find your parents."

Kendall's hands were shaking now. "Why are you doing this?"

"Because you can't keep pretending these things didn't happen. You talk about your parents like they were saints."

"They did their best."

Cassie sighed. "Their best? Remember when you told me about that time they forgot to pick you up from school? You waited for three hours in the rain before walking home alone in the dark."

Kendall swallowed hard. "That was one time."

"It wasn't, though. What about your tenth birthday, when they promised you a party but never sent out any invitations? Or the time they left you and your brother alone all night because they were at the casino and lost track of time."

"They had car trouble that night." Kendall narrowed her eyes. "Why do you even care anymore?" Kendall asked, her voice cracking. "We broke up. You don't get to psychoanalyze me."

"I care because you're still pretending none of it happened. Have you told any of it to your new girlfriend?"

Kendall stood abruptly, nearly falling backward over the bench. "I'm not doing this with you. You and I—we're done."

Cassie reached for her hand. “Ken, wait. I’m sorry. I still care about you, and I can’t believe you’ve moved on so quickly with that ranger woman.”

“*You* left me, Cassie. I didn’t have any choice but to move on.” Kendall paused, tears welling in her eyes. “And whether I choose to tell Ivy or not, digging up old memories isn’t helping anyone.”

“Sometimes you need to remember before you can really forget,” Cassie said softly. “Not just push things down where they hurt you in ways you don’t even realize.”

Kendall stood frozen, caught between walking away and sitting back down. Nature buzzed around them, oblivious to the childhood ghosts suddenly filling the space between two people who had once loved each other.

She took a deep breath and let her pulse calm. “Good luck with your interview.” She pulled her hand free and raced across the grounds to her car. She was not going to let Cassie get into her head and ruin this opportunity for her.

Chapter Twenty-seven

The engine of Ivy's truck hummed as her dad's words ran through her head. *Your mother and I are looking forward to meeting this girl who makes you so happy.* There was no way around lying to her parents. They were bad at keeping secrets even when they tried.

"Don't look so worried." Kendall gave her a sideways smile. "I know how to converse with parents. I have two of my own, you know."

"This will be more than conversing. My parents will be suspicious since I haven't talked about you." She passed the curtain of large pine trees concealing the house and pulled into the drive, then killed the engine. It was a modest one-story, ranch-style home with decorative landscaping and a couple of raised garden beds on the south side.

Kendall unfastened her seat belt and turned sideways in her seat. "Do you always discuss your love life with your parents?"

"Not every aspect of it, but they usually know when I'm dating someone." Ivy exited the car, circled the front, and opened Kendall's door for her.

Kendall slid out of the seat, dropping the short distance from the running board to the ground. "So, we stick with the plan and tell them you were unsure of how this would work out since I don't live here." She hopped eagerly toward Ivy, clasping her hands in front of her chest. "And now I'm here, and it's splendid."

"Splendid?" Ivy grinned.

"Yes. Splendid." Kendall took Ivy's hands and interlaced their fingers.

Ivy sucked in a deep breath. "Splendid indeed." She took in the beautiful blond vision in front of her. Dressed in jeans, boots, and a simple brown, cable knit sweater, Kendall glowed. She released one of her hands and led Kendall to the door of her parents' house. The thought of being romantically involved with Kendall was very appealing, even exciting. Not a bad option at all, considering her track record with women. But whether her parents would believe the match was yet to be seen.

The door opened before they reached the porch, Ivy's dad standing in the doorway.

"Move out of the way, Lance, and let them in. It's cold out there." Her mom motioned for them to come inside.

They entered, and everyone seemed to stall in the living room. That was Ivy's cue to begin the big lie. "Mom, Dad, I'd like you to meet someone very special." She held out her hand in front of Kendall. "This is Kendall. We've been dating a few months now, and I wanted you to finally meet her." Her stomach rumbled. She'd never lied to her parents about anything like this before. Sure, she'd stayed out late in high school and fibbed about where she was, but that was harmless stuff. This was such a huge deception.

Kendall held out her hand. "It's nice to meet you Mr. and Mrs. Patterson. I've heard so many wonderful things about you both."

"Please. It's Lance and Karen." Karen took Kendall's hand between both of hers and squeezed it. "It's very nice to meet you too, Kendall. We didn't even know Ivy was seeing someone." She grinned. "She's been keeping you a secret."

Ivy's dad chimed in. "Yes, this is quite a surprise. Glad to see she's found someone that makes her happy, though." He shook her hand. "How did you two meet again?"

"We actually met at a mutual friend's party," Kendall said. "I know Noah Cramer well, and he lives nearby. I was in town visiting for a week, and he had a barbecue. We really hit it off talking about our favorite books and movies."

"I asked her out while she was here, and we've been communicating ever since," Ivy said as she smiled at Kendall. "I care about her a lot." More huge lies. Ivy barely knew Kendall.

"Yes. We clicked immediately, and things have been great since then." She turned to Ivy. "It was such luck that Ivy boards her horse with Noah and his girlfriend Taylor, or we might never have met."

"Well, that is just lovely." Judging by her tone, Ivy's mom wasn't convinced. "We'll have to get to know you better over dinner tonight. I want to hear everything about the girl who stole my daughter's heart."

"Something smells delicious," Kendall said. Ivy could see that she knew how to charm her way into her mother's good graces.

Karen offered Kendall and Ivy drinks before dinner, and they made small talk in the living room about Kendall's job, her family back home, and how she met Ivy.

Soon Karen announced that dinner was ready. They gathered around the dining table, passing around roast chicken, potatoes, and green beans.

"So, Kendall, what are your career goals?" Lance asked before taking a bite from his chicken leg.

"Well." Kendall set her fork down and took a sip from her glass of wine. "I'm hoping to get the bid on the lodge landscape redesign. That will help boost my reputation some. I'd like to expand my landscaping business. I worked with a partner previously, and decisions didn't always move in the direction I preferred."

"Have you ever thought about working for the lodge?"

"Not really. Decisions would still be out of my hands."

"I mean in an oversight capacity. The state is looking for a Director of Ecoplanning."

"I didn't realize the state didn't contract everything out," Kendall said.

"They wouldn't have to if they could find a good candidate to handle it all for them," Lance said as he focused on getting every bit of meat from the bone.

"I think you should apply," Ivy said, even though she knew she had a great chance of getting the restoration contract.

Kendall shook her head slowly. "I'm not sure I'm qualified for a director role."

"It will be a demanding job," Lance said between bites.

"Are you kidding me?" Ivy raised her eyebrows. "You have over ten years of design experience and have completed several large projects. You're absolutely qualified."

"I don't know. Managing an entire team and department seems intimidating."

"Don't you do that in your own business currently?" Karen asked.

"I do, but I contract a lot of the work out. I've found several companies that I like and work with frequently."

"That just proves that you're great at bringing teams together and motivating others. You've already won over some of the staff at the lodge today. You got along really well with everyone, and Daniel said the group you met with was impressed."

"I guess that's true. But what if I don't get the job?"

"I wouldn't have recommended it if I didn't really think you have a strong chance." Ivy smashed a potato and scooped it onto her fork.

"Even if you don't get this one, going through the application process will be great experience in aiming for other director roles," Karen said.

"I'm not sure that's the type of role I'm aiming for." Kendall speared a green bean and bit off the end.

"The interview experience alone would be valuable," Lance said, dropping the picked-clean chicken bone to his plate.

"True. It would give me an idea of what the state is looking for in a director. Maybe I'll apply for it and see what happens."

"That's awesome. I'm happy to help in any way." Ivy was actually excited at the prospect. "Maybe we can practice some interviews or work on your resume. You have an excellent shot at landing this." She was really playing this up, being as supportive as she could to make this whole relationship believable.

"Thanks so much for the encouragement and offer to help, Ivy. I'll start putting my resume together when we get back to your place."

Chapter Twenty-eight

"Thank you so much for dinner. It was delicious," Kendall said, glancing over her shoulder at Ivy's parents standing in the doorway as she and Ivy stepped off the porch and walked to Ivy's truck. She wasn't pretending; dinner *had been* delicious. Kendall had eaten so much roast chicken her stomach was ready to pop. Ivy's mother was a fantastic cook.

She'd felt Karen's skepticism through the evening, though. Lance was in lockstep with her, pelting Kendall with questions about when and where she and Ivy had met. Thank God, Noah lived in the area, and they could use him as common ground. Once they'd gotten all of their questions out of the way, the evening had been quite enjoyable.

Ivy tugged open the passenger door, held out her hand, and waited for Kendall to grasp it as she got in. She'd never been treated with such chivalry, and it felt kind of nice. Ivy slid into the driver's side and fired the engine.

"Where's the current director going?" Kendall asked as she fastened her seat belt.

"She's retiring in a couple of months." Ivy put the truck in gear and backed into a three-point turn to head out of the driveway.

"Really?" Kendall was honestly surprised. "She doesn't look old enough to retire."

"She's going on forty years of service. A lot of people working for the state started young and never leave."

"Forty years." Kendall drew the words out as she spoke. "That's a long time." She didn't know if she could make that kind of commitment. "Why so long?"

"Knowing you're doing something to help the citizens of the state can be very rewarding. I love every minute of seeing families enjoy the lodge area. Especially the kids."

Kendall remained silent for a minute. "I guess that would be fun to experience daily. I do love it when I finish a job and the client is pleased with the transformation I've created." She had to admit that it sounded like her dream job. She'd love being in charge of protecting and managing all that beautiful landscape every day.

"Right, and with your background in landscape design, you'd be perfect. Plus, from what you've told me, you've always loved the outdoors and working with nature, so the opening made me think you'd be the perfect candidate."

"Diamond Mountain is such a beautiful park, with its gorgeous views and hiking trails. A director role at the lodge would be an incredible opportunity. Running a park like that has always been a goal of mine." She just hadn't considered working for the state, which, honestly, should've been obvious. She'd always seen herself running something smaller like a private country club or something similar, if not her own business. "What are they looking for in the candidates?"

"According to the job description, they want someone with at least five years of park-management experience and good leadership abilities. A background in conservation and working with park staff teams is important too."

"I don't have that kind of relevant experience. I've worked with a few city municipalities, but not any park management. Other than that, it does seem like a good fit."

"They're also looking for someone to handle the budgets, staff, and maintenance. All key things that you've done in your business. The job description is usually full of wants, not necessarily what they will accept in experience. You really should apply. You'd be perfect for it." Ivy looked straight ahead at the road. "And you could move closer to Noah and the mountains." She squeezed the steering wheel. "And I'm here too…I mean to help you with anything you need."

Warmth spread through Kendall. It seemed like Ivy was getting comfortable with her—maybe even liked her more than Kendall had expected. "Okay. You've convinced me. This seems like an opportunity I shouldn't pass up. I'm going to work on my resume and application letter tonight. Maybe this could be the next step in my career." She wasn't sure, though. This was an unknown path, one she'd never considered, with all new people. "Wish me luck."

"You don't need luck. You've got skills, but I'll keep my fingers crossed for you." Ivy looked both ways before turning onto the main road. "Part of the hiring committee even knows and respects you already."

Kendall laughed. "I appreciate that, but considering our relationship, fake as it may be, you'd have to recuse yourself when it came time to make a choice."

"I wasn't talking about me. Several of the people you've been interacting with at the lodge will be involved, including Daniel, the director." Ivy smiled. "Plus, I plan to talk you up to everyone else in the meantime." She reached across the console and squeezed Kendall's hand.

Kendall appreciated Ivy's support more than she could convey. Her own family had been supportive in the past, but mostly because they needed the additional money for support.

What if she wasn't ready for that kind of responsibility? She didn't have as much management experience as some of the other candidates probably did. Even though she'd been hiring and managing contractors for a few years, directing an entire department felt like a huge step up. Overseeing so many employees and major projects sounded really stressful. She could barely keep up with her current workload. Saying yes to this role would be biting off more than she could chew. Why was she even worried about this? *They're never going to pick me anyway. I don't have the perfect resume for a director role.* She was sure she hadn't even been working in landscape design that long compared to other applicants. She'd just be wasting her time applying when they'll clearly find someone more qualified.

Her insecurity was kicking her ass big-time. *I'm going to embarrass myself in the interview. What if they ask me some complicated leadership question I don't know how to answer? Or what if I say something stupid without thinking first? That's exactly the kind of mistake that would ruin my chances completely of getting the job or this bid.*

Did she really have what it took to be a leader at this level? Would she be able to handle all the responsibility? Maybe she'd just been lucky so far and fooled Ivy into thinking she was director material. If she got this job, it wouldn't take long for everyone, including Ivy, to realize she was under-qualified and in way over her head. Applying would just be setting herself up for failure and Ivy's disappointment.

Chapter Twenty-nine

They were almost to the house when they saw something flicker on the side of the road—an animal of some kind struggling in the bushes. Ivy pulled onto the shoulder. "Wait here." She clicked on her high beams and took a pair of canvas gloves from the console before she got out of the truck, leaving it running. Just what she needed to top off her night with Kendall. She walked slowly to the area where they'd seen the reflection. There it was, a small raccoon sitting in front of the bushes. She shined her flashlight in the bushes surrounding the area, spotted another flicker, and kneeled to see what it was. Momma raccoon. She must be hurt, or she'd have moved out of sight by now. She stood, and after assessing the area to assure there were no other animals, Ivy went back to the truck.

Kendall rolled down the window. "What is it?"

"Baby raccoon."

"All alone?"

"No. Injured mother is in the bushes. Looks like she might have been hit by a car. I can't tell for sure." That was most likely the case since she didn't run.

"Oh, no. What are you going to do?"

"I'll capture them both and take them to a local rescue shelter." Ivy headed to the back of the truck and took her medium-sized animal crate from the bed. Then she checked the contents to make sure she had something warm to wrap the mother in. The kit would snuggle up next to her.

She tugged on her gloves before she took the small blanket from the crate and set it a short distance from the mother raccoon. She didn't move, which meant she *was* hurt, as Ivy suspected, and probably couldn't escape quickly. She approached the animal slowly, bringing the crate with her. Her best bet was to try to gently herd her inside it. She didn't have a broom or anything similar to move her toward the container, but it didn't look like she'd run. She laid the blanket over her and quickly wrapped up the raccoon, which resisted slightly but seemed resigned to being handled. Ivy moved her into the crate and closed the door, removing the blanket as she did so. Now for the kit. It wouldn't be as difficult to wrangle since its first instinct was to stay with its mother. Ivy captured it and placed it inside the crate as well.

After she closed the door, she shone her flashlight around the area to see if any other kits were nearby. She didn't see any but would come back tomorrow during daylight hours to check. She held the handle of the crate tightly as she walked back to the truck, pulled open the door, and placed the crate between them on the console before she climbed into the driver's seat.

Kendall peered into the crate through the small slats on the side. "Will you take her tonight?"

"Yeah. My friend Shauna is the local vet. She accepts emergencies any time. I'll drop you off first." Ivy slipped off her gloves and fastened her seat belt before she grabbed her phone from her jacket pocket and hit a button. It rang twice before the line connected through the car's audio system. "Hey. I've got an injured momma raccoon and a little raccoon kit for you. Mom was probably hit by a car."

"Is it bad?" Shauna's voice rose in concern.

"I didn't see any lacerations. Maybe a broken leg. She didn't run from me."

"Bring them on. I'm still in the shelter," Shauna said.

"Thanks. Should be there in about fifteen—twenty minutes." She hit the end button and slipped her phone into her pocket.

"Can I come with you?" Kendall asked.

Ivy raised her eyebrows. She hadn't expected that request. "Sure." She smiled as she put the truck into gear. "Shauna doesn't live too far from here. She's also a licensed wildlife rehabilitator."

"Didn't even know there was such a profession."

When they arrived, Ivy put the truck in Park and took the crate with her as she exited before she rounded the front of the car to open the passenger door. Kendall had already pushed open the door and hopped down from the cab. "I would've gotten that for you."

"You have your hands full." Kendall followed her to the house.

Shauna met them at the door and took the crate from Ivy. "I'm glad you found the mother too."

"You taught me well."

"What? What exactly did she teach you?" Kendall seemed curious.

"Sometimes young animals only appear to be alone. An adult is typically nearby watching and will return when a perceived threat moves on."

"Oh. So, we should leave them alone?"

"Yes. And notify me or your local wildlife rescue."

"So, what do you do with them when you find them abandoned?"

"Depending on the age, a raccoon kit needs to be fed three to eight times a day. That works out to about every two to four hours in a twenty-four-hour day. In addition to that, baby wild raccoons can't eliminate on their own when they're small and before their eyes are open, so they need to be gently rubbed in the genital and anal areas to make that happen. It also can't maintain its own body temperature, so it needs to be kept warm." Shauna talked as she assessed the animals. "Thankfully this momma will survive and, even with a broken leg, can care for its baby."

"Wow. That's fascinating."

"Are you new to the area?" Shauna asked as she wrapped the raccoon's leg "I'm pretty familiar with most people around here and haven't seen you around before."

"She's here to bid the lodge beautification project," Ivy said.

Shauna straightened. "Really? Where do you live?"

"A few hours away, in Oklahoma," Kendall replied.

"How long are you in town?"

"Depends on whether I get the bid."

"You staying at the lodge?"

Kendall shook her head. "With Ivy." She moved closer and placed her hand on Ivy's back. "We're kind of involved." She let the fake information spill out easily.

Shauna tilted her head and glanced at Ivy. "Really?"

Ivy hadn't thought about how Shauna would take the news. They'd met long ago and had actually dated at first, but when it didn't work out, they'd become good friends. She hoped Shauna wouldn't take this as some sort of betrayal of their friendship. There was no turning back now. "We've been seeing each other since the summer."

Shauna raised an eyebrow. "I had no idea. You've been keeping secrets from me. Guess we're going to have to schedule a coffee date."

"Just waiting until it became more serious before we made it public." She hoped Shauna would accept that explanation and let it go, but she probably wouldn't.

"Right." Kendall said. "It's been mostly long distance until now."

Kendall rattled off their cover story with the passion of someone who'd actually experienced it. Ivy had to admit it was a fantasy that most people would embrace, but it still made her nervous.

"Hmm," Shauna said as she curved her lips into a smile. "Sounds like a fairy-tale romance." She glanced at Ivy. "I hope it works out for the best."

Ivy nodded as she glanced at Kendall. "Me too."

"So, tell me more about rescuing injured animals." Kendall attempted to change the subject.

Shauna started splinting the raccoon's leg again. "Often, animals may seem to be distressed, but an adult animal will find and care for them. Eventually, when they're released, momma raccoon will teach the kit all the skills it needs to survive in the wild. Forage for food, climb, seek a den, and, most important, avoid predators and humans. Even when baby raccoons are handled a lot when they're young, they become wild quickly as they grow."

"I'm impressed. Sounds like you're doing wonderful things for animals here."

"Thanks. It's not much, but it's what we can accomplish with grants and donations."

"You can apply for grants?" Kendall seemed honestly surprised by that tidbit of information.

Shauna nodded. "Yep. We're waiting for approval on a large one that will be used to enlarge the facility. We've had more intake this year than in the past and have run out of habitat areas."

"I'd love to help out." Kendall glanced around the room. "How can I volunteer?"

"There's a flyer on the front counter with a QR code." Shauna checked to make sure the baby was comfortable with the momma. "Or you can volunteer when you're in town."

"Not sure she'll have time while she's here working on the project bid," Ivy said. She didn't need Shauna getting cozy with Kendall. Even if this wasn't real, that would only complicate things. "You ready?" She glanced at Kendall.

"Yeah." Kendall smiled at Shauna. "If I get the contract, I'll definitely set some time aside to volunteer."

"Sounds great." Shauna smiled widely. "Looking forward to getting know you." She grabbed Ivy by the arm. "You and I need to catch up—soon."

Ivy flattened her lips. "Sure. I'll call you." She'd known that was coming and wasn't looking forward to that conversation. This lie was getting a whole lot bigger than she'd realized.

CHAPTER THIRTY

Kendall watched Ivy as she drove. Earlier, she'd stayed in the car as Ivy had instructed and watched intently as Ivy took what looked like a baby blanket from the crate and gathered the small animal in it before she placed the little one in the crate and closed the door. Then she'd gathered the baby raccoon and put it in with the mother. Kendall was in awe of Ivy. Most people would have driven on by, never giving the animals a second thought, but Ivy hadn't hesitated to save the raccoons.

She could really fall for this woman. In fact, if love at first sight truly existed, she actually was falling. When Ivy parked in front her house, she didn't wait for Ivy to open the door for her again. Instead, she pushed it open and walked quickly to her front door.

"Kendall, wait." Ivy rushed after her. "Are you okay? Did I do something wrong?"

Kendall spun around. "No." She shook her head. "You didn't do anything wrong." *You did everything right.* "I'm just tired. Taking in the awfulness of the raccoon's injury along with the miracle of how Shauna saved her leg was just a lot."

"It can be overwhelming sometimes." Ivy stepped onto the porch. "I know we talked about hanging out after dinner, but I can take you to Noah's if you'd rather go there."

Kendall moved to the door. "No. I want to stay for a while." She let out a sigh, still thinking through the past hour. "What you did tonight—stopping to pick up those raccoons—was wonderful. Most people would've driven right by without noticing them. I probably would've. Stopping to rescue them seemed so easy for you. Like second nature."

"It's part of my job. I've learned how to help animals in distress." Ivy's easy answer made the situation even worse.

"I know. You're just so different than I imagined when we first met." *So much different.*

"Yeah, well, to be honest, when I saw you get out of your car that day, the first thing I thought was, I want to meet her." A blush came over Ivy's face. "The trash was just an opportunity." She reached behind Kendall to unlock the door and open it, and Kendall caught a whiff of her cologne. Sweet and spicy all at once. Just like Ivy.

"So, you reprimanded me?" Kendall laughed, still blocking the doorway as she decided what to do next. "All you had to do was say hello," she said softly as she studied Ivy's lips. A ripple of arousal trickled through her. This was the perfect opportunity to taste them, but Kendall needed to stick to their agreement. No kissing or touching of any kind unless it was for show. She turned and sped inside but stopped at the bathroom door and turned around briefly. "Thank you so much for tonight. The dinner and everything after were wonderful." Ignoring her instinct to take this relationship or whatever it was to the next level, she slipped inside the bathroom and closed the door. She sat down on the toilet but couldn't pee. Closing her eyes, she took in a couple of deep breaths to calm herself. Why was she so turned on by Ivy? Was Ivy turned on as well? She had to be—the darkness that had come over her eyes had given her away. This whole situation should be giving her anxiety, but instead it was exciting her more than any real relationship she'd ever had. This was a whole different secret she had to keep.

When she opened the bathroom door, the scent of popcorn filled the air.

"You want to watch a movie? I picked out one that could be an Academy Award contender."

"Sure. Sounds great." Anything to get her mind off the throbbing between her legs. Otherwise, it was going to be a long night.

"You'll love it. I promise," Ivy said, her eyes bright with enthusiasm as she settled onto one end of the couch, patting the cushion beside her invitingly. It was getting impossible to say no to Ivy when she got excited about something. Kendall wanted to make her happy just to see her excitement, but she had told herself to keep some distance between them or she would never get through this night without kissing her. When she took a seat at the end of the couch, Ivy hadn't protested. She'd simply set the popcorn on the cushion between them. Perhaps she was feeling the discomfort as well.

The glow of the television painted the darkened living room in soft, shifting colors. On the screen, the movie played on, a drama Kendall wasn't familiar with at all. She was fairly tuned in to popular movies but hadn't heard any Oscar buzz about this one. From the start, the slow pace made Kendall skeptical that it would make the cut.

They'd started the evening on opposite ends of the couch, a bowl of popcorn between them, but as the movie progressed and the popcorn disappeared, the distance had gradually lessened. Now, nearly an hour into the film, Kendall's eyelids grew heavy. The dialogue faded into a pleasant murmur as the warmth of Ivy's body next to hers became more immediate than the story unfolding on screen. She blinked slowly, fighting the waves of drowsiness that washed over her.

"Are you even watching?" Ivy whispered, nudging her gently.

"Mmhmm," Kendall mumbled, straightening up momentarily. "The guy just...you know...with the thing..." She had no idea what was happening in the movie, but the cozy warmth between them had disappeared, and Kendall wanted it back.

Ivy rolled her eyes but smiled, returning her attention to the movie. Kendall tucked her legs beneath her, inadvertently shifting closer to Ivy in the process. Warm and soft, this was the perfect spot.

CHAPTER THIRTY-ONE

The glow of the television cast shifting patterns of light across the living room as the film played on, its dialogue now just background noise. Ivy had chosen the movie, some indie drama with beautiful cinematography that had been on her watch list for months, but her attention had shifted entirely to Kendall, whose head had gradually settled onto her shoulder during the past fifteen minutes.

Ivy glanced down, careful not to move too suddenly. Kendall's eyes were closed, lashes casting faint shadows on her cheeks in the dim light. Her breathing had slowed to the steady rhythm of sleep, one hand still loosely clutching the forgotten popcorn bowl balanced precariously on her lap.

Ivy reached over and delicately rescued the bowl, setting it on the side table without disturbing Kendall. The movement caused Kendall to stir slightly, mumbling something unintelligible before shifting position. Instead of waking, Kendall slid her head closer and found a resting place in the crook between Ivy's arm and chest. She stiffened for a moment, surprised at how nice it felt, then relaxed as she heard Kendall's breathing deepen into the steady rhythm of sleep again. Her weight settled against Ivy's side, warm and unguarded.

Ivy glanced down at Kendall's peaceful face, her features softened in slumber, dark lashes resting against her cheeks. She hesitated, then carefully adjusted her position, allowing Kendall's head to slide into a more comfortable spot in the bend of her shoulder. Kendall stirred briefly, murmuring something unintelligible again before settling back into a deep sleep.

Ivy froze, unsure whether to wake her or let her sleep. After a moment's hesitation, she relaxed back into the couch cushions. The soft weight of Kendall's head against her felt comfortable, even natural. With a slight smile and a contented sigh, Ivy tentatively ran her fingers through Kendall's soft, blond hair. Warmth rushed through her when Kendall leaned unconsciously into her touch.

The movie continued, forgotten now as she watched the gentle rise and fall of Kendall's chest. "I knew you wouldn't make it through," she whispered affectionately, her words lost beneath the film's soundtrack.

On the television screen, the movie continued its journey toward some emotional climax that Ivy had lost track of twenty minutes ago. The protagonist was saying something profound about life and love, but Ivy found herself more captivated by the peaceful expression on Kendall's sleeping face.

She lowered the TV volume and ran her hand slowly across the back of the couch, seeking the throw blanket she kept draped there and then carefully spread it over Kendall's shoulders. The rhythmic rise and fall of Kendall's breathing synced with the quiet soundtrack of the film, creating a moment of perfect tranquility in their otherwise chaotic lives.

Outside, rain began to patter against the windows, creating a soothing backdrop to the moment. When the movie ended, she would move Kendall to the bedroom to sleep alone, but for now, she was perfectly content to be her pillow, to share this quiet moment of vulnerability neither of them had planned for but both, perhaps, had secretly wanted.

Ivy rested her head back against the couch, continuing to absentmindedly stroke Kendall's hair. The plot of the movie had been lost, but it could wait for another night. This moment, with the soft lamplight, the forgotten film, and Kendall peacefully asleep next to her, was worth savoring until the credits rolled.

Chapter Thirty-two

Ivy slipped in and out of the bedroom quietly. Kendall was still sound asleep and hadn't stirred as she'd opened the closet and chosen her uniform for the day. She'd taken a moment to watch her sleep and then realized that was kind of creepy. She didn't know what she would've said if Kendall had awoken and found her standing in the room.

Once she got out onto the porch, she stretched her arms above her head. The couch wasn't as comfortable as she remembered. She rarely fell asleep there after she'd bought a new mattress last year. The couch was old and broken-in perfectly for movie watching, and she hadn't thought about replacing it until this morning, when she'd woken up hanging halfway off it.

She couldn't see a dust trail from the road as Susan approached, but she could hear the rocks crunching beneath the tires of her red Toyota RAV4. It had all-wheel drive, which was sometimes needed on the mountain, and it got great gas mileage. It was a cute little SUV, and Susan had been very proud when she'd purchased it not long ago.

Ivy jerked on the handle, but the door was locked. Susan smiled and hit the unlock button on her door.

"Sorry," Susan said as Ivy climbed into the seat.

"Thanks for coming by to get me." She fastened her seat belt.

They were almost to the lodge when Susan spoke. "You're awfully quiet this morning. Something's on your mind."

Ivy glanced over briefly and then back at the road. "Is it that obvious?"

Susan smiled. "We've been friends for a long time. I can read you like a book with extra-large print."

Ivy sighed. "It's Kendall."

Susan reached across and squeezed Ivy's knee. "What about Kendall? Did something happen?"

Ivy shook her head. "No. That's the problem. Nothing's happened, but I really like her. She's beautiful, and fun, and just easy to be around."

"So, I thought you and Kendall agreed to fake this whole relationship thing."

"We did—we are. We were watching a movie, and she fell asleep." Ivy shifted uncomfortably in her seat. "I put her in my bed, and I slept on the couch."

Susan widened her eyes. "That sounds cozy."

"It was. That's the problem. I think I might be falling for her."

"Whoa." Susan dragged out the word. "Since when?"

"I can't pinpoint the exact moment, but last night we had dinner with my folks, and then she went with me to the wildlife rescue."

"She met Shauna?" Susan didn't wait for an answer before pelting her with the next question. "What'd she think about her?"

"Yeah." Ivy sighed. "She convinced her to volunteer while she's here, if she gets the landscaping contract. I hate to say it, but I felt a little jealous."

"Wow." Susan said excitedly. "Who knew it would only take a couple of days to hook you."

"I know, I know. I've been trying to talk myself out of it. This whole relationship is supposed to be fake, and if Kendall gets the contract, she'll kind of be my coworker. We have that no-dating policy at work, and, besides, she just got out of a long relationship with Cassie."

"Is that why you snuck out early and left her your truck to drive?"

"Yes. She fell asleep on me last night. I don't think I could handle being alone in the truck with her this morning. I'm not confident that I wouldn't spill my feelings to her. That would probably scare her off, and we agreed to no touching or kissing unless someone was watching."

"Well, that kiss I witnessed looked like more than something in a contract. Has Kendall given any signs she might feel the same way?"

"Maybe." She shrugged. "I caught her looking at me across the table a couple of times last night, but I'm not very good at reading whether her actions are real or for show." She sighed.

"And after dinner she fixed my coffee exactly how I like it without me asking. I don't even recall telling her how I take it."

"That's something, though."

"Or she just paid attention and was simply being nice. Kendall's nice to everyone."

"Not that nice. I bet she doesn't memorize everyone's coffee order." Susan frowned. "She hasn't brought me any."

"Even if she does feel something, we have an agreement, and I don't think I should break it. Plus, we could be working together."

"Agreements get broken. Policies change. Jobs change. Feelings like you're having don't come around often for you."

"What if I'm misreading everything and make a fool of myself?"

Susan reached for Ivy's hand. "Then at least you'll know. Isn't knowing better than wondering for a week, month, or year?"

Ivy chuckled. "When did you get so wise?"

Susan smiled as she put the SUV in Park. "Around the same time you got so scared of taking chances. This isn't like you, Ivy."

Ivy let out a breath. "You're right. It's not."

Susan turned to Ivy and raised her eyebrows. "So, what are you going to do about it?"

"Talk to her." She rubbed the back of her neck. "I'm not sure when, and it won't be a grand declaration. Just a conversation. See where it leads."

"There's the Ivy I know." Susan slapped her on the leg.

"If this blows up in my face, I'm blaming you."

Susan laughed. "Fair enough. But if it works out, I expect to be your matron of honor." She pushed open her door.

"Let's not get ahead of ourselves." Ivy rolled her eyes as she got out of the SUV. "Now, I need you to get me coffee just the way I like it."

"You picked the wrong girl for that. She's back home snuggled up in your sheets—*alone*."

"Yeah. Don't remind me."

"Oh, and by the way, Daniel said he wants her to come back for another interview with her next week to meet the regional director." Susan grinned. "So you'll get the opportunity to feel this out a little more…maybe even feel her out a little more." She laughed. "And that no-dating policy is really more of a guideline that's been broken multiple times."

The tingle in Ivy's belly returned like a raging tsunami. Ivy had really wanted to crawl into bed with Kendall last night, even if only to hold her close, but she didn't know what Kendall was feeling and certainly didn't want to offend her if she wasn't feeling the same way. Now she'd have the chance to find out.

CHAPTER THIRTY-THREE

The alarm hadn't gone off. That was Kendall's first thought as consciousness crept in, her eyes still closed against the morning light filtering through the partially drawn curtains. Kendall reached out, finding only empty sheets. The bed felt too spacious, too cool on the left side where Ivy's warmth should be. Wait—how did she get into Ivy's bed? The last she remembered they were on the couch. She bolted up and rubbed her eyes. "I fell asleep on Ivy."

She opened her eyes, squinting against the brightness. No impression on the pillow remained—no sign at all that Ivy had slept next to her. Disappointment set in as she remembered the evening. She'd squandered a perfect opportunity by falling asleep, though it was partly Ivy's fault for picking the slowest-paced movie ever.

"Ivy?" she called, her voice still thick with sleep. Nothing but silence answered her.

Kendall pushed herself up, brushing tangled hair from her face. The digital clock on the nightstand read 9:17 a.m.—far later than either of them usually slept. Ivy would have already been up and at work for a couple of hours.

A yellow sticky note clung to Ivy's pillow. Kendall peeled it off, recognizing the neat, precise handwriting immediately.

Emergency at work. Didn't want to wake you. Leftover pizza in fridge if you're hungry. Call you later. - Ivy

Kendall sighed, letting the note drop to her lap. Last night had been wonderful, and she'd hoped they'd be having breakfast together, enjoying the secrecy of their fabricated relationship over coffee and blueberry pancakes—Ivy's specialty, as she recalled from their extensive conversations. She felt like she'd known Ivy for months, yet it had only been a few short days.

She swung her legs over the side of the bed, toes curling against the cool hardwood floor. The cabin felt too quiet, too still. Kendall wrapped herself in Ivy's robe that she found hanging on a hook on the bathroom door. She pressed the collar to her nose, inhaling the faint spicy scent of her cologne still lingering in the fabric.

After heading into the kitchen she found the coffee already made, kept warm in the thermal carafe. A clean mug sat beside it with another sticky note.

Made it strong, just how you like it.

Kendall knew the thoughtfulness should have been enough. But as she poured the coffee, watching the dark liquid swirl in the mug, disappointment settled heavy in her chest.

The same way it always did on mornings like these from her past, when Cassie's side of the bed was empty, and the day stretched ahead without her. Though Ivy was so much more considerate than Cassie ever was.

Kendall carried her coffee to the window, looking out at the yard already buzzing with birds and wild bunnies. She pressed her forehead against the cool glass. How many more mornings would she wake up alone before she found her special someone? Could Ivy possibly be that person?

"I'm glad you called about lunch," Ivy said as she ran her finger across the crease of the napkin in front of her. "Since I didn't get to see you this morning. I mean, getting called in early and all."

"I'm glad you were free. I know you're usually very busy." Kendall fidgeted with her napkin as the server placed their plates on the table. "I got an email from Daniel. They want to talk to me again next week." She glanced at Ivy, who was already reaching for her fork, then at the array of condiment bottles between them—ketchup, mustard, and hot sauce, all nearly full.

"That's awesome. I knew they'd want to see more of your plans. Are you planning to go home for a few days?"

"I think I might just stay, if that's okay with you." It would look weird if she left.

"It's absolutely okay with me." Ivy smiled widely and then hesitated for just a beat. "I mean, to keep up appearances and all." She quickly veered her gaze to her burger. “This looks amazing,” she said, adding lettuce and tomato to her burger. “I’ve been craving this all morning.”

Kendall nodded, glancing down at her Denver omelet, but her attention drifted to the condiments after Ivy used them. After adding a line of ketchup to the top of her hash browns, almost unconsciously, she began rearranging them, grouping them closer to her side of the table.

“So, anyway,” Ivy said, “how’s the presentation coming?”

“Do you think they’d mind if we took these?” Kendall asked, ignoring Ivy’s question and gesturing to the condiment bottles.

Ivy paused mid-bite. “Took what?”

“The condiments.” Kendall tapped the ketchup bottle. “They’re practically full.”

Ivy’s brow furrowed. “You want to steal the ketchup?”

“It’s not stealing,” Kendall said quickly. “I mean, we’re paying for the meal, right? And they just throw these out when they’re almost empty anyway.” She laughed, trying to sound casual. “My parents always had us take them. It’s just practical.”

“I don’t think—”

“When I was little,” Kendall said, “we’d go to diners, and my dad would bring this big purse—well, it was my mom’s, but he carried it—and we’d all help collect the jelly packets and creamers. Once, my brother got an entire bottle of maple syrup into his pocket.” She smiled at the memory. “Mom would ask for extra sauce packets whenever we got takeout too. We had containers on our fridge door full of them.”

Ivy set down her burger. “That’s interesting.”

“It’s just being resourceful. My parents taught us not to waste anything.” She pointed to Ivy’s plate. “Like, see how you left that half of your burger? We never left anything. Mom would say, you either eat it all, or it comes home with us.”

“I’m not done eating.” An awkward silence fell between them as Ivy looked at the condiments, then at Kendall’s face. Her expression softened. “My grandfather used to save the honey butter packets from restaurants,” she said. “He had a whole drawer of them.”

“My parents…” Kendall stopped. Started again. “When I was growing up, we never left anything behind. At restaurants, my parents would take all the sugar packets, ketchup, everything. They grew up poor, and I guess old habits die hard.” She laughed quietly. “They’d make us clean our plates completely. Take home every leftover, even if it was just a spoonful. One time, my dad got into an argument with a waiter who tried to take my plate before I’d finished the last two green beans.”

Kendall looked up, expecting judgment, but found only understanding in Ivy's eyes.

"My grandmother kept every rubber band that came into the house," Ivy said. "She had a drawer full of them. Never bought one in her life, and my mom still washes and reuses Ziplock bags." She picked up the remainder of her burger. "My dad used to turn the heat down so low in winter we could see our breath indoors." She took a bite and wiped her mouth. "I think he still does that."

Something loosened in Kendall's chest. "I've been trying so hard to be normal."

"Normal's overrated," Ivy said as she stood and grabbed a couple of to-go containers from the counter and scooped her remaining fries into one. "And wasteful, apparently."

Later, after they got up from the table with packed to-go containers of leftovers carefully tucked inside a paper bag, Kendall stood, staring at the three condiment bottles lined up on her counter.

"Let me help you with those," Ivy said as she picked them up and set them in the bag. "Just in case Noah and Taylor don't have any." She smiled and motioned Kendall in front of her and followed her into the lobby. "I have to get back to work, but I'm looking forward to hearing more about your parents when we have dinner tonight."

Kendall warmed at the thought. "Me too. I'll have Noah help me bring your truck up later this afternoon." Ivy was turning out to be much more understanding than she expected.

"Don't worry about that. Susan can drop me off," Ivy said as she opened the door for her.

They exited through the front door of the lodge, and after Ivy walked Kendall to her Bronco, she watched Ivy go back into the lodge. Once she was out of sight, Kendall fired up the truck and then said, "Hey, Siri. Call Mom."

"Calling Mom," Siri said, and the phone rang through the speaker.

"Hi, Mom," she said when her mother answered. "Just wanted to say thank you."

"For what, honey?" her mother asked, clearly surprised.

Kendall looked at the bag of leftovers sitting on the seat next to her. "For teaching me that everything has value," she said quietly. "Even the small things. Especially the small things."

CHAPTER THIRTY-FOUR

Ivy set two cups of coffee and a handful of creamer containers on Susan's desk before she dropped into the chair next to it. "You won't believe what happened at lunch today," she said, taking the lid off her coffee.

Susan looked up from her laptop. "What now?"

"So, I had lunch in the restaurant with Kendall, right? The burger was amazing, as usual." She shifted in her seat. "She zoned in on my half-eaten burger and said I shouldn't leave it."

Susan scrunched her eyebrows together. "What was that about? Were you finished?"

"No. I was just taking my time, but then she told me that her parents had this strict rule about never leaving food on their plates. Either they ate everything or took it home. No exceptions."

"Well, that makes sense. Food waste and all that. Kids don't always finish their dinner," Susan said with a shrug as she closed her laptop. "Did she explain it at all?"

She told me it's just what her family always did. And apparently, when they dined out during her childhood, her parents specifically instructed all the kids to take every condiment from the table. Can you imagine?"

Susan's eyebrows rose. "What, like they were stocking their home kitchen?" She opened a couple of creamer containers and poured them into her cup.

"Exactly. And she said when they'd get takeout, they'd specifically ask for extra packaged condiments too. Like, deliberately collecting them."

"I mean, I get taking the occasional extra ketchup packet, but not much else." Susan stirred her coffee slowly, watching the cream swirl into caramel spirals. "Otherwise, it gets put in a drawer, and I end up throwing it out anyway."

"Combined with everything else? It seems like her parents were really intense about getting their money's worth."

"Maybe they went through some hard times? My grandparents who lived through the Depression had some similar habits." She relaxed into her chair. "How'd you react?"

"I told her about my grandma and her rubber-band collection and how my mom reuses Ziplock bags."

"Your grandma will never have to buy another rubber band for the rest of her life." Susan laughed. "Did that lighten the mood?"

"A little, but she was pretty focused on taking the condiment bottles."

"Did you stop her?" Susan took a sip of her coffee.

Ivy shook her head. "I put them in the bag for her. Who am I to mess with her childhood trauma, right?"

Susan smiled. "Good move. Could be more to that story than you realize."

"True." She sighed. "I really like her, and I'm not sure what to think about the whole situation."

"I'm surprised this hasn't come up before." Susan said skeptically. "Think she's been hiding it from you?"

Ivy pulled her eyebrows together. "I guess I could've missed it, but I haven't seen her take any before."

"At least she's being honest with you." Susan shrugged. "Better to find out now and deal with it early, right?"

"Right." Ivy nodded slowly, thinking about their dinner dates. Specifically, dinner at her parents'. Nothing unusual there at all. Maybe the rules were different when eating at someone's house.

"Well, you'll be glad to know that June has moved on."

"Oh, yeah?"

Susan nodded. "Seems there's a new waitress at that little bar in town, and she just happens to like girls."

"Good," Ivy said resolutely. "You know I didn't want to hurt her, but I just couldn't date someone that young."

"Plus, you already had something going with Kendall." Susan winked and picked up her cup. "If I'd known how adamant you were about the age gap, I wouldn't have encouraged you to see June."

"Is that what blindsiding someone with a setup is called now? Encouragement?" The woman had been relentless.

"Ha." Susan laughed. "I guess I did get a little overzealous, but it all worked out in the end, right?"

CHAPTER THIRTY-FIVE

After Kendall exited the Uber, she added the tip for the driver on the app in her phone. She wasn't comfortable driving Ivy's truck, it was too big, so she'd left it at the cabin. Plus, she needed to have her own transportation from Ivy's place tonight. As Kendall opened the door and entered the living room, Taylor was coming out of the bedroom with Noah trailing her. "The way you worry about her is unhealthy. She's a grown woman and can stay where and with anyone she wants." Taylor glanced at her as she passed and went to the door.

Uh-oh. Bad timing for sure, Kendall thought.

Noah stopped short when he saw her. "Where have you been? I've been worried sick about you."

Kendall had seen the multiple missed calls and texts on her phone this morning but hadn't responded. "I was at Ivy's. We watched a move and fell asleep on the couch."

"This isn't working for me," Taylor threw over her shoulder as she pulled the door closed. Her anger was evident.

"What happened?"

"Taylor read a study about people who get back together with their previous loves later in life. She said that the study showed that those couples have a seventy percent likelihood of staying together for good."

"Oh, Cowboy." She let out a slow sigh. "Did you tell her that's never going to happen with us? I like women. A lot." She'd been there for less than a week and hadn't realized she was causing issues between them.

"I did, but she's jealous and wants you out of here."

"Okay. I'll make other arrangements today." She didn't want to come between the two of them.

"That's not what I want, though. The truth is, you're still my best friend, and I like having you here…like this. Talking about old times." He took a few steps toward Kendall. "Sneaking around like this is kind of like high school all over again."

"Yeah. I guess it is." She smiled and moved around to the other side of the couch before he could get any closer. The whole situation had become really uncomfortable—really quickly, and she couldn't tell whether he was being truthful about his feelings or not. "You *really* need to understand that there is no chance of anything between us other than friendship."

"I know that now. I wasn't sure at the time. Thought the odds were against us, but we could've given it a shot." He looked sad, which made Kendall's stomach drop. He was still hoping.

"It would've all been a lie, and I couldn't do that to you." She plucked several pieces of clothing from her bag and rushed into the bathroom. Taylor was right. She needed to find another place to stay. "I need to shower and get to work."

When she came out of the bathroom, Noah was gone, thankfully, but Taylor was waiting for her.

Taylor stood with her arms crossed. "We need to talk."

Kendall held up her hand. "No need. I'll get dressed and be out of here in few minutes." She headed into the bedroom, gathered her belongings, and put them in her bag. When she went back into the living room Taylor was standing in the same position. "I don't want to come between you and Noah. That wasn't my intent—at all. I just needed a place to stay."

"Everything was fine until you showed up."

"Was it? Really?" She didn't want to shine a light on their problems, but clearly they had some if Noah was longing for something long past.

"It will be. I want you to stay away from him while you're here."

"Listen. I can't guarantee that. We've been friends for a long time, but I can't control Noah any more than you can."

"Well, then I might let your little secret with Ivy spill out in conversation sometime."

"How's that going to help you?" Taylor had more moxie than she thought. "It'll just make things worse when Noah finds out." Kendall dropped her bag. "I can help you with Noah."

Taylor remained silent for a moment, seeming to think about that statement. "How?"

"I'm his best friend. I know everything about him, including why he's been reluctant to commit to you."

"I'm listening."

"You need to become someone he can't live without."

"Well, how do I do that with you hanging around?"

"It's not about me. It's about you and the things you do together. Do you like the things he likes?"

Taylor shrugged. "Not really. All he talks about is sports and cars. My life is the horses and the ranch."

"Have you tried liking them? You know, going to a car show with him once in a while."

"No. I just don't get it."

"They're actually kind of fun. Especially the antique shows." Kendall always enjoyed them but didn't know how to make them more attractive to Taylor. "There's usually some test drives or ride-alongs, and there's always food and beer." Kendall tilted her head. "You like food and beer, don't you?"

Taylor nodded. "Probably more than I should."

"And sports are easy once you learn the game."

"I don't know. They seem pretty complicated. So many innings and yards. Too much to remember."

"Once you find a favorite team it'll get easier. I can help you with that too."

"Okay. I'd appreciate that." She smiled slightly. "What else?"

"You need to cool the baby talk for now. He's not ready for that, and the more you talk about it, the more he's looking at the big picture. "

"He told you that?" She put her hands on her hips. "My big picture involves babies."

"I understand, but you need to work on getting your relationship solid first, or it's not going to last with or without babies."

Taylor crossed her arms again and flopped onto the couch. "I don't want to wait until I'm in my thirties."

"How old are you?" She already knew because Noah had told her.

"I'll be twenty-seven in April." Taylor was clearly counting her fertility years.

"Plenty of time." She sat beside Taylor on the couch. "Let's get you and Noah solid first and then work on the baby timing." She raised her eyebrows. "Okay?"

"Okay," Taylor said softly.

She didn't want to put a wedge between Noah and Taylor, and she definitely didn't want him to have any false hope about rekindling something from their past. Admittedly, he was her best friend, and she did love him, but not in the way he would want or need. She wanted to help Taylor make him see a future with her.

CHAPTER THIRTY-SIX

Ivy opened the door, expecting to see Kendall, but was surprised to see her father. "Hi. What are you doing in my neck of the woods?"

"Your mother asked me to come by and deliver an invitation to you and Kendall for dinner again Sunday." Ivy's dad walked farther inside and scrutinized the cabin. "After the mix-up with the room reservations at the lodge, I though Kendall was staying with you."

"She is, but she's gone to visit Noah. They're friends, remember? They haven't seen each other in a while and wanted to catch up." She hoped he didn't wander into the bedroom and see Kendall hadn't left any of her things. She was going to have to have a conversation with Kendall about staying here with her, which would be inconvenient since there was only one bedroom.

"Right. You didn't want to go along?"

"No. The four of us are getting together later in the week. I thought they could use some quality time. Thought it might be awkward if I was there."

He nodded. "Yeah. Talking about old times with people you don't know can be boring." He raised an eyebrow. "Could've been a good time to get to know more about Kendall's past, though. Make sure she's the right girl for you."

"She's the right girl, Dad." She said it without hesitation, but she wasn't sure of anything right now. Especially about lying to her parents.

The door opened as her dad walked toward it.

Kendall appeared. "Sorry I'm late. I got caught up talking to Taylor." She crossed the room to Ivy. "I was going to show her some of my designs but couldn't find my tablet. Have you seen it?"

Ivy shook her head as Kendall turned back to her dad. "It's nice to see you again, Mr. Patterson."

"You as well." He tipped his head. "Well, then, I need to get going. Your mother plans to see you for Sunday dinner, as usual." He stopped and turned slightly as he reached the door. "And she expects you to come along as well, Kendall."

Ivy nodded. "Understood."

"I hope you like pot roast." He turned toward the door.

"Love it. Is there anything we can bring?" Kendall asked.

"Just yourselves." He headed outside, pulling the door closed behind him.

Kendall rubbed her forehead. "I think this just got more difficult."

Ivy shook her head. "I don't think he realized you're not living here."

"That might have to change." Kendall took in a deep breath. "I can't stay with Noah any longer. It's causing tension between him and Taylor."

"Oh. I'm sorry to hear that." Ivy rolled around the options in her head. Only one bedroom here, but there was also a couch.

"Do you think there's any room at the lodge? Maybe I could sleep in the event area?"

"No. That's not allowed." Ivy needed more information. "What happened with Noah?"

"He seems to be using our high school relationship as a guide to fix whatever issues he has with Taylor."

"I didn't know they were having trouble."

"Taylor's jealous of me, and I don't blame her. I'd feel the same way if my significant other's ex showed up and took root in my house. I don't want to be the reason for their breakup."

Ex? That was news to Ivy. "Did you ever think you had a chance to go the distance with him?" She was genuinely interested.

Kendall shook her head. "No. The probability of us making it was slim to none. I mean, he's a great guy for the right woman, but I always knew something was missing."

"Were you confused?"

She nodded. "At first. I always thought there would be something to tell me when I found the right person. You know, sparks…heat…chills… some sort of sign. We could kiss for hours, and he would get all worked up, but nothing was happening with me."

"When did you figure it out?"

"I didn't right away. I thought something was wrong with me. Then one day I saw this girl—this magnificently gorgeous girl with the most confident swagger—and the sight of her sent something through me. A searing hot jolt to my midsection I hadn't experienced with Noah. Ever."

Ivy had been abruptly reminded of that feeling only a few days ago, when Kendall arrived at the lodge. "So did you break up with Noah and date her?"

Kendall shook her head. "Sadly, she was straight. But after that, I was honest with Noah. Told him all about how watching her made me feel. He was pissed at me for a long time after we broke up. Then he hooked up with that same gorgeous girl. They dated for a while, maybe for about six months. Then they split up, and our friendship went back to normal. We never talked about it, but I think he did it to get back at me, which was fine. I deserved it."

"You can stay here with me. I'll sleep on the couch."

"Are you sure? I don't want to put you out or anything. I can just go home for a few days."

"No. I'd rather you stay. Honestly, it'll probably be easier than explaining why you went home." If nothing else, it would alleviate some of her dad's suspicions. "You won't have to sneak around anymore, which will improve our odds of not being discovered as frauds."

Ivy would have to figure out the sleeping arrangements later. It wouldn't be appropriate for her to put Kendall on the couch. It also wouldn't be comfortable for Ivy to have breakfast in Kendall's bedroom if she did put her in the living room. The cabin had only so much private space.

CHAPTER THIRTY-SEVEN

Kendall's mind wandered as she tried to focus on her landscape-design presentation. Despite her best efforts, she kept thinking about Ivy and their living situation at the cabin. Leaving Ivy in the living room last night while she slept in the bedroom had been awkward, and she was gone again before Kendall woke this morning, having left sweet notes about coffee and food and a key to the cabin on the table.

She felt a twinge of guilt about imposing on Ivy's hospitality. "I should do something to thank her," she said aloud, tapping her pen against her notepad. "A warm meal seems like the perfect gesture—something comforting after a long day working outside in the brisk fall weather." She glanced out the window at the gray, cloudy haze. The cold had come in on the mountain quickly following the short phase of Indian summer.

The decision made Kendall smile to herself. Creamy mushroom pasta—one of her specialties and hopefully something Ivy would enjoy. Her mom had taught her how to cook it when she was younger. She remembered the nearly empty refrigerator at the cabin and made a mental note to leave the lodge early, giving herself time to stop at the market. Scratch that. She would go now. She could work on the presentation at the cabin, or it could wait until tomorrow. Tonight was going to be about connecting with Ivy and expressing her gratitude with a home-cooked meal. As she packed up her materials, Kendall felt a flutter of anticipation.

Later, she pushed her cart down the produce aisle, consulting the mental recipe she'd been perfecting since lunch. The fluorescent lights of the small mountain-town grocery store cast everything in a harsh glow, but she barely noticed as she focused on her mission.

"Mushrooms, obviously," she murmured to herself, selecting a package of cremini mushrooms, then adding a handful of wild ones that looked particularly good. She held them up briefly, imagining how they'd taste sautéed with garlic and herbs.

The rest of the items came together quickly: heavy cream, good parmesan cheese, fresh garlic, shallots, a bunch of thyme, and a crusty loaf of bread from the bakery section. On impulse, she added a bottle of her namesake white wine and a small bunch of wildflowers wrapped in brown paper near the checkout area.

As she loaded the bags into her car, Kendall felt another surprising flutter of nerves. "It's just dinner," she told herself, but the thought of living with Ivy after all the pretense they'd been spinning made it feel like something more.

The drive to Ivy's cabin took her along winding mountain roads, trees pressing close on either side. As daylight faded, shadows stretched across the pavement. Kendall rolled down the window, letting the crisp, pine-scented air fill the car. The groceries rustled in their bags on the passenger seat beside her.

When she finally turned onto the narrow dirt road leading to the cabin, the trees opened up to reveal glimpses of the lake below, its surface shimmering with the day's last light. The cabin appeared around the next bend, sturdy logs with a wide porch and windows that glowed with warm light.

Kendall parked in front of the cabin, taking a deep breath, hoping she was reading the signals from Ivy correctly. She gathered her bags and made her way up the steps to the porch before slipping the key into the lock, twisting the knob, and letting the door swing open.

Kendall went directly to the kitchen, a cozy space with open shelving and a small island. There, she unpacked her ingredients and arranged them on the counter in the order she planned to use them. Last, she pulled out the wildflowers and opened a few cabinets until she found a Mason jar large enough to arrange them in. She filled it with water and set it on the table, a beautiful centerpiece for dinner later.

As Kendall began to chop garlic and slice mushrooms, the day's tension began to melt away. The cabin's kitchen was small but well equipped with various cooking utensils, and within minutes, the air filled with the rich aroma of mushrooms cooking in butter. Outside the kitchen window, the sky was dark, rain threatening to fall soon, turning the glass into a mirror that reflected her shattered appearance. She'd need to make time to remedy that fact before Ivy arrived home.

The pasta sauce simmered on low heat, filling the cabin with rich, earthy aromas. Kendall gave it one final stir before covering the pan. Perfect timing. She'd have just enough time to freshen up before Ivy returned home from work.

"Twenty minutes, tops," Kendall murmured to herself, wiping her hands on a kitchen towel. She surveyed her handiwork: the table set with mismatched dishes she'd found in Ivy's cabinets, wildflowers arranged in the Mason jar, and candles that were perhaps too obvious, though she'd added them anyway.

In the small bathroom, Kendall splashed water on her face and studied her reflection. The day's work showed in the slight smudges beneath her eyes. She retrieved her makeup pouch from her overnight bag and began touching up. Nothing too dramatic. Just enough to feel put together. A swipe of mascara, a touch of blush, a dab of tinted lip balm.

"What are you even doing?" she asked her reflection. Her stomach fluttered with a nervousness she hadn't felt in years. "It's just dinner with your fake girlfriend."

But it wasn't, not really. Something unspoken seemed to be happening between them, something that lingered in glances held too long and conversations that stretched into the early morning hours, and a pretend kiss that was off the charts.

Kendall rummaged through her duffel bag and pulled out a soft green sweater she'd picked up at a boutique in town, one that brought out the color of her eyes. She changed quickly, trading her loungewear clothes for the sweater and a pair of comfortable jeans.

Back in the living room, she adjusted the dimmer on the lights, then immediately turned it back up. "Too obvious," she told herself, though she left the candles burning.

She wandered to the large windows overlooking the lake. Dusk had settled, painting the water in deep blues and purples. Somewhere out there, Ivy was walking the trails—a nightly ritual she'd mentioned that helped her clear her mind from the day.

What if she was misreading everything? What if Ivy had offered her cabin purely out of necessity to keep this ruse alive? Kendall pressed her forehead to the cool glass. Could she go forward with this? She closed her eyes as the tingle ran through her again. She knew what might happen if one of them said something—anything—to acknowledge the current that seemed to be running between them.

"Just give me a sign," Kendall whispered to the darkening landscape. "Something to let me know I'm not imagining whatever this spark is between us."

The sound of footsteps on the porch steps made her heart leap. She moved away from the window and pretended to be adjusting something on the table. The door opened, bringing with it a gust of cool evening air and the faint scent of Ivy's cologne, weakened by the long day.

"It smells amazing in here," Ivy said, closing the door behind her. She unwound a scarf from her neck, her cheeks flushed from the cold. She gazed at the candlelit table, then at Kendall. Her smile softened. "You look beautiful."

"Thank you," Kendall said, suddenly self-conscious.

Ivy stepped closer, her gaze lingering. "That sweater. The color looks great on you." She reached out, lightly brushing Kendall's sleeve. "It brings out the blond in your hair." She slid her hand up and took a strand of hair between her fingers gently before quickly retreating. "Sorry. That sounded silly."

"No. It wasn't silly at all." Warmth spread through Kendall's chest. Ivy had complimented her, not something someone who wasn't interested would do. "The pasta's ready whenever you are," Kendall said softly. "But there's no rush. Just need to put the bread in the oven."

"Let me wash up," Ivy said, her gaze still holding Kendall's. "And then maybe we can open that wine you bought?" She moved toward the bathroom, then paused in the doorway, glancing back over her shoulder. "I'm really glad you're here, Kendall."

As Ivy disappeared into the bathroom, Kendall finally released a long breath. Maybe, just maybe, those words were the sign she'd been looking for.

CHAPTER THIRTY-EIGHT

Ivy stood at the window of her cabin, watching raindrops race down the glass. Behind her, Kendall moved around the kitchen, humming as she prepared dinner for their continued relationship refinement. They'd been fake-dating for less than a week now—not necessarily long enough to convince Kendall's ex that she'd moved on, but long enough to make her parents stop the blind-date setups.

It had all seemed so simple when they'd made the arrangement. They weren't friends; they were barely acquaintances. Ivy had found Kendall attractive, and that's why she'd approached her the day she arrived. At the time she'd stepped into that conversation with Kendall and Cassie, she hadn't foreseen any complications. They both needed a convenient plus-one. But now that was all changing because of the real chemistry between her and Kendall.

"You're quiet tonight," Kendall said, appearing at her side with two glasses of wine. Her shoulder brushed against Ivy's as she handed her one.

"Just thinking." Ivy accepted the glass, careful not to let their fingers touch. She'd been doing that a lot lately, creating distance where before there had been an easy closeness. She had to protect her heart.

"About?"

"This." She gestured vaguely between them. "All of this."

Kendall leaned against the window frame, studying her. "Having second thoughts about our arrangement?"

"Not exactly." She took a sip of wine, buying time. "It's just getting complicated."

"How so?"

Ivy turned back to the window, unable to meet Kendall's eyes. "You know how when you repeat something enough times, it starts to feel real? Like when you practice a signature that isn't yours?"

The kitchen timer beeped, and Kendall straightened. "Hold that thought."

Ivy watched her walk away, noting how familiar her movements had become. The way she ran her hand through her hair when concentrating. The half-smile that appeared when something amused her. The gentle way she touched Ivy's elbow in crowds to keep them connected.

None of it was real. Every touch, every glance, every whispered inside joke had all been carefully choreographed for their audience. But somewhere along the way, her heart had forgotten to maintain the distinction.

Kendall returned, leaning against the counter. "You were saying? About signatures?"

Ivy set down her wineglass with a decisive click. "I think I need to step back."

"From…?"

"This. Us." She gestured between them again. "The fake relationship."

Kendall went still. "Did I do something wrong?" Her forehead wrinkled.

"No." Ivy's laugh sounded brittle even to her own ears. "You did everything right. That's the problem."

"I'm not following. What is the problem then?"

Ivy took a deep breath. "You're too good at pretending, Kendall. And I'm…" She paused, searching for words that wouldn't reveal too much. "I'm starting to forget where the act ends."

Understanding dawned in Kendall's eyes. "Ivy—"

"Don't." She held up a hand. "Please don't be nice about this. It'll just make it worse."

Kendall set her glass down and stepped toward her, but she backed away.

"We said no complications," she reminded Kendall. "That was the deal. And this—" she pressed a hand to her chest, trying to suppress the painful uncertainty searing her heart, "—this is definitely a complication."

"What if I want complications?" Kendall asked quietly.

Ivy froze. "What?"

"What if I stopped pretending days ago?" Kendall bit her bottom lip.

The rain tapped against the window, filling the silence between them. Ivy's heart swelled as her carefully constructed walls began to crack. "You don't mean that," she whispered.

"I do." Kendall stayed where she was, not pushing into her space. "But I didn't know how to tell you without scaring you away. I thought maybe you felt it too, but then you started pulling back, and I thought I might be wrong."

"I got scared," Ivy admitted. "This wasn't supposed to happen."

"I know." Kendall smiled softly. "Best laid plans and all that."

Ivy wrapped her arms around herself. "So, what now? We can't just flip a switch and make this real."

"Why not?" Kendall asked. "We already know we work well together. The only difference would be—"

"Everything," Ivy said. "The stakes would be everything."

Kendall nodded, looking serious. "You're right. And if you want to end our arrangement completely, I'll respect that wish. But I'd rather figure this out together than walk away from something that could be real."

The timer in the kitchen beeped again, more insistently this time. Neither of them moved.

Ivy wanted nothing more than for this to be real, but she couldn't say that to Kendall. "Dinner's going to burn," she said softly.

"Let it," Kendall replied, her gaze never leaving Ivy's. "Some things are more important."

Ivy was wavering, teetering on the edge between safety and possibility. She'd become so good at pretending that being genuine felt like the bigger risk now. "I need time," she finally said. "To figure out what's real and what's just habit." *Or the fantasy of what could be.*

Kendall nodded, disappointment flickering across her face before she masked it. "I understand."

She turned toward the kitchen, and a sudden panic rose in Ivy's chest. This wasn't what she wanted either—this polite distance, this careful retreat. "Kendall," she called after her.

Kendall looked back, hope written plainly across her face.

"I'm not saying no," Ivy said. "I'm just saying not yet. We need to take it slow."

Kendall's smile made her heart skip. "I can work with that," she said.

As Kendall moved to salvage their dinner, Ivy remained by the window for a moment, watching the rain before she set her glass on the table, and went into the bedroom to change. For the first time since this charade began, she allowed herself to imagine what it would be like if this—all of this with Kendall—was actually real.

CHAPTER THIRTY-NINE

Kendall placed the last dish on the table, adjusting it slightly before stepping back to survey her work. The pasta with mushroom cream sauce, a variation on her grandmother's recipe, sat steaming gently beside a small salad and fresh bread. She'd even found candles earlier, though she hesitated before lighting them. Too much maybe, considering their conversation.

"Something smells incredible," Ivy said, emerging from the hallway. She'd changed into an oversized national parks sweatshirt that hung loosely on her, the sleeves rolled up several times.

Kendall's heart did that strange flutter again. "It's nothing fancy. Just something my mother taught me." Pasta was cheap and easy. They'd had it often when she was a child, her mother always reminiscing about her grandmother as she prepared it. She wished her grandmother was still around to taste her masterpiece.

After the words they'd exchanged by the window—hesitant admissions of feelings that had been building for days—a new tension filled the air between them. Kendall had nearly dropped the wooden spoon when Ivy's fingers brushed against hers while tasting the sauce.

"Your mother must be an amazing cook," Ivy said as they settled at the table. She twirled pasta around her fork and took a bite, closing her eyes. "Oh, wow."

Kendall watched Ivy's expression, a warmth spreading through her chest that had nothing to do with the wine they were sharing. "She'll like you," she said softly.

Their conversation flowed easily throughout dinner, despite the newly acknowledged current running beneath their words. They talked about work, about books, about Ivy's upcoming junior ranger classes. But their frequent gazes lasted longer than before, and Kendall found herself noticing details she'd overlooked. The small scar near Ivy's eyebrow, the way she gestured with her hands when she got excited.

"Movie?" Kendall suggested as they finished clearing the dishes. "How about that superhero one you mentioned wanting to see?" Those movies weren't her favorite, but Ivy loved them.

"Perfect."

In the living room, Ivy's small couch suddenly seemed impossibly tiny. Kendall settled on one end, hyperaware of the space between them as Ivy sat down. Not too close, but close enough that she could smell the faint scent of Ivy's cologne.

As the opening credits rolled, Kendall pressed herself firmly against the armrest, maintaining a careful few inches' distance. She'd placed a throw blanket between them, an offering Ivy could take if she wanted.

Twenty minutes into the film, Ivy reached for the blanket, unfurling it over her legs. "Mind if I share? I'm always cold."

"No. Not at all," Kendall said, her voice slightly higher than normal.

Ivy extended the edge of the blanket toward her, an invitation that Kendall accepted after a moment's hesitation. They still weren't touching, but the shared blanket created an intimate space that made Kendall's skin tingle with awareness.

Onscreen, the hero was making improbable leaps between buildings. The complete opposite of what was happening between her and Ivy. Kendall couldn't focus. She was cataloging every shift in Ivy's position, every small laugh at the film's attempts at humor.

During a particularly tense action sequence, Ivy gasped and instinctively moved closer. Their shoulders brushed, and Kendall felt the contact like an electric current. She didn't pull away, but she didn't lean in either, maintaining that careful equilibrium as her heart raced.

"Sorry," Ivy whispered, glancing sideways with a small smile that suggested she wasn't sorry at all.

"It's okay," Kendall whispered back, not moving away.

They stayed like that, shoulders barely touching, through two more action sequences. Kendall gradually relaxed, though her awareness of Ivy never diminished. This new territory between friendship and something more was both terrifying and exhilarating.

When the hero finally saved the day, Ivy turned toward her. "Thank you for dinner. And for…" she gestured vaguely between them, "not making things weird after what we talked about."

Kendall smiled, finally allowing herself to lean near just slightly. "Is this weird?"

"No," Ivy replied, dropping her gaze briefly to Kendall's lips before looking at her again. "This is nice." You want to watch another one?

Kendall nodded, and Ivy clicked on the sequel.

As the beginning credits rolled, neither moved to turn on the lights. In the blue glow of the screen, they remained side by side on the couch, the careful distance between them narrowing by inches as the night continued.

CHAPTER FORTY

After seeing what was in Ivy's pantry, Kendall had to go to the store again to pick up some real food. No one could survive on tuna, instant noodles, and macaroni and cheese alone. Sure, Ivy had peanut butter and jelly too, but Kendall liked actual cooked food for dinner.

She pulled up to the metal-roofed store, grabbed a cart from the line at the front of the building, and went inside. She remembered how the store was laid out and rushed down the first aisle to the meat area to pick up a small pork roast, then zoomed down the canned vegetable aisle to grab a couple of cans of sauerkraut. She then spun the cart around and headed to the produce section to pick out an onion and some potatoes. She was thrilled to have discovered the slow cooker in one of the cabinets under Ivy's counter, and, if she could get all the ingredients, she'd be able to pick up everything, get back home to Ivy's, and sear the roast before placing it in the slow cooker. Then she'd have a full dinner ready before Ivy got home from work.

She hurried through the aisle to the produce department, grabbed a large bag of Jonathan apples, and dropped it into her cart. Halfway down the aisle she stopped. What was she doing? Her family wasn't here with her, so she didn't need ten to twenty apples. She needed only enough for herself, maybe more if Ivy liked them as well. She took the bag from her cart, placed it back on the center kiosk, and chose four apples from the bulk bin. That would be enough get her through the week unless Ivy did indeed like them. In that case she would be back here sooner rather than later.

She turned around to head to the potatoes and stopped short. Kendall hadn't expected to run into anyone she knew at the grocery store, considering she hadn't been in town very long. She'd left the lodge early and had driven the thirty minutes into town specifically to avoid familiar faces. Her relationship with Ivy was still new and fragile—something she wanted to protect from curious eyes and probing questions.

But there she was, examining avocados with clinical precision in the produce section: Shauna Jones, the veterinarian she and Ivy had taken the injured raccoon to after they'd found it on the side of the road. She recognized her immediately—the dark, curly hair pulled into a messy bun, the practical clothes that somehow still managed to look stylish.

She considered abandoning her half-filled cart and making a quick exit, but Shauna looked up before she could retreat.

"Hi. It's Kendall, right?" Her smile was warm and genuine as she approached. "It was so nice chatting with you the other night."

Kendall nodded. "And you're Shauna." She shifted awkwardly, suddenly very aware of the carton of ice cream and bottle of wine in her cart. "Nice to see you again. I was really impressed at how you handled those raccoons."

"Just doing my job." Shauna smiled.

Ivy's told me a lot about you." Not true, but she didn't know what else to say.

"Has she?" Shauna's eyebrows rose slightly. "That's interesting, because she's been suspiciously quiet about you."

She felt heat creep up her neck. "Well, we haven't been together for that long. I mean, it's still kind of new."

"New?" Shauna's expression changed, curiosity sharpening her features. "I thought you two had something going on since summer?"

"Yeah. That's right. She hasn't… She stammered, caught off guard by her own story mix-up…"mentioned anything about us?"

Shauna shook her head, dropping an avocado into her basket. "Not a word. And we've been friends since high school. We usually tell each other everything."

Shauna's slightly hurt tone made her stomach twist with guilt, though she wasn't sure why she felt responsible for Ivy not letting her in on a relationship that wasn't even real.

"It *really is* still kind of new, being long distance and all," she explained, trying to sound casual. "We were just mutual acquaintances before that. You know how it is. You know someone who knows someone, and then you're finally in the same place at the same time and meet."

"That's exactly why I'm surprised," Shauna said, leaning against the produce display. "Ivy's usually so private about her personal life at work. For her to start something with a colleague, which looks like you might turn out to be…" She studied her with new interest.

"It wasn't planned," she admitted. "As she said, we met at Noah and Taylor's cookout and just hit it off. That same night, there was a crazy thunderstorm, and we spent all night talking. Neither of us had any idea I'd be in a position to actually do any work at the park in the future."

"The one that knocked out power to half the park? That was quite a storm."

She nodded, remembering the story they'd come up with about being at the cabin, how Ivy had built a fire and they'd talked through the night as rain pounded the roof. It almost felt real now. "Things just happened naturally after that."

Shauna's expression softened. "I've known Ivy for a long time, and I've never seen her let anyone get close very quickly. She's always so cautious."

"I know," she said quietly. "I'm trying to be patient with her pace." Something in her tone must have convinced Shauna, because her posture relaxed.

"Well, this explains why she's been turning down our usual Sunday hikes. I thought she was just busy with work."

That was a fortunate unrelated occurrence. She felt a pang of anxiety. "I hope she's not avoiding you because of me. I would never want to come between friends." Seems that wasn't the case anyway. Why was Ivy cancelling on Shauna?

"Oh, don't worry about that." Shauna waved dismissively, but Kendall could see she was processing this new information. "It's just strange she hasn't mentioned anything. Ivy and I have never kept secrets."

She shifted uncomfortably. "Maybe she was just waiting for the right time? Or making sure it's serious before making an announcement?" *Or not expecting me just to drop in on her life and want to play house.*

"Maybe." Shauna nodded slowly, clearly not entirely convinced. "Or maybe she's worried about what I might think."

"Why would she worry about that?"

Shauna looked directly at Kendall. "The last person Ivy dated was my research partner. It ended badly. Really badly." She paused. "I introduced them."

"Oh." The single syllable felt inadequate.

"Just…be careful with her, okay?" Shauna's voice had lost its interrogative edge, replaced with genuine concern. "Ivy acts tough, but she's more vulnerable than she lets on."

"I know," she said softly. "I'm not going anywhere." Those words were truer now than ever. She wanted to see this possibility through.

Shauna studied her for a long moment, then nodded, apparently satisfied with what she saw. "Good. Well, I should finish up here. Tell Ivy to call me, would you? She owes me a hike or two and probably dinner."

Kendall promised she would, and they parted ways with an awkward but friendly good-bye. She grabbed a bag of potatoes and an onion as she pushed her cart toward the checkout, but she couldn't help but wonder what other parts of Ivy's life she had yet to discover—and whether she should tell her about this encounter with Shauna or let her explain their relationship to her friend in her own time.

She turned the cart around. "Hey, Shauna. Why don't you come for dinner tonight? I mean, if you're not busy."

"Not busy at all." Shauna smiled. "I'd love to."

"Great. I'll see you at six, then." She spun the cart around. Some secrets, she was learning, were meant to be kept. But some revelations weren't hers to make.

Chapter Forty-one

Ivy removed her muddy boots before entering the cabin. She was beat. Her day had been long and cold as she searched the trails for lost hikers, and her legs were feeling it. She'd barely had time to stop and sit on the trail momentarily to scarf down a sandwich for lunch before she'd had to get back to it. Multiple people were searching, but she couldn't rest until they were found. Thankfully, they'd been found and no one had been hurt. They were just navigationally challenged.

"Hey there, ranger. Thought you might need some caffeine. Hot and black, just how you like it." Kendall handed her a piping hot cup of coffee.

Ivy smiled as she took the cup. "You're a lifesaver. Been on my feet since dawn. Three lost hikers and a family of raccoons in someone's cooler today."

Kendall leaned against the counter. "Never a dull moment in your world, huh?"

"That's why I love it." She walked closer to the kitchen. "What smells so good?"

"I put a pork roast in the crockpot. I hope that's okay."

"That's more than okay. It's fantastic." Ivy hadn't had home-cooked meals except on Sundays at her parents' house before Kendall arrived, and she imagined her waistline was beginning to show it. She lifted the lid off the crockpot and took a glance. It looked different from what she was used to. "What's that in there with it?"

"Sauerkraut and onions." Kendall took the lid from her and placed it back on the slow cooker. "Just the way my mom always made it."

"I haven't had it that way before." Ivy glanced at the potatoes and gravy cooking on the stove.

"Oh. How do you make it?"

Ivy picked up the bottle of white wine on the counter and smiled as she examined the label, Kendall Jackson. "With potatoes, carrots, and celery in the oven." That was how her mom always made it.

"Like a beef pot roast?" Kendall raised her eyebrows. "I remember you said you liked my brand of chardonnay." She grinned as she pointed at the bottle.

"I do." She set the bottle back on the counter. "And, yes. Just like that. Didn't realize there was another way to make it." She clearly needed to get outside her comfort zone and find some new recipes.

"Historically, there's a tradition of eating pork and sauerkraut for luck on New Year's Day. Its origins can be traced back to Germany."

"Is that when your family usually has it? Are you German?" Ivy hadn't really wondered about Kendall's lineage.

"Nope to both. My family doesn't have a New Year's tradition. We usually have whatever sounds good at the time." She poked a fork into a potato. "This is one of my favorite dishes because it's the ultimate hearty meal for a cold evening. The pork is perfectly juicy and tender after simmering with the sauerkraut and onions."

Ivy noted the extra place set at the table. "Are we expecting company?"

"I ran into your friend, Shauna, at the grocery store."

Ivy was caught off guard. "Shauna? Oh. That's a coincidence." A weird coincidence. Why was Shauna at the market during the middle of her workday?

"I didn't see her and almost ran right into her." Kendall turned off the burner under the potatoes. "She started asking questions about us and didn't seem to be convinced that this is real." Kendall motioned between them with her hand before she picked up the pan and drained the potatoes in the colander in the sink.

Ivy laughed. "That sounds like her. She's known me for a long time. What did she say?"

"Well, after the third-degree about my intentions, I worried about how to make her trust us, so I thought what better way than to show her, so I invited her to dinner." She put the potatoes in the pan again and carried it back to the stove. "I thought it might be nice." She tossed a hunk of butter into the pan. "But I sense she's not thrilled about us."

Ivy sighed. "She's always been protective. Especially since that disaster with her friend Alex."

"She made that clear." Kendall widened her eyes. "Then she did this thing where she stared at me for a full minute without blinking."

Ivy groaned. "Oh, god. The Shauna Stare. She thinks it's her superpower."

Kendall smiled as she popped the beaters into the mixer. "It's kind of effective, not gonna lie. She definitely loves you, Ivy. Said you deserve someone who appreciates your dedication to Diamond Mountain."

Ivy chuckled. "That's oddly specific. Look. I'm sorry if she made you uncomfortable. Shauna's just seen me through some rough patches."

"Hey, I get it. Actually, I respect it. Shows what a good friend she is. And that you're worth looking out for." She stuck the mixer into the pan and turned on the motor, whipping the potatoes.

Ivy touched her on the shoulder. "So, you invited her to dinner? You're brave." Facing the problem straight-on. That was refreshing.

Kendall shrugged as she turned off the mixer. "I figure if I can handle your stories about bear encounters, I can handle Shauna." She gave her a sideways smile. "Besides, anyone important to you is worth getting to know."

Ivy smiled and took Kendall's hands. "Thank you for understanding. And for the coffee."

Kendall popped the beaters out of the mixer. "Fair warning, though. I have plenty of questions for her as well."

"Oh, no. We're cancelling."

Kendall narrowed her eyes. "Not a chance, ranger. Not—a—chance." The words flowed slowly from her tongue.

"Just kidding. Ask away." Ivy squeezed her hands before she let them go. "No secrets here. I'm an open book."

They both laughed as Ivy headed into the bedroom to change her clothes. She really didn't want Shauna giving Kendall the good, bad, and the ugly of her past relationships, but she could suffer through one dinner of truth-or-dare.

CHAPTER FORTY-TWO

Ivy drummed her fingers nervously against the kitchen counter as she lifted the lid of the crockpot with her other hand. The rich aroma of comfort food filled her small cabin, but her thoughts were elsewhere. Shauna would arrive at six, and tonight would be a test to see if their so-called relationship could stand the scrutiny of one of her oldest and dearest friends.

She'd hoped for a nice, easy evening at home, but that plan had been shattered by a casual run-in at the grocery store. Kendall had said that the encounter had been awkward enough, but when Shauna had been skeptical about them as a couple, Kendall knew the best thing to do was to invite Shauna to join them for dinner. Tonight, their carefully constructed fake relationship might just crumble into dust, which should be easy, considering the biggest secret of all was that she was falling hard for Kendall.

"Don't worry so much. It'll be great," Kendall had said. "Any friend of yours is someone I'd love to spend time with."

The doorbell rang, startling Ivy from her thoughts. She glanced at the clock on the wall. Shauna was early, as usual.

When she opened the door, her best friend stood there with a bottle of wine and a smile that seemed more forced than natural. She was obviously playing nice to be polite.

"I brought reinforcements," Shauna said, holding up a bottle of Kendall Jackson Chardonnay. "Your girlfriend's brand." She grinned.

"You didn't have to come," Ivy whispered as she accepted the wine. She set the bottle on the counter as she went into the kitchen.

"Are you kidding? After meeting Miss Perfect the other night and then running into her in the produce section, wild horses couldn't keep me away." Shauna stepped inside, surveying the cabin with the critical eye of someone looking for evidence at a crime scene. "You cleaned. You never clean unless you're seriously interested."

Ivy's cheeks warmed. "It's not like that." It was but it wasn't.

"You changed your sheets too, didn't you?" Shauna raised an eyebrow.

"Shauna," Ivy hissed, mortified.

Her friend's expression softened slightly. "After what happened with Alex, I just need to make sure this girl isn't another charmer with wandering eyes."

"Kendall isn't Alex." Ivy turned to the stove, stirring the mashed potatoes with more force than necessary. "And besides, whose fault was that?"

"I know." Shauna held up a hand. "I never should've let you go out with her." Shauna helped herself to a glass of water. "So, tell me everything you haven't told me already about Kendall."

"There's nothing more to tell. We met at that cookout at Noah and Taylor's place."

"Right. The one I couldn't attend due to an emergency at work." Shauna tilted her head. "Why didn't you tell me about her back then?"

Ivy shifted against the counter. "I didn't think it was going anywhere. She lives out of state." She put the spoon on a plate by the stove and returned the lid to the pot. "Since then, we've been talking a lot over the phone, and when she came across the landscape opportunity at the lodge, it seemed meant to be." She hoped Shauna bought that story. Ivy wasn't one to have long discussions on the phone, a fact that Shauna knew from experience.

"Nice," Shauna repeated flatly. "The most random get-together in existence."

Before Ivy could defend herself, Kendall came out of the bedroom. Her stomach flipped.

"Here comes your girl now." Shauna gave her a look. "Don't worry. I'll behave."

Ivy's stomach bounced again at the thought of Kendall being her girl. She took a deep breath before turning to see her. Kendall stood there, her blond hair looking slightly windswept, wearing a pair of skinny jeans and one of Ivy's flannel, button-down shirts. She wore it unbuttoned to the second button, sleeves rolled up, with the bottom tied at the waist.

"Hey," Kendall said, her smile making Ivy momentarily forget her anxiety. "Most of my shirts are in the laundry. I hope you don't mind me borrowing one of yours."

"No. Not at all." Ivy took in the whole picture of her. "Looks much better on you than it does on me." Behind her, Ivy heard Shauna make a small noise that could indicate either approval or skepticism.

Dinner began with an uncomfortable silence, broken only by the clink of cutlery against plates. Kendall, to her credit, seemed unfazed by Shauna's scrutiny, answering her increasingly pointed questions with good humor.

"So, Kendall," Shauna said, mixing a bit of sauerkraut with her potatoes. "Ivy mentioned your ex is here, also bidding the landscape project. How long ago did that relationship end?"

Ivy choked on her wine. She hadn't mentioned that situation at all. Shauna must have been getting her information from Susan, who seemed to keep everyone informed about everything that happened at the park.

Kendall nodded, apparently unruffled. "Sometime in the spring. I don't remember the actual date. It was mutual, but I still try to block those things out as much as I can. We just had different visions for our futures."

"I hear there's going to be a meteor shower tomorrow night." Ivy said, trying to change the subject.

"Oh yeah? That's cool." Shauna glanced at Ivy before she returned her attention to Kendall. "Children?" She was relentless.

"None," Kendall answered. "Though I'd like to have several someday, with the right person." She glanced at Ivy, who quickly averted her eyes to her plate, suddenly finding her mountain of mashed potatoes fascinating.

"Interesting. And you plan to move here if you get the landscape contract at the lodge?"

"Shauna," Ivy said, keeping her voice calm. "Maybe we could talk about something else?"

"It's okay," Kendall said, touching Ivy's hand lightly. "I don't mind. I'm actually looking forward to being here on a more permanent basis."

Shauna's expression shifted almost imperceptibly, which led Ivy to believe she accepted Kendall's response. "That's good to know."

As the evening progressed, Ivy watched with a mixture of horror and reluctant appreciation as Shauna put Kendall through what amounted to a full background check disguised as dinner conversation. Yet something unexpected happened around dessert—Shauna laughed at one of Kendall's terrible puns, a genuine laugh that Ivy recognized as unforced.

When Kendall excused herself to go to the restroom, Shauna leaned across the table. "Okay, so she's not so terrible," she said.

"That's some high praise," Ivy said dryly.

"She looks at you when you're not talking. Most girls pay attention only when a woman is speaking directly to them. She notices you even when you're quiet." Shauna rolled her eyes. "Weird, right?"

Ivy laughed. She hadn't realized that fact. "So, I have your approval?"

Shauna shrugged, but her expression had softened. "You don't need it. But for what it's worth, she seems genuine. Unlike Alex."

"Again, your fault."

"I know. I know." Shauna shook her head. "Next time I'll be more selective about who I introduce you to."

"Hopefully there won't be a next time." Ivy was honestly hoping for that.

Shauna gazed at her for a minute, then sighed. "Just be careful, Ivy. You fall hard, stupid fast."

"I know my track record," she said, rearranging the food on her plate. "But this feels different."

"That's what you said last time." Shauna frowned.

"And we were both wrong last time," she said. "But I'm asking you to trust me now. And maybe, just maybe, give her a chance?" Ivy raised her eyebrows slightly.

Shauna held Ivy's gaze for a long moment before nodding. "For you, I'll try. But if she hurts you—"

"You'll be the first one I call for help burying the body," Ivy said with a small smile.

When Kendall returned, the atmosphere had shifted to a lighter tone. Shauna began sharing embarrassing stories from their early days, referring to unflattering pictures in full-on Xena garb taken at multiple cosplay parties, making Ivy groan and Kendall laugh. By the time they were lingering over coffee, the initial tension they'd all felt had dissolved into something comfortable.

Later, as Kendall helped clear the table, Shauna pulled Ivy aside in the kitchen.

"If she hurts you, I'll still destroy her," she whispered, but there was less conviction in her threat now.

Ivy smiled. "I know."

When they said good night, Shauna gave Kendall an unexpected hug that lasted a beat longer than necessary—a silent communication that Ivy knew contained both warning and tentative acceptance.

As the door closed behind her friend, Ivy turned to find Kendall watching her with amusement.

"She's intense," Kendall said.

"I'm sorry about that. She's just protective."

"Don't be sorry," Kendall replied, stepping closer. "It means you're loved. That's never something to apologize for."

Ivy felt something settle inside her. A quiet recognition that perhaps, just perhaps, Kendall might be someone worth keeping around. Someone even Shauna could approve of.

"Now," Kendall said, taking her hand, "why don't you show me some of those Xena cosplay photos."

"I think I might still have the costume in the back of my closet."

Kendall raised her eyebrows. "Even better."

CHAPTER FORTY-THREE

Ivy was at the sink rinsing her coffee cup when her dad drove up. She quickly ran to the couch and moved the makeshift bed elements to the bedroom.

"Ivy, is that you?" Kendall rubbed at her eyes. "Is everything okay?"

"Yeah. My dad just pulled up." He'd never shown up at her door this often. "It's early. Go back to sleep." Ivy rushed back through the living room, threw on her coat before she went to the door, pulled it open, and stepped out onto the porch. "What's going on, Dad? Everything okay with Mom?"

He nodded. "You gonna invite me in?"

Ivy didn't step aside. "I was just on my way out to work."

He glanced at his watch. "A little early, isn't it?" He was right. It was earlier than usual.

"I have some paperwork to catch up on." Ivy had tossed and turned most of the night. Her couch wasn't that uncomfortable, but having Kendall in such close proximity made sleep difficult.

"Is there anything you want to tell me about Kendall?

"I think you and mom pretty much grilled her at dinner."

"Yeah. Sorry about that. You know your mom has to know everything." He smiled.

"Not to blame her, but," Ivy laughed, "that's probably why I haven't been able to keep a girlfriend for more than a few months."

"In all fairness to your mother, she has your best interests at heart."

"I know that, Dad. What's this all about?" Ivy already had an idea.

"You seemed to learn as much about Kendall as we did the other night. I think you enjoyed it, but it was new to you."

"Sure. I don't know some things yet, but we haven't been together long enough for me to learn everything about her."

"I'll give you that." Her dad sucked in a deep breath. "Just don't hurt your mother. If this isn't exactly what you say it is, she'll be crushed."

Ivy heard the door click open behind her. "Good morning, Mr. Patterson." Kendall's voice was gravelly, and it had the usual response on Ivy's metabolism. Kendall came closer and tucked herself under Ivy's shoulder. Ivy's pulse zipped into a faster pace as her stomach did a quick somersault.

"Good morning," Ivy's dad glanced at Kendall and cleared his throat. "You'd better get inside out of the cold." He moved toward his truck. "Ivy, you and I can finish this conversation later. Just remember what I said." He waved his hand at the grass. "It's time to put down some pre-emergent weed killer. Once I get mine done, I'll come over and do yours."

"I will, and thanks, Dad." Ivy waited for a few minutes as her dad backed up and drove down the gravel driveway to the main road. She hadn't noticed until just now that Kendall was wearing only an oversized T-shirt—one of Ivy's.

"What was that about?" Kendall asked.

"Just some stuff going on with my mom." She motioned Kendall toward the door before she reached in front of her and turned the knob.

"He suspects, doesn't he?"

"He did, but I think your appearance might have convinced him otherwise." Ivy took the throw from the couch and wrapped it around Kendall's shoulders. "You want some coffee?"

"I'd love some."

CHAPTER FORTY-FOUR

Kendall spread her documents across the coffee table in Ivy's cabin, running her fingers through her hair in frustration. Sketches of garden designs, contractor quotes, and photos of overgrown pathways formed a chaotic collage that somehow needed to become a coherent presentation by tomorrow morning.

"Earth to Kendall? You've been staring at that same page for five minutes." Ivy sat on the couch next to her, two steaming mugs in hand. "Made you some cocoa."

"My savior." Kendall sighed, accepting the mug gratefully. "I'm drowning in this presentation. The next meeting's tomorrow, and I still can't make a convincing case for why the state should spend six figures on landscaping when the interior renovations have already gone over budget." She flipped her pen onto the table. "As much as I want to, I'm not going to be able to go to your parents' house for dinner tonight."

"Don't worry about that. I've already cancelled."

"How did your mom take it?"

"She was disappointed, but I told her there'd be plenty more Sundays for dinner." Ivy set her mug on the side table and scanned the scattered papers. "Mind if I take a look?"

"Please." Kendall gestured to the disorganized mess before her. "I've got cost projections, design concepts, and contractor bid estimations, but I can't make it all click."

Ivy picked up a photo of the lodge's current entrance with stalky, overgrown junipers partially blocking the concrete pathway and a weather-damaged pergola porte cochere casting uneven shadows across the faded welcome sign.

"You know what your problem is?" Ivy asked, dropping the photo onto the table. "You're thinking about this as an expense, when you should be framing it as an investment in the lodge's future."

"Boards usually see only dollar signs," Kendall said.

"Then show them bigger dollar signs coming back," Ivy said, reaching for a blank sheet of paper. She drew three columns. "Let's organize this properly. Column one for current problems with quantifiable impacts. Column two for proposed solutions. Column three for projected returns."

Kendall leaned forward, intrigued. "Go on."

"First problem," Ivy said, writing as she spoke, "outdated entrance creates poor first impression. Impact, based on our guest surveys, 38 percent mentioned disappointment with the tired exterior despite loving the guest rooms."

"I didn't think to connect those points," Kendall admitted.

"Second problem: overgrown vegetation blocking natural light in the west-wing rooms. Impact, those rooms rent at a 22 percent discount compared to east wing rooms with similar amenities."

Kendall grabbed her laptop, quickly pulling up occupancy data. "You're right. We're leaving money on the table."

"Third problem: lack of usable outdoor gathering spaces. Impact, we've had to decline seventeen corporate retreat bookings this year that specifically requested outdoor team-building areas."

"How did you know all that?"

"I talk to the sales team at the lodge." Ivy grinned. "Now, what's the projected increase in bookings if you could accommodate those retreats?"

For the next hour, they methodically organized the presentation, transforming it from a landscaping proposal into a business-growth strategy. Ivy helped Kendall calculate potential revenue increases from wedding-venue rentals, corporate events, higher occupancy rates, and premium pricing for rooms with improved views.

"And here's your closer," Ivy said, sliding over a notepad with a timeline sketched out. "Phase the project over eighteen months to spread out the costs, prioritizing the areas with highest revenue impact first. That gives you early wins to show the board before requesting the next phase of funding."

Kendall stared at the reorganized presentation, now a compelling business case rather than a plea for beautification. "This is actually brilliant. How did you see what I couldn't?"

"Fresh eyes." Ivy shrugged. "Plus, even though I'm emotionally attached to the plants, like you, I think they need rejuvenation." She tapped a sketch of an elaborate rose garden. "I do think this should stay in the plan. Just maybe not in phase one."

Kendall smiled, gathering the papers into a neat stack. "I owe you big time."

"Just make sure I get invited to the grand-opening garden party," Ivy replied, relaxing into the couch and picking up her mug. "This isn't only about selling your skills to the committee. It's about selling them the growth of nature and beauty you're going to bring to the lodge."

"Growth," Kendall repeated, feeling confident for the first time in weeks. "I can definitely sell that." She scooted closer and took the mug from the table. "You deserve something special for this." She kissed Ivy's cheek.

"I could get used to this." Ivy blushed. She seemed to be ready to take a baby step into what was bound to happen between them.

CHAPTER FORTY-FIVE

Kendall watched nervously as the board members filed down the back stairs of the lodge. Knowing they would be discussing her proposal soon made her anxiety go through the roof. "They're heading our way."

"Deep breath, Kendall," Ivy whispered. "They're just people who love this park as much as you do."

Kendall nodded, clutching the portfolio containing all her work—sustainable designs that would showcase the park's natural beauty while improving visitor accessibility. She smiled at Ivy, who had quietly championed Kendall's proposal behind the scenes, impressed by her respect for the land's ecological integrity.

As three of the board members, who were engaged in conversation, approached the picnic area where Ivy and Kendall sat, Ivy stood and straightened her khaki uniform.

"Good morning, everyone," Ivy called out. "I'd like you all to meet Kendall Jackson."

The board members turned, coffee cups in hand. Eleanor Reeves, the board president, stepped forward first. Her silver hair gleamed in the morning light, and despite her formal blazer, her hiking boots revealed her true priorities.

"Ah, Ranger Patterson. This must be the designer who proposed the native pollinator corridors." Eleanor extended her hand to Kendall. "I've been quite interested in your sustainability metrics."

"Yes, ma'am," Kendall replied, shaking her hand firmly. "I believe the park deserves solutions that will flourish for generations, not just look good on opening day."

Marcus Chen, the youngest board member and head of the park's finance committee, studied Kendall with shrewd, narrowed eyes. "Your budget projections include a ten-year maintenance forecast. That's uncommon but appreciated."

"The best designs account for their entire lifecycle," Kendall responded, gaining confidence. "I wanted to demonstrate that beauty and practicality aren't mutually exclusive."

The third board member, Dr. Josephine Winters, a retired ecologist, had been quietly observing. She finally spoke, her voice gentle but precise. "I noticed your water management system incorporates indigenous knowledge. What inspired that approach?"

As Kendall explained the research behind the design choices, she could see the board members' expressions soften. This wasn't just another bid to them now. Kendall was becoming a person with vision and passion, not just a name on a proposal. At least that's what she hoped.

When a park volunteer approached, signaling it was time for the board meeting, Ivy raised a hand to gain their attention. "I just want to add one thing. Unlike some of the firms who sent junior associates for the site assessment, Kendall personally spent many hours walking every corner of our park, asking questions about visitor patterns, wildlife habitats, and maintenance challenges."

Eleanor turned to Kendall with a genuine smile. "Thank you for bringing such thoughtfulness to this project. Regardless of the outcome, your approach honors what Diamond Mountain means to this community."

As the board members walked toward the administration building, Ivy gave Kendall a subtle thumbs-up. "You did great. You spoke their language—conservation, responsibility, and respect for this place. That's what they understand."

Kendall exhaled slowly as the board members disappeared into the building where they would start deliberations. "Thanks for that introduction, Ivy. No matter what happens, it means everything to have you in my corner."

Ivy smiled, gazing out at the landscape they both cherished. "The park has a way of bringing the right people together at the right time. Now, how about some coffee to warm you up before I fill your brain with more native plant details?"

CHAPTER FORTY-SIX

Ivy's dad approached. "Hey, kiddo. Sorry I'm late. Traffic was brutal." His normal excuse when he got caught up in something else, considering there wasn't much traffic in the area. She was glad he was late this time. When he'd called this morning to say he'd be by to walk the trails with her today, she wasn't thrilled with continuing their conversation from yesterday.

Ivy smiled. "Dad. I didn't see you there. I was just introducing Kendall to a few of the board members."

Lance glanced at Kendall. "Nice to see you again, Kendall."

Kendall nodded at Lance. "Likewise. Your daughter was just telling me about the native plant species in this area. Her knowledge is better than any Google search I can do."

"Yes. It's impressive." Lance smiled.

"Kendall's portfolio is amazing, Dad. She did that award-winning sustainable garden for the children's hospital in Oklahoma City last year."

"That sounds wonderful. Ivy, can I talk to you?" He glanced at Kendall "Would you excuse us for just a minute?"

"Of course. I'll just review my notes in case they have any questions. Thanks again, Ivy." Kendall walked a few feet away.

Ivy's dad lowered his voice. "Ivy, what exactly are you doing?"

Ivy pulled her eyebrows together. "What do you mean, Dad?"

"I overheard you talking about Kendall's work to those board members." He motioned to the people she'd just left. "Aren't they the ones selecting the winning bid?"

"Yeah. They'll make the final decision. I was simply introducing them to her."

"And singing her praises. I overheard you say that she's the most innovative designer you've ever met and that she's perfectly aligned with our conservation goals. That's hardly neutral, Ivy."

"Well, it's true. Her designs are exactly what this park needs." She *had* seen Kendall's designs and was impressed by them.

"That may be, but aren't other designers submitting bids?" Her dad was being sensible, as usual.

Ivy shifted uncomfortably "Yes…four others." She knew what her dad was getting at.

"Have you introduced them all to the board with the same enthusiasm? Highlighted their accomplishments?"

"No, I haven't." She didn't want to either.

"Honey." He took her by the shoulders. "I know you mean well, but you're giving Kendall an unfair advantage. As a park ranger representing this public space, you have an obligation to remain impartial during the bidding process."

"I'm not on the selection committee, Dad. I'm just sharing my professional opinion." She hadn't done anything more than that.

"Your professional opinion carries weight here. You're respected, and the board trusts your judgment on what this park needs. By promoting one designer over the others, you're potentially influencing a process that should be fair and transparent. Especially considering your relationship with Kendall."

"I didn't think about it that way. I just got excited about her ideas." And her. Kendall was more than Ivy had expected, and she wanted her to have a reason to stay around.

"I understand, but public projects have strict protocols for a reason. Imagine how the other designers would feel if they knew the park ranger was essentially endorsing their competitor before the bids were even reviewed?"

Ivy sighed. "You're right. I should have been more careful about maintaining neutrality. I just genuinely think she's the best person for the job."

"Maybe she is, but that's for the board to decide, based on the merits of all the proposals, not on your recommendation." His expression remained serious and unwavering. "If you feel strongly, there might be appropriate channels for providing input, but it shouldn't involve giving Kendall special access or praise. That looks improper."

Ivy nodded. "I see your point. I need to step back and let the process work as intended."

"That's my girl." Lance smiled "Public service comes with responsibilities, even when they're not always spelled out."

"I should probably talk to my supervisor about this too, make sure I haven't compromised anything." She didn't want to ruin Kendall's chances at the bid even if her intentions were good.

"That's a good idea." Lance squeezed her shoulders before dropping his arms to his sides. "Being transparent about the process shows integrity."

"Thanks for the reality check, Dad. Sometimes I forget that even small actions can have bigger implications."

"That's what dads are for." He grinned. "Dispensing unwanted wisdom and embarrassing you in front of your friends."

"Well, you're one for two today. I'll take it." She glanced at Kendall, who was busy organizing her papers in her bag.

She was going to want to know what her dad wanted, but she wouldn't tell her. She would simply say it was something about her mom and that she was meeting her mother later that afternoon for coffee. That part was true.

CHAPTER FORTY-SEVEN

As Ivy stood at the counter getting their drinks, Ivy turned and watched her mom hum to herself as she scrolled through her phone. They were having their weekly mother-daughter coffee at her mom's favorite café, and her mother had arrived early to secure their usual corner table. Ivy heard something clatter to the table and turned to see her mom clutching her chest.

"Mom? Are you okay?" Ivy rushed to her mom, adrenaline surging through her. "You look pale." The coffee shop suddenly seemed too loud, too bright, and too crowded.

A cold sweat broke out across her mom's forehead and upper lip. "Something's wrong." She tried to say more, but she could only gesture weakly toward her phone.

Ivy picked it up, and her neck heated when she saw what was on the screen. An Instagram notification from Kendall's account. When the hell had they exchanged social media information? Kendall had been tagged in a new photo. Ivy tapped it, expecting to see Kendall and her involved in some kind of park activity. Instead, she saw a post by Cassie, Kendall's ex. She scrolled down to read the caption: "@kendall-jackson-naturedesigner I know your secret! This relationship with the ranger is as fake as it looks! #norealfeelingsthere #youstillloveme."

"Shit. Mom, I can explain—"

"You lied to me?" Karen finally managed to speak, her voice barely above a whisper. "All those stories about Kendall…the dinner plans I changed…the blind dates I canceled…"

"It wasn't like that," Ivy said, sliding into the chair across from her. "Well, I mean, it was, but—"

"My heart is racing. I don't know what's happening to me." Karen gripped her arm.

"Mom?" Ivy tried to remain calm but couldn't stop her voice from rising with urgency. "Mom, you're scaring me."

Ivy's mom gripped the edge of the table, her knuckles white. "I can't—I can't breathe," she gasped.

"Someone call 911!" Ivy shouted, her voice high with panic. "My mom needs help! I think she's having a heart attack."

"Ivy," Karen managed between rapid breaths, "why would you lie to me?"

"I'm sorry, Mom. I just wanted you to stop with the setups. You were so happy when I mentioned Kendall, and then it just spiraled."

A server rushed over with a glass of water. Ivy gently rubbed her mom's back as a few other patrons looked on with concern.

"Slow breaths, Mrs. Patterson," the server said calmly. "In through your nose, out through your mouth."

Karen closed her eyes. "I can't focus. My chest feels like it's being crushed, and my fingers are tingling." She took in a deep breath, and gradually her breathing began to normalize.

"I thought—" Karen's voice broke. "I thought we told each other everything."

Ivy's eyes welled with tears. "I know. I'm so sorry, Mom. It started as an innocent thing, but then you got so excited about me finally dating someone. I just didn't know how to tell you."

Karen took a shaky sip of water. "So, Kendall's in on this too?"

Ivy nodded and bit her lip. "But don't blame her. Kendall's great, and we've become really close friends. We just made it look real to keep the story going."

"And I'm the audience," Karen whispered, her hand still trembling around the water glass.

"I just needed you to stop trying to fix my love life. I know you mean well, but those women you kept setting me up with? We had nothing in common." Ivy felt like this wasn't the time to go into it, but her mother wouldn't let it go.

Her mom's breath hitched again, but she clearly fought to keep it steady. "I only wanted you to be happy."

"I know," Ivy said softly, taking her mother's hand. "But I need to find my own way there. Find my person myself." She'd never expected her mom to find out about it at all.

Her mom sucked in a short breath. "The room is spinning."

"It's okay, Mom. Just breathe in through your nose and out through your mouth," Ivy said, but her mom didn't seem to be able to follow her simple instruction. Each breath she took was short and labored.

"I feel like I'm dying," she gasped.

"You're not dying," Ivy said firmly, watching the fear flicker in her eyes. "You're having a panic attack. Remember what Dr. Lambert said? Try to focus on something in the room. Help is on the way," Ivy told her. "Just stay with me, okay?"

CHAPTER FORTY-EIGHT

Minutes stretched into an eternity as Ivy's mom's breathing didn't improve. She slumped against her, and Ivy could feel her trembling.

When the bell above the door jingled, relief washed through her. Two EMTs entered, equipment in hand, their movements calm and practiced. A woman with a tight gray bun and a younger man with short dark hair walked toward them.

"What's your name, ma'am?" the woman asked Ivy's mom as she knelt beside them.

"Karen," Ivy said, answering for her. "Karen Patterson. I'm her daughter, Ivy."

"Hi, Karen. I'm Rita," the woman said, taking Karen's wrist to check her pulse. "Can you tell me what happened?"

Karen tried to speak but couldn't seem to get enough air. Rita placed an oxygen mask over her face while her partner set up monitoring equipment.

"She has anxiety," Ivy explained, her voice small and distant to her own ears. "But it's never been this bad before."

Rita nodded, all business. "Her heart rate is elevated, blood pressure is up too. We're going to take her in to be safe." They helped Ivy's mom onto a stretcher. As they strapped her in, her eyes, which were wide with fear, found Ivy's.

"I'll be right behind you, I promise," Ivy said, squeezing her hand before they took her out the door.

In the parking lot, she watched them load her mom into the ambulance, the oxygen mask fogging with each breath.

The younger EMT noticed her hovering. "Are you coming with us?" he asked and waved her forward.

Ivy nodded, climbing inside the ambulance and sitting beside her mom. The heavy doors closed with a thud that felt oddly final somehow.

Inside, the ambulance was all sharp angles and equipment that Ivy was familiar with due to her EMT studies. She'd assisted with rescues before and watched as others were loaded into rescue vehicles, but she'd never experienced something this personal before. Everything she'd learned so far had been lost when her mother had clutched her chest.

Rita worked efficiently, attaching monitors, while the younger man drove and spoke into the radio. Numbers flashed on screens, indicating that heart rate and blood pressure were still somewhat elevated.

"Is she going to be okay?" Ivy asked, hating how insecure she sounded. It had all the signs of a panic attack, but at this moment Ivy was unsure if she was right.

"Her vitals are stabilizing," Rita said. "Sometimes anxiety attacks can mimic heart attack symptoms. They call it panic disorder. But we'll run tests at the hospital to make sure nothing else is going on."

Ivy nodded. "I'm familiar with them."

Her mom's eyes were closed now, and her breathing seemed less labored. She took her hand. It was cold. She'd never seen her mother so vulnerable. Even with her anxiety, she'd always been the strong one. And now here Ivy was, watching her, looking so small and fragile on the stretcher. As the ambulance sped toward the hospital, Ivy realized that the roles she and her mother held had shifted without warning. For the first time, her mom needed her to be the strong one. She squeezed her hand, a silent promise that she'd be up to the task.

The ambulance swayed as it moved through traffic, siren wailing overhead. It was strange how ordinary moments, like having coffee, could morph so suddenly into something else entirely.

"Does your mom have these episodes often?" Rita asked, breaking into her thoughts.

"Sometimes. But not like this." Ivy's lies had thrown her mother into a full-blown panic attack. Would she ever forgive her?

Rita nodded, making a note on her clipboard. "And who can we call for you?"

Ivy rubbed her head. "My dad. We need to let him know before he hears about it from someone else." Word traveled fast in small towns.

As her mom's panic attack subsided, Ivy relaxed, but her chest was still filled with a dull ache that had nothing to do with her own racing heart. It was guilt for lying to her mother, a different kind of ache altogether.

She could only imagine how she had felt reading that Ivy's relationship with Kendall, the girlfriend she'd only recently been introduced to, was a complete sham.

The ambulance slowed as it rolled into the emergency room entrance. Rita stood and opened the back door of the vehicle as the younger man came around to help her get the gurney inside.

After she exited the ambulance, Ivy followed closely and tripped on an uneven part of the sidewalk. She twisted to try to tumble sideways but landed hard. Her shoulder burned with pain as it absorbed the shock. *Fuck!* Now wasn't the time to get careless.

The young male emergency tech rushed over. "Are you okay?" He extended his hand. "Here. Let me help you up."

Ivy took his hand. "I'm all right. Just a little embarrassed." She'd walked across that raised section many times and hadn't taken a header like that.

"Don't be embarrassed. It can happen to anyone." He brushed some dirt off her sleeve. "Did you hurt anything when you fell?"

"Just bruised my pride a little." Ivy winced as she put weight on her knee. "Tweaked my knee a tiny bit. Nothing serious though." She lifted her arm to rotate her shoulder, but pain seared through her, and she almost threw up.

"Let's get you inside and take a look at you just to make sure."

"I need to check on my mom first."

"They're working on her. She's stable. Here. Sit down on this bench." He walked with Ivy as she limped along, stretching her knee slowly. "I want to check if it's swollen or anything."

Ivy sat and rolled up her pant leg to find a raspberry the size of a golf ball across her kneecap. "Not terrible. Hopefully it won't swell too much."

The tech felt around her knee. "You got lucky. It doesn't seem very serious." He slid his hand to her ankle, moved it around. Maybe you should stay off it for a bit, just in case."

The pain in her knee was minimal, as was the throbbing in her shoulder. "At least I didn't face-plant on the ground."

The tech glanced at her face. "I wouldn't say that."

Ivy touched her cheekbone and winced. "So much for hiding my clumsiness."

"Come on." He stood. "Let's get inside and check on your mom. Then they can take a look at you too."

CHAPTER FORTY-NINE

Kendall was working on some sketches when the phone buzzed in her pocket. When she saw Ivy's name on the screen, a tingle rushed through her, and she smiled and pushed the green button. "Hey there. I was just thinking about you."

"My mom's been rushed to the hospital. She thinks she's having a heart attack." The panic in Ivy's voice was real.

"I'll be right there." She didn't wait for Ivy to finish explaining. She dropped what she was doing and ran to her car. She had no idea where the hospital was, but she would find it. Thank God for the Waze navigation app on her phone.

Her hands trembled as she gripped the steering wheel, her knuckles white with tension. The hospital parking lot was nearly full, so she didn't waste time looking for a space. She stopped her car in the passenger loading zone, threw it into Park, and rushed toward the entrance. All that mattered was getting inside to Ivy.

The automatic doors parted with a whoosh as she rushed through the entrance, her sneakers squeaking against the polished floor. The medicinal smell hit her immediately, that distinct blend of antiseptic and artificial air that filled all hospitals.

"I'm looking for Karen Patterson," she told the receptionist, breathless. "She was brought in about an hour ago. Her daughter Ivy is with her."

The woman typed something into her computer. "Patterson...yes, she's still in the ER." The woman pointed down the hall "Just through those—"

"Thank you," Kendall called over her shoulder, already hurrying toward the double doors.

The hallway felt endless. Kendall leaned against the wall, trying to steady her breathing before pushing through the doors. She and Ivy had been fake dating for only a week, but in that time, Kendall had grown to like Karen and admired her relationship with Ivy. The thought of losing her—of Ivy losing her mother—was unbearable.

When she finally pushed open the doors, Kendall spotted Ivy immediately. She was pacing the hallway outside the waiting room, still in her park ranger uniform, her usually neat hair scattered about her face.

"Ivy," Kendall called softly.

Ivy looked up, her face a mask of worry that cracked slightly at the sight of Kendall. Without a word, she walked into Kendall's open arms.

"Hey," Kendall whispered, holding her close. "I got here as fast as I could. How is she?"

Ivy pulled back, wiping quickly at her eyes. "They're saying it wasn't a heart attack."

"What is it then?"

"The doctor thinks it was an anxiety attack." Ivy's voice was hollow with disbelief. "We were at the coffee shop, and she collapsed while I was at the counter. I had someone call 911. I didn't know what else to do since she was clutching her chest. She thought it was her heart, and I wasn't sure."

"You did the right thing," Kendall said gently. "But she's okay?"

Ivy nodded. "My dad's in there with her now. They're running tests to be certain, but her heart looks strong. The doctor said anxiety can mimic heart attack symptoms perfectly—chest pain, shortness of breath, the works."

Kendall led Ivy to a row of chairs against the wall. "Has she been stressed lately?"

Ivy shook her head. "She saw a post you were tagged in by Cassie on social media."

"Oh my God. What did it say? I haven't really looked at it since I've been here. I didn't realize Cassie was still following me." Kendall took out her phone and hit the button for the app and found the post. "Shit." Why couldn't Cassie just leave her alone?

"Mom never mentioned anything about it to me either," Ivy said, slumping into a seat. "She's upset that I 'lied to her.'" She made air quotes with her fingers, then let her hands fall heavily into her lap. "I knew this would happen. I should've told her the truth from the beginning."

"Hey," Kendall said firmly, taking Ivy's hand. "This isn't your fault. And the important thing is she's going to be okay." If it was anyone's fault, it was Kendall's for not handling Cassie better. "What happened here?" Kendall touched Ivy's cheek below a fresh scrape.

"When I arrived, I was rushing to get in here and tripped on an uneven part of the sidewalk and fell." Ivy held up her palms. "I tried to catch myself but fell forward. Got a little scraped up."

"Looks like you landed hard." Kendall let her hand drop slowly to Ivy's shoulder and down her arm. "Does it hurt?" She cradled the back of Ivy's hand in hers.

"Not really. My shoulder and knee took the brunt of it."

"Has anyone looked at it?" Kendall stood and glanced around for a nurse. "Let's get you into an exam room and take a closer look."

Ivy shook her head. "It's fine."

"Can I see?" Kendall reached for the hem of Ivy's pants.

Ivy's hands brushed against hers as she reached down and tugged the pant leg up and over her knee. "Looks worse than it feels."

"That needs some attention." She glanced toward the reception desk. "Let me find someone."

"I'm fine." Ivy shoved her pant leg down. "I'll dress it once I get home." She started to stand. "Need to check on my mom."

"Wait here." Kendall placed her hand on her shoulder. "I'll get the nurse. Have her come give you an update."

"Thanks," Ivy said.

Kendall walked to the desk. "Can someone come out and give Ivy an update on her mother?"

The woman rotated her chair and looked behind her. "Sure. Let me ask."

Kendall walked back to Ivy. "They're going to send someone out."

Not long after that, a doctor emerged from the hallway, tablet in hand, and said, "Patterson family."

Ivy jumped to her feet. "Here." Ivy raised her hand. "I'm her daughter."

"Your mother is stable and is resting comfortably. All the cardiac tests came back normal."

"So, it was definitely anxiety?" Ivy asked. Kendall could see the relief wash across Ivy's face. She must have been terrified. Kendall would've been if something had happened to her mom.

The doctor nodded. "We believe so. Has she experienced any major life changes recently? Loss of a loved one, financial difficulties, anything that might trigger excessive worry?"

Ivy hesitated. "I don't think so." She seemed to want to keep that information to herself.

"Well, we'd like to keep her overnight for observation, but you can see her now if you'd like."

After the doctor left, Ivy turned to Kendall, looking lost. "I had no idea this would happen when she found out."

Kendall squeezed her hand. "Why don't we go in together? I'll stay as long as you need me."

"You don't have to—"

"I want to," Kendall said simply. "For both of you."

For the first time since Kendall arrived at the hospital, Ivy's face softened into something resembling a smile. "Thank you for coming," she whispered. "I didn't know who else to call."

"That's what I'm here for," Kendall said, wrapping an arm around Ivy's waist as they walked toward Karen's room. "Besides, your mom and I have a bird-watching date next weekend. Can't have her miss that."

That earned a small laugh from Ivy, the sound a welcome relief in the sterile hospital corridor.

As they paused outside the door, Ivy took a deep breath. "Ready?"

Kendall nodded, and they both stepped toward the room, ready to face whatever came next—together.

Ivy's dad met them as they started through the door. "You should probably wait until tomorrow to see your mother," he said as he shoved his crossed his arms across his chest. "I don't want her upset anymore tonight."

"But, Dad."

"Nope." He held up his hand. "You need to figure out whatever this is that's happening between you two and come clean with your mother. She doesn't deserve this, and neither do I."

Ivy sucked in a deep breath. "I know. I'm sorry, Dad."

"Now go home and get some rest." He put his fingers under Ivy's chin and assessed her injury. "You tend to your own wounds. I'll see to your mother." He turned and went back through the door.

Kendall reached out to Ivy. "Let's go home."

Ivy took her hand and laced her fingers with Kendall's. "Thank you again for coming."

Kendall nodded without a word. She would always come when Ivy called and would stay as long as she needed her.

CHAPTER FIFTY

Ivy stood in the doorway of her mother's hospital room, clutching her phone so tightly her knuckles looked white. Her mom glanced up from her book, reading glasses perched on the end of her nose.

"I'm still furious with you," Karen said, setting her book aside after a long silence. "And humiliated."

"I deserve that." Ivy nodded, wiping away a tear. "What can I do?"

Karen took another deep breath. "For starters, you can tell me the truth. The whole truth. About everything."

"Everything?" Ivy asked, suddenly looking nervous again.

"Everything," Karen said, her gaze now locked with Ivy's. "Starting with why you felt you needed to create this elaborate charade instead of just talking to me and your father."

Ivy took a deep breath. "I'm sorry, Mom. I'll tell you everything."

Her mother patted the edge of the bed. "Lance, maybe you should give us a minute."

"No. Dad needs to hear this too." Ivy crossed the room to sit beside her. Even over the antiseptic hospital smell, the familiar scent of her mom's lavender lotion was comforting as anxiety twisted her stomach into knots.

"I lied to you both," Ivy said, barely above a whisper. "About Kendall."

Her mom's expression remained open, waiting.

"We're not actually a couple. We never were." The words tumbled out now. "When you kept asking if I was seeing anyone, and then you mentioned setting me up with yet another one of your friends' daughters, I panicked. Kendall agreed to pretend to be my girlfriend for the duration of her visit." She kept Kendall's ex to herself for the time being, not wanting her mother to think Kendall had used the situation to her advantage. After all, Ivy was the one who put the whole fake relationship into play.

Ivy stared down at her hands. "I thought it would just be for a little while, until Kendall finished her business and went back to Oklahoma. But the interviews were extended a week, then everyone loved her so much, and you both seemed so happy for me, and it just snowballed."

Her mother was quiet for a long moment before asking, "Why didn't you just tell me you weren't interested in dating anyone?"

"I think she has, several times." Lance spoke up. "I don't think you were listening."

"Dad's right. I have mentioned it." She smiled. "Probably not firmly enough because I know you want me to be happy, and I didn't want to disappoint you." Ivy's voice caught. "The truth is, now I do have feelings for someone. Real feelings. For Kendall."

A tear slipped down her cheek. "What started as pretend for me isn't pretend anymore. Every time we're together, even when we're just practicing being a couple, feels more real than anything I've ever experienced. But for Kendall, it could still be just an act." She was still unsure, even after Kendall indicated she wanted more the other night.

Her mom reached out and tucked a strand of hair behind Ivy's ear. "Oh, honey."

"I'm sorry I lied to you," Ivy said, finally looking up. "I was embarrassed and confused, and I didn't know how to explain it all."

To Ivy's surprise, her mother smiled. "You know, I suspected something was off. Kendall is a terrible actor."

"What? No. She's been perfect—"

"Perfect for you, maybe." Her mom chuckled. "But every time you leave the room, that girl looks at you like she's memorizing you, afraid you might disappear. That's not the expression of someone who's pretending."

Ivy's heart skipped a beat. "You think…?"

Her mom squeezed her hand gently. "I think you should be having this conversation with Kendall, not me."

"You're probably right. I'm just not sure how to make it real." The last thing she wanted to happen was to have Kendall reject her.

"Maybe just tell her. You did a fine job with me."

Her mom was right, but Ivy was afraid of getting her heart broken.

Chapter Fifty-one

Ivy led the way up the narrow path on the mountain, her breath forming small clouds in the crisp autumn air. The forest around them was alive with color. Amber, crimson, and gold leaves were catching the early morning light, a sight Ivy never grew tired of. A gentle mist clung to the ground, giving the woods an ethereal quality.

It had been a few days since her mom had been released from the hospital, but today was the first day she and Kendall hadn't spent the morning with her. At her mother's suggestion, Ivy decided to take Kendall on a hike to one of her favorite places instead.

"Not much farther," she said, glancing back at Kendall. "Eagle Ridge is just past this next bend." The usually put-together, all-business Ivy wore regular hiking clothes and looked even hotter than in uniform.

Kendall nodded, adjusting the small pack on her shoulders. "I still can't believe I've been here many times before and never made this hike." It wasn't surprising since Noah wasn't much of a hiker.

"Most people don't know about it," Ivy replied, pushing a low-hanging branch aside. "My grandfather showed me when I was little. The eagles have been nesting here for generations."

They walked in comfortable silence for a few minutes, the only sounds their footsteps on the carpet of fallen leaves and the occasional call of a black-capped Carolina chickadee. The path grew steeper, and Ivy reached back instinctively, offering her hand to Kendall, who took it, her fingers warmed against Ivy's despite the morning chill.

"Watch your step here," Ivy said, navigating around a moss-covered rock. She didn't let go of Kendall's hand even after they passed the obstacle.

The trail opened suddenly onto a rocky outcropping that jutted from the mountainside. Below them, the valley stretched out in a patchwork of autumn colors, a silver ribbon of river winding through it. The rising sun painted everything in soft, golden light.

"Oh, wow," Kendall said, taking it all in as she tried to catch her breath. "This is incredible."

Ivy smiled, watching her face rather than the view. "Wait till you see the eagles." She led her to the northern edge of the ridge, where a mass of ancient pines grew. After taking out a small pair of binoculars from her pack, Ivy handed them to her.

"Look there," Ivy said, pointing. "Third tree from the left, about two-thirds of the way up."

Kendall raised the binoculars and adjusted the focus. After a moment, she saw light movement within the branches. "I see them. The nest is huge," she said, her voice rising with excitement.

"They add to it every year," Ivy explained, moving closer to her. "That pair has been coming back for at least a decade. And look. You can just make out the newly hatched chicks."

Kendall nodded. "Two of them. They're so big already." She'd never seen anything like this before except on social media. The parks department had installed a solar-powered camera to observe a pair of eagles in California's Big Bear Park. She'd been following them on and off for years.

"They'll fledge soon," Ivy said. "In a few weeks, they'll be taking their first flights."

They sat down on a flat rock close by, shoulders touching, passing the binoculars back and forth as the sun climbed higher, burning away the morning mist.

"It's strange to think about," Kendall said after a bit of silence. "These eagles have been doing this for thousands of years—building nests, raising their young—completely unaware of all the human drama occurring down below them."

Ivy nodded. "That's what I love about coming up here. It puts things in perspective."

"How so?" Kendall asked, turning to face her.

"All our worries, our deadlines, our complications seem so important. But then you see something like this—" she gestured toward the eagles "—something that's part of a life cycle that's been going on since long before we were here and will continue long after we're gone. It makes me feel small in the universe of things, but not in a bad way."

Kendall was quiet for a moment, taking in the depth of Ivy's statement. "I think I understand. It's humbling but also comforting somehow." She couldn't look at Ivy any longer and had to look away. Ivy was smart, sexy, and compassionate, and the impact Ivy was having her on her was too much.

"Exactly," she said softly. "It reminds me that we're part of something bigger."

The mother eagle took flight suddenly, her wingspan impressive as she caught an updraft and soared over the valley. They watched in silence as she circled once, twice, then dove toward the river below.

"I've never seen anything like this outside of webcams," Kendall said, letting her voice fill with wonder. "Thank you for bringing me here."

Ivy smiled. "I've wanted to share this with someone for a long time. I'm glad it is you." The brilliant hue of sunlight warmed her face.

Was it only the sunlight coloring her skin, Kendall wondered. Their eyes met, and for a moment, everything else seemed to fade away. The eagles, the vista, the autumn colors. Kendall reached out, gently tucking a strand of hair behind Ivy's ear, letting her hand linger on Ivy's cheek.

"You know," Kendall said quietly, her heart beating faster. "I think I'm starting to see why this place is so special to you." She sighed, feeling a warmth that had nothing to do with the rising sun.

Ivy leaned into her touch. "And now it will always remind me of you too." When Ivy bit her bottom lip, Kendall's toes curled, and her stomach did a huge somersault.

Kendall took her cue and the opportunity to brush her lips against Ivy's. The kiss was tentative and light, and she was unsure of moving forward, but she felt no resistance, only soft, sweet lips returning contact, urgency slowly increasing. Ivy gave her a green light by slipping her tongue between Kendall's lips, meeting hers. They snaked their arms around each other, and Kendall dug her fingers into Ivy's back as their tongues came into play and the kiss deepened. Her mind exploded with carnal thoughts as the tingle in her belly bounced farther south. There was no faking involved in this kiss. Her body told her to continue, but her mind told her to stop—now. She felt the hot wet drag of Ivy's tongue across her bottom lip as she broke the kiss. Much more of that and Kendall would be going nowhere else this morning but to Ivy's bedroom.

They sat in quiet, comfortable silence for a few minutes before Kendall shifted to put some necessary space between them. “I love this place. If I get this contract, I might never go back to Oklahoma again.”

“I’d be okay with that.” Ivy said. “And more adventures with you. Some of the best adventures happen before dawn.” She held up her phone sideways. “How about we take a selfie?” They leaned closer together and smiled

Kendall could attest to that, only the adventures she was thinking about now were usually conducted in bed. *Did Ivy like sex in the morning? Keep your mind on this nature adventure, Kendall.* She shook the thought from her head.

The sun climbed higher as they sat together on Eagle Ridge holding hands while no one was watching, looking at the eagles and talking sporadically in low, soothing voices. And as the morning wore on, the space Kendall had put between them slowly grew smaller.

CHAPTER FIFTY-TWO

Ivy hadn't wanted to leave Kendall this morning, but when her radio crackled to life, they headed back to the lodge, Ivy changed into her ranger uniform, and another workday in the wilderness began. The first call came from a local trail-maintenance crew. Something about a young deer trapped in some old fencing near the abandoned logging road. Ivy knew those areas well. The forest was slowly reclaiming the remnants of past human interference there.

She adjusted her ranger hat, scanning the dense pine forest around her, and found the deer about a mile down the rough dirt road. A young doe, probably no more than a few months old, had become entangled in an old wire fence, its slender leg caught in a rusted section of wire. The animal was exhausted, having clearly been struggling for hours.

"Easy now," Ivy murmured, approaching slowly. She carried wire cutters and a calming presence that had helped her through countless wildlife encounters. The deer trembled but seemed to sense her careful approach.

With practiced precision, she cut away the wire, speaking softly the entire time. "You're okay. Just gonna help you out." The wire gave way, and the young deer stumbled back, momentarily stunned. Within moments, it found its footing and bounded away into the dense forest, stopping briefly at the tree line to look back, almost as if in thanks.

By midday, the radio chirped again. A group of hikers was lost on the north trail—a winding path that could be tricky even for experienced trekkers. Ivy radioed back to base, then started up the trail, her GPS and emergency kit at the ready.

She found the group about two miles in. Four college students, appearing tired and slightly panicked. "You folks look like you could use some help," Ivy called out, her friendly tone immediately cutting through their anxiety.

They hadn't realized how far they'd wandered from the marked trail. Ivy pulled out her map, showing them exactly where they were. "See these ridge lines? They're your best landmarks. At this time of day, always keep the sun at your back, to the west, and you'll find your way to the lodge."

She walked them to the main trailhead, pointing out trail markers and sharing stories that made the hike feel shorter than usual. By the time they reached the visitors' center, they were laughing, their earlier panic seemingly forgotten.

As the afternoon waned, Ivy made one last stop in town. The local outdoor-supply store had a small selection of camping gear. She picked out a set of thick, comfortable cushions that were soft enough to make the truck bed comfortable for stargazing.

"Kendall's going to love these," she murmured to herself, imagining the night ahead. They'd been talking about spending the evening watching the Leonids meteor shower, and these cushions would make their impromptu stargazing setup perfect. She rolled the truck-bed cover back halfway and slid the cushions into the truck bed before she rolled the cover over the top and secured it tightly. The weather app on her phone said there was a possibility of showers this evening. She hoped they didn't last long or they would ruin her plans.

The drive back to the cabin was quiet, filled with thoughts of the woman who had come into her life by chance and had filled it with comfort. The setting sun painted the forest in shades of gold and deep green as it set on another day of protecting, guiding, and connecting with the wilderness she loved so deeply.

As she pulled up to the cabin, her stomach bounced as she saw Kendall in silhouette in the window, probably working on her latest landscape design. Home—in every sense of the word.

CHAPTER FIFTY-THREE

The cabin was quiet except for the soft crackling of the wood stove and the distant call of an owl. Ivy sat propped against the arm of the couch, her fingers tracing lazy patterns on Kendall's arm as she lay nestled against her.

Kendall's work clothes were draped over a chair, replaced by one of Ivy's soft flannel shirts. Her sketches from her proposed lodge project were spread across the small desk by the window, illuminated by a single reading lamp.

"Tell me about your day," Ivy murmured, her voice low and warm. Her hand never stopped its gentle movement—a touch that was more comfort than anything else.

Kendall shifted slightly, her head resting on Ivy's shoulder. "The playground design is coming together. I'm trying to incorporate natural elements—fallen logs for climbing, stone formations that blend with the existing landscape. Something that feels like an extension of the forest, not something imposed on it."

Ivy pressed a soft kiss to the top of Kendall's head. "Sounds like you're doing what you do best. Making spaces feel like they've always belonged."

The compliment hung in the air, soft and meaningful. Kendall's hand found Ivy's, their fingers intertwining. Outside, a light rain began to tap against the cabin windows—a gentle rhythm that seemed to match the quiet intimacy of the moment.

"How was your day?" Kendall asked, knowing Ivy's ranger shifts could be unpredictable.

Ivy's fingers continued their soothing motion. "Rescued a young deer caught in some fencing. Helped a group of hikers who got turned around on the north trail. Nothing extraordinary, but one of the good days."

Kendall lifted her head to meet Ivy's eyes. No words were necessary. They both understood that good days meant days spent doing exactly what they were meant to do, in the places that felt most like home.

The rain continued its soft percussion against the window, a quiet accompaniment to their shared silence. Kendall savored these moments alone with Ivy. Soon they would go to the diner for dinner, be on public display again, acting as though it all mattered more than it did, and knowing it mattered more than it should.

The neon sign of the diner cast a warm glow across Kendall and Ivy's booth by the window that was still dotted with raindrops from the light cloudburst earlier. The red vinyl seats squeaked as Kendall shifted, scanning the laminated menu even though she'd ordered the same Denver omelet with a side of bacon she'd had the last time she was there with Ivy.

"You know, eventually you'll have to try something different," Ivy said, folding her menu and setting it aside. Her dark curls were pulled into a messy bun, a few strands framing her face.

Kendall shrugged. "When I like something, I stick with it. I don't see you ordering anything different."

"Why mess with perfection? Besides, their French toast is amazing."

"You'll never know how good the omelet is if you don't—" She froze mid-sentence, her eyes fixed on something over Ivy's shoulder.

"What?" Ivy asked, turning to follow Kendall's gaze.

Kendall put her hand on Ivy's. "Don't look, but June just walked in," she whispered, slouching lower in her seat.

A tingle of jealousy shot through Kendall as the young, very attractive waitress walked through the diner's entrance wearing tight jeans and a leather jacket, hair falling in perfect waves down her shoulders. The same June who'd been not-so-subtly pursuing Ivy for weeks before Kendall and Ivy had started their fake relationship to ward off unwanted romantic attention.

Ivy groaned. "Seriously? We came here specifically to get away from the lodge so we wouldn't run into her or anyone else."

"Well, she's here now," Kendall said, watching as June scanned the diner. The moment their eyes met, Kendall knew they'd been spotted. "And she's coming over."

"Hey, Ivy," June said, appearing beside their booth with a smile that seemed to be reserved only for Ivy. "Didn't expect to see you here. And you're Kendall, right?"

"Right," Kendall replied, forcing a smile. "What brings you to this part of town?"

"Meeting some friends for dinner," June said, gaze drifting back to Ivy. "It's been a while since we've talked. How've you been?"

"Good," Ivy said. "Just busy with work and, you know, life."

"We should catch up some time," June said, leaning slightly closer to Ivy. "Maybe coffee next week?"

Something tightened in Kendall's chest—another pang of jealousy, which was ridiculous because this was all supposed to be pretend… until a few days ago. Before she could think too much about it, Kendall reached across the table and took Ivy's hand in hers.

"Sorry to interrupt," Kendall said, thumb stroking over Ivy's knuckles, "but I think our food's coming soon, babe."

Ivy looked momentarily startled but recovered quickly. "Right, thanks, honey." She turned her hand to intertwine their fingers, and Kendall tried to ignore the way her heart skipped at the contact.

June's smile faltered slightly. "Oh, so you two really are together?"

"Almost six months now," Kendall added, the lie rolling easily off her tongue. She brought Ivy's hand to her lips and pressed a quick kiss to her knuckles, surprising even herself with the gesture.

Ivy's cheeks flushed. "We're actually celebrating tonight," she added, leaning into the charade with unexpected enthusiasm. "Kendall just got promoted at work."

"Congratulations," June said, her smile not quite sincere. "Well, I should go find my friends. Good seeing you both."

As June walked away, Kendall started to pull her hand back, but Ivy held on.

"Wait," Ivy whispered. "She's still watching."

They remained like that, hands clasped across the table, until their waitress arrived with two plates. Only then did they reluctantly let go.

"Nice touch with the hand kiss," Ivy said quietly, picking up her fork. "Very convincing."

"The celebration was a good addition," Kendall said, suddenly very interested in cutting her omelet into perfect triangles. "Quick thinking."

A beat of silence passed between them, filled with something neither of them seemed ready to acknowledge.

"Do you think she bought it?" Ivy finally asked, stealing a piece of bacon from Kendall's plate—a habit Kendall pretended to hate but secretly found endearing.

Kendall glanced over at June's table, where June was pointedly not looking in their direction. "Definitely. You're officially off her radar."

"Good," Ivy said, but something in her voice made Kendall look up. Their eyes met across the table, and for a moment, Kendall wondered if either of them knew exactly what was real anymore.

"So," Kendall said, clearing her throat, "tell me more about this promotion I apparently just got."

Ivy laughed, and just like that, the moment shifted back to comfortable territory—or what passed for it these days. "Well, for starters, you're now making enough to pay for dinner."

"Is that so?" Kendall raised an eyebrow, fighting a smile.

"Absolutely." Ivy nodded solemnly. "It's tradition. The newly promoted always pay."

As they fell into their familiar banter, Kendall tried not to think about how natural it had felt to hold Ivy's hand, or how much she'd wanted to lean across the table and kiss more than just her knuckles. After all, some lines weren't meant to be crossed—even if crossing them felt increasingly inevitable.

CHAPTER FIFTY-FOUR

What was left of the day's light had faded through the window, leaving behind a deep indigo canvas dotted with the first few stars of evening. Ivy leaned forward, her elbows on the table, watching Kendall finish eating the last of her omelet.

"Hey," Ivy said, suddenly feeling nervous. "I was thinking. There's this spot I know, up on Diamond Mountain Peak. You can see the whole valley from there, and on clear nights like tonight, the stars are so vivid, it's incredible."

Kendall glanced up, pushing a strand of her blond hair behind her ear. "Yeah?"

"Yeah. I've got some cushions and blankets in my truck. I thought we could drive up, maybe hang out in the truck bed for a while, and catch the meteor shower." Ivy suggested, trying to sound casual despite the flutter in her chest. "If we were a little younger, I'd suggest we pick up a six-pack on the way," she said with a grin, trying to hide her nervousness.

Kendall's lips curved into a smile. "That sounds perfect, actually. I could use some star therapy after being cooped up with paperwork all day."

Twenty minutes later, Ivy's pickup wound its way up the mountain road, headlights cutting through the darkness. Kendall sat beside her, window slightly cracked, the cool night air tousling her hair. They drove mostly in comfortable silence, the radio playing softly beneath the sound of tires on gravel.

When they reached the lookout point, Ivy backed the truck toward the edge, giving them a panoramic view of the valley below. Tiny lights from the town twinkled in the distance.

"This is gorgeous," Kendall said, eyes wide.

Ivy hopped out, rolled back the cover, and lowered the tailgate. "Wait till you see what's above us."

Together they arranged cushions and blankets in the truck bed, creating a nest of comfort. Ivy pulled herself up first, then offered Kendall her hand. Their fingers lingered together a moment longer than necessary before they settled in, shoulders touching as they lay back.

Above them, the night sky sparkled with countless stars, a brilliant canvas stretching endlessly above the mountain valley. A vast ocean of stars. The Milky Way stretched across the darkness, a luminous river of light.

"Wow." Kendall turned to Ivy, the soft moonlight catching the golden highlights in her hair. "I've never seen the stars be so clear before," she whispered, her breath creating a small cloud in the cool night air.

"One of the perks of mountain life," Ivy said, her voice equally soft, as if speaking too loudly might disturb the stars themselves.

They pointed out constellations to each other, creating new ones when the real ones eluded them. Ivy found herself watching Kendall more than the sky, memorizing the way starlight reflected in her eyes.

"Look. The meteor shower." Kendall pointed to the sky.

Ivy glanced up to see a dazzling display of silvery light streaking across the night sky but was drawn back to the excitement in Kendall's eyes.

"It's spectacular." Kendall kept her eyes glued to the sky for the better part of fifteen minutes until the shower faded. "How does that happen?"

"Meteor showers?"

Kendall nodded. "What makes them so beautiful?"

Ivy loved that Kendall was so curious. "When Earth passes through the debris trail of a comet, it results in a higher concentration of individual meteors that appear to come from one specific point in the sky. The spatter or stream of light that you just saw is what's known as the radiant."

"I've never seen anything like that before."

"Probably because you live in a metropolitan area. They're easier to see in dark clear skies. This particular meteor shower hasn't happened since 1966."

A slight chill crept into the air, and Kendall moved closer, pulling one of the blankets over them both.

"Better?" Ivy asked.

"Much," Kendall said softly. Their faces were just inches apart now, breath mingling in the cool air.

Ivy's heart pounded as she felt Kendall's hand find hers beneath the blanket. The moment hung between them, fragile and electric.

"I've been wanting to do this since we shared that mind-blowing kiss on our walk this morning," Kendall murmured, leaning closer.

"Me too." Ivy whispered as their lips met, tentative at first, then with growing confidence. Ivy moved her hand to Kendall's waist, drawing her closer. She could taste the sweetness of the syrup they'd had with dinner, could feel Kendall's smile against her mouth. Every ounce of emotion she'd walled up inside crashed right through the dam. As the kiss deepened, every nerve ending fired—every inch of her skin tingled. She couldn't remember a time when she'd been kissed so thoroughly.

When they finally broke apart, both slightly breathless, Ivy pressed her forehead against Kendall's.

"That was…" Ivy didn't have the words to explain how she was feeling.

"Overdue," Kendall said with a soft laugh.

They lay together, trading slow kisses beneath the canopy of stars, the world below forgotten. Ivy traced the line of Kendall's jaw with her fingertips, still not quite believing this was happening.

Eventually, Kendall shivered despite the blankets and their shared warmth.

"We should probably get in the truck," Ivy suggested reluctantly. "It gets pretty cold up here once it's fully night."

Kendall nodded but made no move to get up. Instead, she captured Ivy's lips in another kiss, this one deeper, more urgent than before. "Or," Kendall said when they pulled apart, her voice husky, "we could go back to the cabin and continue this somewhere warmer."

Ivy smiled, tucking a strand of hair behind Kendall's ear. "I like the way you think."

They gathered the blankets and cushions quickly, stealing glances and touches as they worked. As Ivy closed the tailgate, Kendall pressed against her from behind, arms wrapping around her waist, lips finding the sensitive spot just below her ear, and the throb between her legs skyrocketed.

"If you keep that up, we're going to end up naked right here in the truck." Ivy said, turning into Kendall's arms. A soft breeze floated through Kendall's hair, carrying the sweet scent of her citrus shampoo into her nose, igniting all her senses again.

"Then I guess I'll have to behave. For now," Kendall said with a mischievous smile. But she didn't. As soon as they got into the truck cab, the space between them dissolved quickly and deliberately. Kendall's hand rested on the worn leather seat, fingertips just touching Ivy's. Then their lips met in a gentle, tender kiss that tasted of heat and mountain air, of possibility and connection. "I suggest you put this truck in gear and get us down the mountain fast," Kendall said with a lick of her lips.

The drive back down the mountain seemed to take both an eternity and no time at all. Whatever was happening between them had been building since they met—a slow, sweet tension finally finding release.

As the cabin came into view, lights glowing warm against the darkness, they exchanged a look of shared anticipation. Whatever tomorrow would bring, tonight belonged to them—to this unexpected connection beneath an endless sky of stars.

Chapter Fifty-five

As soon as they were inside, Kendall lost all her willpower when Ivy pulled her into another steaming kiss. Their tongues moved like they'd been dancing together for years.

"I've been waiting so long for this," Kendall whispered against Ivy's lips.

"You have?" Ivy's voice was soft and uncertain.

"Uh-huh. Since the moment we had our first pretend kiss." She remembered that day perfectly. Ivy's mahogany hair had been lightly tousled by the wind, her cheeks tinged with a tad of pink. Kendall's anxiety had almost stopped her from suggesting it.

"We were on the trail. I was so nervous, my hands were all hot and sweaty."

"They were? I didn't notice. All I remember is when you turned around and smiled at me, my world shifted." She moved up to her ear and whispered, "God, you were gorgeous." A ranger uniform had never looked so good.

"I have to admit, my world shifted a bit that day as well." Ivy smiled softly.

Finally, Kendall was certain she hadn't been the only one who felt the connection. She tugged Ivy's flannel shirt from her pants and slipped her hands underneath. The soft, bare skin she felt was warmer than she expected. Ivy was hot, sizzling, even. She skimmed her fingers over Ivy's ribs and felt her quiver, a sensation Kendall thoroughly enjoyed.

Ivy covered Kendall's mouth with hers and kissed her deeply, tongues mingling gently, bringing her arousal higher. She broke the kiss with a growl and trailed small nibbles across Kendall's cheek to her neck before tugging Kendall's sweater over her head and tossing it to the floor. Kendall created a small space between them to take in the intoxication overcoming her. She hadn't thought she'd ever be here, in this moment with Ivy.

"You're so beautiful," Ivy whispered as she traced the valley between Kendall's breasts with her fingers. "Is this okay?"

"Yes," Kendall whispered and let out a soft moan. It was so much more than okay.

Ivy slipped her thumb beneath the band of Kendall's bra, pushing it up just enough to flick her nipple between her fingers. Kendall couldn't hold in the gasp as the touch sent the most incredible jolt coursing to her clit. She kicked off her shoes and quickly unbuttoned her jeans and let them fall to the floor, and Ivy did the same but struggled to remove her boots. Kendall took charge, quickly untying each boot as Ivy leaned on the bed, and when Ivy stood to work the buttons on her shirt, Kendall assisted, kissing each bare spot as it appeared as they worked their way down.

When they fell onto the bed, Ivy took control, and Kendall let her. Every inch of her needed to be touched, sucked, licked. One swipe of Ivy's tongue across Kendall's nipple made her squirm beneath Ivy as a jolt zapped through her. Every part of her was hypersensitive. If she kept this up, she was going to explode before Ivy even got between her legs. Ivy seemed to sense that possibility and gave her nipple one more twirl before she abandoned it and moved lower.

The first touch of Ivy's tongue almost sent her tumbling into orgasm immediately, but Ivy slowed her pace to an almost halt. She opened her eyes to find Ivy watching her, the look in her eyes dark and steamy. If she was asking for permission, Kendall would gladly provide it.

"More of that, please," she breathed in a whisper.

Ivy didn't waste any time giving her just that. She moved in between Kendall's legs and let out a moan as she pressed her mouth against the hot wetness waiting for her. She knew exactly what to do and where to touch her, taking her somewhere she hadn't been in a very long time, if ever. The heat of Ivy's mouth between her legs had Kendall on the verge of letting go, and when Ivy pushed her tongue inside and back up across her clit, Kendall didn't hold back. She tumbled into orgasm as a light show more intense than any meteor shower blurred her vision. Ivy held firm, stroking her tongue across Kendall's clit repeatedly until she couldn't take any more and reached to stop her. Ivy laced their fingers together and pressed her hand to the sheets as she slipped a finger inside and continued the rhythm with her tongue. Suddenly, without warning, another orgasm took her. A rush of sweet, hot, pleasure shot through Kendall, electrifying her as she let the deeper, more intense, climax overtake her.

When the orgasm subsided, Ivy rested her head on Kendall's thigh momentarily before she crawled up next to Kendall and kissed her gently. The warmth that enveloped her when she saw the tears welling in Ivy's eyes overwhelmed her. It was clear that Ivy was feeling emotional, and Kendall's heart told her she felt the same.

"I...That was—" Ivy couldn't seem to find any words.

"I know." Kendall held her closer and pulled the blanket over them. She couldn't quite find the words to describe what she was feeling either.

"I need to be honest with you." Ivy lifted her head and shifted her weight onto her elbow to make eye contact. "I haven't been with a lot of women, and I haven't felt like this with anyone before." Ivy swiped the tears from her cheeks. "I know that's a lot of information. Probably too much."

Kendall turned toward her, wiped the remaining moisture from her face. "It's not too much. It's what I hoped for. I haven't been with many women either, and when I have been, it's been because I really care about them."

Ivy smiled, and all the bells and whistles went off in Kendall. No one had ever made her react the way Ivy did. She pushed Ivy back onto the bed and kissed her before trailing her tongue from her ear to her collarbone. The taste of Ivy's skin was a sweetness she'd been craving for too long.

Ivy let out a soft moan, and Kendall was instantly wet. Kendall glanced up, caught by Ivy's gorgeous green eyes, the yellow starbursts in them more vivid than she'd seen before. Ivy moaned louder when Kendall slid a finger between her folds and felt the glorious hot wetness, swirled her finger in it. Soon her fingers were deep inside. Ivy raised her hips, her breasts heaving with each stroke. This was only the beginning. Kendall wanted much more of this.

Within minutes, Kendall had moved between Ivy's legs to finish with her mouth what she'd started with her fingers. She licked and stroked as Ivy grasped fistfuls of bedsheets and arched into her, beginning to quiver. She let out a cry, and Kendall forged on as the orgasm ripped through her. She slowed her rhythm, and Ivy's hips collapsed against the bed.

As she lay between Ivy's legs, her head on Ivy's thigh, she couldn't resist lightly flicking the swollen clit she'd just brought to orgasm. Ivy bounced with tiny spasms and softly moaned, a sound Kendall was becoming quite fond of. Kendall's name flew from Ivy's lips in a whimper. With that, Kendall grabbed her ass and crushed her mouth against her again to make Ivy come hard and fast. She was enjoying this moment to the fullest.

Then she lay there still feeling the beats of Ivy's body as each aftershock went through her. Every muscle felt like jelly, spent in the most glorious way. She crawled up beside Ivy, kissed her lightly, and laid her head on Ivy's chest. Any awkwardness that had remained between them was completely gone now. When Kendall had journeyed up the mountain, she'd been looking forward to three blissful days of nature but had now experienced so much more than she'd ever imagined.

Chapter Fifty-six

Ivy was nervous as she drove up to the veterinary clinic. It was just past noon, and Ivy had picked up takeout from the Thai restaurant in town. It was Shauna's favorite, and she needed something to soften the news she planned to tell her. She sat in the truck for a few minutes, thinking about the changes that had happened between her and Kendall over the past few days. The memory of this morning's lovemaking filled her head. Ivy had felt as though she'd just drifted off to sleep when she was awakened by light touches circling her belly button. She'd glanced at Kendall's fingers and then at Kendall. As soon as they made eye contact, Kendall chuckled.

"I didn't mean to wake you." Kendall grinned and kissed her softly. Then her lips were on Ivy's neck, her hand drifting slowly across her stomach, her fingers tripping lower, gliding lightly across Ivy's clit, teasing her mercilessly.

Heat rushed through her as she remembered the warmth of Kendall's mouth on her breast. She'd sucked in a deep breath as Kendall's tongue had circled her nipple and flicked it back and forth, sending sharp jolts through her. She'd squeezed her breasts together, dividing her time between them. Ivy had wriggled beneath her. She couldn't take much more. Kendall had seemed to read her and moved slowly down her body, the warm wetness of her tongue igniting each and every sense as she went. Sex had never felt this good.

She'd quivered when Kendall's tongue had moved to her clit, flicking at it, making it swell with anticipation. Heat rose quickly within her, and she hadn't been able to stand it anymore. She'd pleaded with Kendall to make her come, and she had. A jolt shot through her as she recalled Kendall's hot breath against her. She'd bucked as Kendall's fingers had entered her, curling inside her. Her mind had fragmented into blinding shards of color as the staggering orgasm overtook her, and she'd let out a cry as she grabbed a fistful of sheet to ride it out.

Kendall had rested her head against Ivy's thigh as she'd stroked a finger slowly through her folds. Ivy had put her hand to her forehead as an occasional jolt still hit her. Then Kendall had crawled up next to her and kissed her tenderly on the lips before she drifted off to sleep.

Contentedly satisfied, Ivy had lain in bed that morning with Kendall curled up next to her, asleep. Just moments earlier there had been no words, just the sound of soft kisses and caresses as Kendall had explored her. Feelings were bubbling to the surface that she hadn't experienced before. Ivy shook herself out of her dreamy state. How was she going to explain all this to Shauna?

She pushed open the truck door and grabbed the bag of food from the passenger seat. Shauna was finishing some work at the front desk when Ivy walked into the clinic. "Hey. I brought lunch. Thai from that place you like." She held up the bag.

Shauna looked up from the computer with a smile. "You're a lifesaver. I haven't eaten since I had a granola bar at seven a.m."

Ivy set the food on a small, white table in the break room while Shauna washed her hands.

"So, how's everything going with Kendall?"

"I'm not quite sure how to tell you, but I've been keeping a secret from you and everyone else."

Shauna narrowed her eyes. "What's going on, Ivy?"

"I've been lying to you about Kendall." Ivy's voice lowered, worry seeping into her chest. This fake relationship felt more real than ever, but it had started as a lie, and there would be backlash. After her parents, Shauna would be the first of many to snap that whip.

Shauna shook her head. "I knew something wasn't right from the start."

"I'm sorry. I didn't intend to lie to anyone. I was trying to help Kendall get out of a situation with her ex, and it just happened."

Shauna took a seat at the table. "Sounds like a dangerous arrangement. You're playing with fire, Ivy."

"I know, and I'm not sure what to do." Ivy's voice cracked.

"Honestly, you don't seem to have had any trouble convincing your family and friends that you're madly in love with Kendall."

Ivy focused on opening the food containers. “Yeah. About that.”

Shauna paused as she dipped food onto her plate. “What happened? Did your parents figure it out?”

Ivy sighed, pushing a container of pad Thai toward Shauna. “Yeah. My mom found out and had a major panic attack. We both thought she was having a heart attack.”

“Is she okay?”

Ivy nodded. “She’s fine.” She dropped her head back. “She was just so happy that I’ve finally found someone.”

“So, what’s the problem now that she knows?” Shauna took a bite. “Oh.” Shauna’s voice lowered. “It’s not just playing house for you, though, is it? You have real feelings for her.”

She nodded. “I don’t know how or when it happened, but everything has changed, and I feel much more than friendship for her.”

Shauna touched her arm. “I saw the infatuation in your eyes that night you brought the raccoons in.”

“She’s so different from what I imagined. I mean, I didn’t even really like her at first. Thought she was a spoiled middle-class girl who’d been given everything in her life.”

“And she’s not?” Shauna didn’t seem upset, just genuinely interested.

“No.” She shook her head. “That couldn’t be further from the truth. She’s been supporting her family in some way or another since she was sixteen.”

“That’s a lot of responsibility.” Shauna took another bite of her food.

“I know. I can’t imagine having all that on me at such a young age.”

“You can’t save her, if that’s what you’re trying to do.” Shauna gave her a supportive half smile.

“I’m not.” Ivy shook her head. “She’s got a real shot at getting the contract on the landscape redesign at the lodge. She’s got some great ideas.”

“For what it’s worth, I think it’s changed for her too. Saw that the other night at dinner.”

“Really?” Hope bled into her chest, pushing out the worry. “I think I’m falling for her,” Ivy said quietly.

Shauna nearly choked on her food. “I’m sorry, what?”

“I know it’s ridiculous. This was supposed to be temporary. Just to get through her having to interact with her ex and stop the setups from my folks.”

"But now?" Shauna studied Ivy. "I can see you're actually smitten with her."

Ivy dropped her fork onto the plate. "Pretty obvious, huh?"

Shauna laughed softly. "Ivy, I haven't seen you light up talking about someone like this since…well, ever."

"Right." Ivy groaned. "Now when she holds my hand for show, I don't want her to let go. When she puts her arm around me at family dinners, I lean into it. Last night we were practicing our couple story for my aunt's interrogation and ended up talking until almost two a.m." She pushed her plate away. "But we had an agreement. A few months of pretending and then a mutual breakup after the holidays. No complications."

"Eat." Shauna pushed her plate back to her. "Does Kendall know how you feel?"

Ivy nodded. "I took her to the peak to see the meteor shower a few days ago, and one thing led to another."

"You dog. You set it up." Shauna laughed. "She didn't have a chance."

"I did want it to happen, but she made the first move."

"Okay." Shauna added more food to her plate. "So, you know now that she has feelings for you too."

"She's been so professional about the whole thing. She even has a spreadsheet of relationship milestones to make our story believable."

"A spreadsheet?" Shauna raised an eyebrow. "That's…thorough."

"That's Kendall. Everything planned out to the last detail."

"You're pretty organized yourself. Sounds like a perfect match." Shauna took a bite of her pad thai and chewed. "You know, people who need that much control are often hiding something."

"What do you mean?"

"I mean, who agrees to be someone's fake girlfriend for a few months? Someone who either really needs the money or…"

"Or?" Ivy felt hope rise in her chest.

Shauna shrugged. "Or someone who wanted an excuse to spend time with you."

The clinic phone rang, and Shauna got up to answer it. "Just something to think about. And, Ivy? That look on your face right now. That's how I knew. Be careful, my friend. It might be only a few hours away, but she lives in a different state."

CHAPTER FIFTY-SEVEN

Kendall adjusted the strap of her messenger bag as she walked along the path not far from the lodge. She'd left Ivy hours ago because Ivy had plans for lunch with Shauna, and Kendall didn't want to intrude on that. Back at the lodge, the board was deciding the fate of the final bidders. The last of the landscape design proposals were finally complete. She'd spent so many hours on this project—sustainable trail systems, native plant restoration, the whole vision for revitalizing the park. She'd outlined it in phases, just as Ivy suggested. She didn't know what she would've done without her help.

Her phone buzzed. Cassie. Again. The third call this week. Kendall let it go to voice mail, but moments later, a text appeared:

I'm at our spot. We need to talk. Now.

Our spot? When Cassie had been here for the initial presentations, she'd met her once at a picnic table near the campgrounds, but that wasn't a pleasant experience, and she'd never consider any place in this park their spot. Her shoulders tensed. She'd avoided Cassie since they'd met at the coffee shop when she was here before. She'd abandoned their partnership, and Kendall wanted nothing to do with her, but something in the message's urgent tone made her change direction, heading toward the campgrounds.

As she came around the bend to them, the picnic table appeared just as she remembered it—dappled sunlight, wildflowers scattered across the grass nearby. Cassie sat on the table with her feet on one of the benches, her blond hair catching the light. She looked up as Kendall approached, her smile not quite as attractive as it used to be.

"I was beginning to think you weren't coming," Cassie said.

"What do you want, Cassie? I have work to do."

"Ah, yes, your big park project. The one I've been aced out of since you've been working on yours with Ranger Ivy." Cassie's voice took on an edge. "Quite cozy, the two of you."

Kendall kept her expression neutral. "She's been helpful. She knows the park better than anyone."

"A bit too helpful, don't you think?" Cassie stood up, crossing her arms. "She's been giving you access to restricted ecological surveys, sharing internal park documents, and letting you into closed areas for your little site visits."

A cold feeling spread through Kendall's chest. *How could she know about anything that Ivy shared with her?* "None of that is true."

"Of course it is. I know because I've become friendly with someone in the Parks Department administration. She mentioned how strange it was that a freelance landscape architect had access to so much privileged information." Cassie took a step closer. "Information that's supposed to stay within the department until the official bidding process is over."

"Ivy would never—"

"Break protocol? Violate department ethics? Play favorites?" Cassie's smile widened. "Maybe the Parks Committee would be interested to know about that before they make their decision."

Kendall clenched her hands into fists. "This is low, even for you."

"Is it? I'm just concerned about procedural integrity." Cassie raised her eyebrows. "After all, I don't have access to that information, and I doubt anyone else does either."

"This is about us, not Ivy. She did nothing wrong."

"That's not what the ethics board will think." Cassie brushed an invisible speck from her sleeve. "I heard she's working on some EMT certification too. It would be a shame if something derailed that."

Kendall took a deep breath. "What do you want, Cassie?"

"What I've always wanted. A chance to talk. A real conversation about what happened between us." Her voice softened slightly. "Dinner. Tonight. Just to talk."

"And if I refuse?"

Cassie shrugged. "Then I make a call. My friend is very interested in department ethics."

Kendall looked away, watching a bird flit between branches. Winning this contract was everything she'd worked for, but she couldn't risk Ivy's career.

"Fine," Kendall finally said. "Dinner. But that's it. And you leave Ivy out of this completely."

"Perfect." Cassie's smile returned to its full wattage. "I'll text you the details. And Kendall? Wear something nice."

As Cassie walked away toward the lodge, Kendall pulled out her phone. She needed to warn Ivy and figure out exactly how much trouble they might be in.

"Wait." Cassie's voice startled her. She'd turned around. "I'm sorry. That's not really the way I wanted to do this. I want us to work on this contract together, if you're willing."

"What? Why would I do that?" She would just be setting herself up for a lot of work and disappointment.

"I don't like the way things ended between us." Cassie sat on the bench and patted the spot next to her. "Can we talk about it? Maybe resolve a few things?"

"What's there to resolve? You set the terms for everything." Kendall felt like she'd been gut-punched. "You acted like the breakup and our partnership dissolution was clean." Like it hadn't mattered to her at the time.

"Clean?" Cassie let out a low chuckle. "There's nothing clean about being broke. All those years, all that work—and now what? I've got nothing."

"I'm not swimming in money either." Kendall rubbed her forehead. "You did this, not me. *You made love to me and moved out the next weekend.* I was blindsided. You found another woman and moved on with your life—*with her.*"

"Yeah. Well, that's done." Cassie's voice rose as she stood. "Sex doesn't cover expenses." She moved closer. "You walked away with half our assets, and I was left scrambling to stay afloat." She poked a finger in Kendall's chest. "And you were just going to try to snag this cash-cow contract for yourself."

Kendall held her temper. "I wasn't the one who walked away. You did. The park contract would've been *our* cash cow if you hadn't left me." Who knew if she'd even get the contract.

Their eyes locked. Years of shared history, professional intimacy, and personal betrayal hung between them—unspoken but palpable.

Cassie flushed with anger and desperation. Kendall watched her, with her arms crossed, a mixture of defiance and hurt flickering in her eyes. The remnants of their once-shared life hung in the silence between them. Admitting she was wrong had never been easy for Cassie.

"You don't understand." Cassie's voice cracked, a raw edge of panic cutting through her words. "Everything we built is gone now. The partnership, the investments, all of it—collapsed."

"Again, you did that. Not me." Kendall knew the financial implosion wasn't just about money, but about trust, about the dreams they'd jointly constructed and then Cassie had systematically dismantled.

"You understand what this means, right? Everything we built is gone. I'm gone unless you get this contract and share it with me. I have nothing left," Cassie said, her hands trembling slightly. "Nothing."

"I can't do that, Cassie. I don't trust you anymore." Kendall remained stonily silent, fighting to keep her gaze steady. The finality in Cassie's statement hung in the air. This declaration of defeat she'd never expected from Cassie revealed more about their fractured relationship than any elaborate explanation could. Their partnership had been more than a business arrangement. It had been a complex emotional landscape now reduced to this desperate confrontation at a picnic table in a public park, with everything—and nothing—between them.

CHAPTER FIFTY-EIGHT

The campground area had been quiet, with most campers enjoying the trails. Late-afternoon sunlight was filtering through the trees as Ivy checked the area around the restrooms for obstacles and trash. She'd heard Kendall and Cassie engaged in a heated conversation but couldn't find a way to escape, so she'd opted to remain out of sight.

Cassie rounded the corner, eyes wet with tears. She stopped short before plowing into Ivy. "You heard all that?"

Ivy nodded. She hadn't meant to eavesdrop, but she'd gotten trapped behind the restrooms and couldn't find a way to get away without being seen.

"I know you've been working with Kendall on the landscape-restoration proposal." Cassie quickly wiped her eyes.

"I may have provided some park information to her."

Cassie took a deep breath. "I need to be direct with you. Kendall isn't who you think she is."

Ivy pulled her eyebrows together. "What do you mean?" She was willing to listen to what Cassie had to say to avoid more conflict but wasn't sure she could trust her.

"She's using you. Not just professionally, but romantically. I know Kendall. This contract means everything to her design firm, and she'll do anything to get it, including getting involved with you to improve her chances." Cassie clearly had no idea that the whole plan for the fake relationship was Ivy's idea.

"That's a serious accusation. You two have a history, I assume?" Ivy knew the story, maybe not the whole story, which she'd just received a deeper glimpse of from what she'd overheard.

"We were together for four years. I know her tactics. She's charming, persuasive, and, when a professional opportunity is on the line, she becomes laser focused. This park contract? It's her biggest potential project this year." Kendall had told Ivy the exact opposite. Cassie had conveniently reversed the roles between them.

"And you're telling me this out of...what? Concern? Jealousy?" Ivy didn't believe her.

"Honestly? A bit of both." Cassie's voice softened. "I don't want to see you get hurt, and I don't want to see the park get a design from someone who's more interested in winning than in genuine restoration."

"I appreciate your concern. But Kendall's proposal has real merit. I've reviewed it extensively." Ivy had seen Kendall's proposal with the actual environmental-impact assessments. Kendall had also told her how Cassie designed just enough to look responsible, but her real goal was always future construction contracts, not beautification.

"Just be careful. Professional admiration and personal interest can look very similar with her, and I'm sure your assistance wouldn't look good to your boss." Cassie raised her eyebrows. "Isn't that considered a conflict of interest?" Seemed Cassie was good at making threats.

Tension hung in the air, unresolved. "Noted," Ivy said.

"Kendall and I aren't done yet. We're still together. I know we've been keeping things low-key lately because of everything that happened with the partnership, but we never actually broke up completely."

"Kendall never mentioned you were still together. In fact, she said you broke up with her, and I think I just overheard that as well."

"She might say otherwise, but she's still in love with me. And honestly, that's why I wanted to talk to you directly. I'm not upset. I just thought you deserved to know the truth about where things stand."

"I appreciate that. But I can take care of myself."

"I didn't want you to get caught in the middle without knowing what's really going on. This is awkward. I feel terrible."

"Please don't. Thank you for being honest with me." She had no intention of hanging Kendall out to dry, even if this all had started as a fake relationship.

"I know this is uncomfortable, but I'm hoping we can move past it. Our friendship matters to me."

What friendship? She'd interacted with Cassie twice, and neither time had been friendly. "I'll definitely take a step back if needed, but I'll have a conversation with Kendall first." All the things Kendall had told her about Cassie were true. She was a charming narcissist to the bone and seemed ruthless to boot.

"Can you and I just figure out how to handle this going forward without letting Kendall know about this conversation?"

"I'm not sure that's possible. Kendall and I don't keep secrets."

Cassie narrowed her eyes. "Once she gets this contract, you don't stand a chance."

"Maybe not, but I need to address that possibility with Kendall. I'll let her make that decision," Ivy said as she turned and walked across the grass to check the recently vacated camping pad. She had to get away from this horrible woman before she lost her temper. That would only make the situation worse.

Ivy sat alone in the booth at the diner. She'd contacted Kendall and asked her to meet. She hadn't told her what she needed to talk about because there was no way she could or would put a conversation like this in a text. She watched as Kendall drove up in her blue Ford Bronco SUV and pulled into a parking space. Ivy's stomach clenched as Kendall bounced out of the car with a smile on her face, as usual. This was going to be a difficult conversation.

Kendall slid into the booth across from Ivy. "Hey. What's up? Your text seemed urgent."

Ivy took in a deep breath. "I need to talk to you about something. I ran into Cassie today after you met with her." Ivy fidgeted. "I also overheard part of your conversation."

"Oh. I didn't see you." Kendall straightened and raised her eyebrows. "What did Cassie have to say?"

"She was trying to warn me not to get involved with you. She seems to think you two are still together."

"What? That's not—"

"She specifically mentioned that you and she aren't done yet, that you're still together, and that you both have been keeping things low-key and never actually broke up completely." Ivy sighed. "If you're working through things, that's fine. You just need to be honest with me." She'd be disappointed but wouldn't get between them. The sinking feeling in her stomach told her it wouldn't be easy getting over Kendall, though.

Kendall ran her fingers through her hair. "Ivy, it's not what you think."

Ivy leaned forward and laced her fingers together on the table. "Then what is it, Kendall? Because you told me that you and Cassie were done. Your exact words were completely over."

"We are. It's complicated—"

"Is it?" Ivy's voice rose "Because it seems pretty simple from where I'm sitting. Either you lied to me or you're lying to her."

"Cassie threatened your job if I don't have dinner with her. She wants to talk. I want her to get closure. It's nothing romantic on my side at all."

"Closure doesn't usually involve making future plans together, which she also mentioned."

"She's twisting things. Can't you see that? I've told you how manipulative she can be."

"I know what we're doing started as something fake, but now it's real, at least it is to me, and I don't want to end up the laughingstock of the lodge—the rebound while you figure things out with her."

"You're not that at all. This is real for me too. I really care about you. That's the only reason I agreed to meet with Cassie. I'm not getting back together with her, but I don't want her to hurt you."

"It sounds like she didn't get that from your conversation."

Kendall reached for Ivy's hand. "I swear, Ivy. It's completely over with her. I'll talk to her again."

Ivy pulled her hand away. "That's what concerns me. Why does it need another conversation if it was already done?"

"I'm trying not to be cruel, but if she's living in some sort of fantasy world where she thinks it's a possibility, I will make it crystal clear to her that it isn't."

"Being honest isn't cruel, Kendall. Leading someone on is."

"I never meant to lead anyone on, especially not you."

"Maybe not intentionally. But I need more than good intentions. I need honesty."

Kendall's voice rose in panic. "What are you saying?"

"I'm saying I need time to think. And you need to figure out what—and who—you actually want. Because you can't have us both."

"Ivy, please." Kendall was begging. "I won't see her tonight. I won't see her ever again."

Ivy slid out of the booth. "Let me know when there's no confusion about where things stand with Cassie. Until then, I think we should take a step back." She left Kendall sitting alone.

CHAPTER FIFTY-NINE

Kendall had texted Cassie immediately after Ivy had left her at the diner. Cassie was angry when she'd told her she wasn't going to meet her, but Kendall didn't care. She had no interest in rekindling any kind of partnership with her. Now, she waited at the cabin, pacing in front of the window. Ivy hadn't responded to any of her texts or calls all afternoon, and now it was getting dark, and she wasn't home yet. Her stomach twisted when she saw the dust cloud in the distance. There she was.

Ivy pulled her truck into the driveway and got out slowly. Not the usual eagerness to race inside that Kendall had seen in recent days.

Kendall pulled the door open before Ivy got to the porch. "Where have you been? I've been worried."

"I had some things to catch up on."

"So many things that you couldn't answer a single text?"

"Cell service was bad."

Now Ivy was just making excuses, but Kendall wouldn't press her. Clearly, she needed time to think about the lies Cassie had told her. "You know everything Cassie said isn't true."

"That's the point. I don't, and I should. My dad even pointed out how I've been giving you special treatment."

"I didn't ask you to do that." She'd never expected anything professionally from Ivy.

"When she told me about your plan to get the bid any way you can, I didn't know what to think."

"I told you. There's no plan." What could Cassie have possibly told her?

"Right. You also told me that you two aren't getting back together, but Cassie thinks otherwise."

"There's no way that's happening." Before Ivy had come into her life, she'd had no idea what a real relationship was supposed to be like. She couldn't even stand to be around Cassie now.

"You know, you should've just told me to begin with. You didn't need to sleep with me. I would have helped you anyway."

"I didn't sleep with you to get the contract. I slept with you because I wanted to. I like you…a lot." More than she'd ever intended when this whole fake relationship had started.

"The cabin is yours for the night. I have the night shift at the lodge."

"I know that's not true. You would've told me that earlier if it were."

"I need to study if I'm going to pass my EMT Certification test." She shoved a couple of books into her backpack and headed toward the door. "I won't be able to focus here. I haven't been able to since you arrived."

"Ivy. You have to believe me. Nothing is going on with Cassie. She's just trying to mess with you because she knows she doesn't have a chance at the bid or with me."

"Maybe." Ivy pulled open the door. "I need a little space tonight. I'll see you in the morning." She didn't look back before she closed the door behind her.

What could she do to convince Ivy that she was telling the truth? She pressed her hand to her forehead. She was lying so much to everyone that she didn't know the difference anymore. She packed up her stuff and zipped her suitcase before she hit the button on her phone for Noah. She wasn't staying here alone…she hated being alone.

"Do you have room for one more tonight? I really need to figure some things out."

"I need to check with Taylor, because she's still uncomfortable with our past."

"That's fine. Check with her. Tell her everything. I don't care anymore."

"Oof. What happened?"

"Nothing major. Only I might have just lost the best thing that's happened to me in a very long time."

"I'm at work, but just go over. I'll handle Taylor."

CHAPTER SIXTY

Taylor came to the door quickly. "Hey. You look like you've had a rough day."

Kendall dropped her bag in the entryway. "The worst day ever."

"What happened?" Taylor actually seemed concerned. "Noah's text just said you had an emergency and were coming over."

Kendall let out a heavy sigh as she tried to hold in the tears. "It's Ivy. She won't talk to me, won't answer my calls…I'm pretty sure we're over."

"Over? Whoa. Back up." Taylor drew her eyebrows together. "I thought this whole relationship was fake?"

"It was at the beginning, but things have changed. Ivy is so much more than I expected. I really like being around her—being with her."

Taylor dipped her head and raised an eyebrow. "With her?" She whispered as though they were in a crowded room sharing a secret.

Kendall nodded. "Yeah. We slept together and it was perfect."

"Huh." Taylor bit her lower lip. "I didn't see that coming." She held up her hands. "I mean, I'm glad it happened but just didn't expect it." She motioned toward the kitchen table. "Come on in and sit down. I'll get us some wine."

Kendall went through the events of the past week, how Ivy and she had gotten closer and eventually slept together.

"So, you two were solid last week. What happened?"

Kendall rubbed her temples. "Cassie happened."

Taylor widened her eyes. "Your ex? I thought she was out of the picture."

"She was, but as you know, she showed up for this bid at the lodge." Kendall paused. "She left, but she came back and begged me to get back together with her, and when I said no, she decided to tell Ivy all kinds of lies."

Taylor leaned forward as she handed Kendall a glass of red. "What did she say?"

"That I've been sweet-talking Ivy—no, using her to get an advantage on the bid, and that, get this." She set the glass on the table harder than she intended. "We're just taking a break and are still together." She let out a bitter laugh. "She casually mentioned how we've stayed in touch and how special our connection still is. Made it sound like we've been seeing each other behind Ivy's back."

"But that's not true, right?" Taylor asked. Seemed she was fact-checking for her own sake.

Kendall drew her eyebrows together. "Of course not. I mean, Cassie did reach out to talk, and I did meet with her because I was afraid of what she might do if I didn't. That's what started this whole thing. Apparently, Ivy overheard enough of the conversation for Cassie to manipulate it so that she thinks I was considering getting back with her."

"You didn't explain it to Ivy after you met with Cassie?"

"I didn't have time." Kendall held her hands out in front of her and let them drop to the table. "Ivy ran into her right after our conversation."

"Why did Cassie want to meet with you in the first place?"

"She threatened Ivy's job. Said she'd go to her boss and claim she's giving me an unfair advantage."

"Oh." Taylor drew the word out as she relaxed into her chair. "Is she…giving you an advantage?"

"I don't think so, but I guess, not knowing the whole situation, her boss might see it that way." Kendall blew out a breath. "I've screwed myself two ways now, haven't I?"

"Kinda looks that way." Taylor winced. "But you haven't slept with Cassie, right?"

"No," Kendall said quickly. "Nothing happened or was going to happen. But I didn't have a chance to tell Ivy about our conversation before Cassie told her, and Cassie made it sound like there's been this ongoing thing between us."

Taylor took a sip of wine. "You kept secrets. That's why Ivy's upset."

Kendall's voice rose. "There weren't any secrets." Her tone dropped. "Well, maybe there were, but I didn't want Ivy to worry about her job."

"Kendall, come on. You know that's not how this works. If you had to hide it, it was relevant."

"I know that now. I wanted to protect Ivy. What am I going to do?" She took a gulp of wine and tried to swallow the lump in her throat. "I think I'm falling in love with her. I can't lose her over something so trivial, over Cassie's games."

"First, you need to be honest with yourself about why you chose to meet with Cassie," Taylor said thoughtfully. "If you can't be honest with yourself, you can't be honest with Ivy."

"I guess, at first, part of me wasn't ready to let go completely," Kendall said quietly. "Not because I want to be with Cassie, but because of becoming single again."

Taylor nodded. "Endings are hard."

"Yeah. And Cassie was such a big part of my life for so long. *Almost four years.* It felt wrong to just erase her."

"That's understandable. But you need to decide what matters more, holding on to the past or building your future with Ivy."

"It's Ivy. I want her. It's been Ivy since I met her."

"Then you need to tell her that. And everything else. The whole truth."

"What if she doesn't believe me? What if it's too late?"

"Then give her proof." Taylor shrugged. "Show her your messages with Cassie. Those can't be friendly, right?"

"No. Not friendly at all." Any messages between them had been all business or filled with contention.

"Delete Cassie's number in front of her if you think that's what she needs. But most importantly, tell her why you weren't upfront in the first place. Your fear of her losing her job and you losing her. Honesty like that is exactly what might make her believe you."

Kendall sucked in a deep breath. "You're right. Complete honesty. No matter how much it hurts."

Taylor placed her hand over Kendall's. "And give her time. Trust isn't rebuilt overnight. You might need to be patient."

Kendall nodded. "I'll do whatever it takes." Including removing herself from the landscape project. "Do you think I should confront Cassie about this?"

Taylor shook her head. "No. This isn't about Cassie. This is about you and Ivy. Engaging with Cassie just gives her power over your relationship."

"Okay. I'll find Ivy in the morning and talk to her. No more texts, no more voice mails for now." She took another drink of wine.

"Definitely a face-to-face conversation." Taylor smiled. "Just remember, vulnerability isn't weakness. It's the only way back to trust." She rubbed Kendall's shoulder. "Your room is ready for you if you want to stay."

"You don't mind?" This was certainly an about-face.

"No. Not at all. I'm sorry about booting you out. I overreacted a bit." Taylor smiled lightly. "Noah and I had a long talk, and things are better." She hadn't been wrong about the situation, but Kendall hadn't been encouraging Noah in any way.

"Thanks, Taylor. I really appreciate you working through this with me. I don't know what I'd do without you."

"Probably something stupid." Taylor laughed as she stood. "Noah should be home soon. You want to help me finish making dinner?" She went to the refrigerator and took out some lettuce.

"Sure." Kendall had no idea if Ivy would accept anything she planned to say, but she had to at least try.

CHAPTER SIXTY-ONE

The embers in the stone fireplace had dimmed to a soft orange glow, casting long shadows across the lodge's great room. Ivy lay curled under her jacket on one of the worn leather couches, her ranger hat sitting on the coffee table. The sound of boots on hardwood floor stirred her awake.

"Ivy?" Her dad's voice was gentle with concern. "Honey, why are you sleeping out here?"

Ivy blinked, disoriented, then sat up quickly when she recognized her father. Lance Patterson had been the head park warden at Diamond Mountain State Park for twenty years before semi-retiring to an advisory role. He still made his early rounds most mornings out of habit.

"Dad." She rubbed her eyes. "What time is it?"

"Just after five." He sat beside her, the couch creaking under his weight. "I was checking the campsites before the next storm hits. Dispatch said you logged out last night but never clocked back in at home."

"The lodge was empty, and I had paperwork to finish anyway." Ivy sighed, pulling her knees to her chest. "I just needed some space to think." And she couldn't go to see any of her friends because they were unpredictable. She didn't need advice. She needed time to sort through the facts.

Lance studied her face. The shadows under her eyes must have told him she'd been crying. "This about Kendall?"

Ivy laughed bitterly. "You were right to be skeptical of her. I should've trusted your instincts."

"What happened?" her dad asked, his weathered face creased with worry.

Ivy stared at the dying fire. "She played me, Dad. The whole time. The landscaping contract for the lodge renovation. Turns out she'd been angling for it since day one. Dating the park ranger who helps oversee contractor requirements was just part of her plan. Pretty convenient, huh?"

Lance was quiet for a moment. "You sure about that?"

Ivy nodded. "According to Cassie Clark, they're still together. She said Kendall told her she had an inside track with me." Her voice cracked. "I know it's only been a short time, Dad, but I thought—I really thought we had something."

Lance put his arm around her shoulders. "I'm sorry, honey."

"I feel so stupid," Ivy whispered. "I introduced her around and recommended her company based on her portfolio, her commitment to sustainability. I believed in her work. Now it looks like I was duped and gave her special treatment."

"You didn't know," Lance said firmly. "And your recommendation is only one of many factors in that decision."

"I should have seen it. The questions she'd ask about work, always so interested in the plants and contract details."

Lance squeezed her shoulder. "People who manipulate others get good at hiding their true intentions. That's on her, not you."

They sat quietly for a moment, watching as the last ember faded to ash in the fireplace.

"What are you going to do?" Lance finally asked.

"I plan to file a conflict-of-interest disclosure with the department. Full transparency." Ivy ran a hand through her tangled hair. "I'll recuse myself completely from any participation with the award committee."

Lance nodded, pride evident in his eyes. "That's my girl. Integrity first."

"Doesn't make it hurt any less," Ivy admitted.

"No, it doesn't." Lance stood, offering his hand. "Come on. I've got coffee in the truck. Then you're coming home with me. Your mom's making her famous buttermilk pancakes."

Ivy managed a small smile. "With the real maple syrup?"

"Is there any other kind in a park ranger's house?" Lance asked, teasing her. "The couch at the house is more comfortable than this old thing. Door's always open if you need it."

As they walked out into the predawn light, Ivy took a deep breath of pine-scented air. "You know what the worst part is? After finding out all that, I still miss her. How messed up is that?"

"Not messed up at all," Lance said quietly. "Feelings don't have an on-off switch. But they do change with time." He gestured to the mountains around them, their peaks just catching the first light of day. "Nature teaches us that, doesn't it? Everything changes. Seasons turn. Wounds heal. And sometimes, what looks like an ending is really just making space for something new to grow."

Ivy nodded, the knot in her chest loosening just a fraction as they headed toward the parking lot, side by side in the growing light.

Chapter Sixty-two

"Thank you for meeting with me, Director Martinez." Cassie's voice was sickeningly sweet, as it always was when she approached strangers who could benefit her. "I wouldn't normally come directly to you, but I'm concerned about something that could affect the park's landscape contract bidding process."

"Of course, Cassie. Have a seat. What seems to be the issue?" Kendall, sitting in the next room, recognized the director's voice.

"Well, I've noticed that Park Ranger Ivy has been spending a lot of time with Kendall, one of the landscape designers bidding for the contract. At first, I thought they were just friendly, but it's become pretty clear they're romantically involved."

"I see," Director Martinez said, "and you're concerned this relationship might impact the bidding process?"

"Exactly." Cassie's voice rose. "The other day, I overheard Ivy introducing Kendall to several board members. She was going on and on about Kendall's previous projects and design philosophy—practically giving her a personal recommendation. Meanwhile, other bidders like me hardly got any face time with the decision makers and have been eliminated from the running."

"That's a serious concern." The director's voice lowered. "Can you give me specific examples of what you witnessed?"

"Sure. During the site walk-through, Ivy repeatedly mentioned Kendall's work at the Oklahoma Children's Hospital as a perfect example of native restoration. Then at the pre-bid meeting, Ivy made sure Kendall sat next to the procurement officer and even highlighted aspects of the RFP that aligned with Kendall's specialty areas. It feels like she's using her position to give Kendall an unfair advantage."

"I understand why you're upset by this. Our bidding process needs to be fair and transparent. Have you discussed your concerns with Ivy directly?"

"No, I haven't." Honestly, I was worried about potential backlash. I depend on park contracts for my business. And I didn't want to create tension with someone who has influence here."

Kendall's neck heated, and she clutched the folder in her lap as she listened in on their conversation. It was all lies. Ivy had introduced her, but she hadn't given her any special seating or highlights about the RFP.

"I appreciate you bringing this to my attention," the director said. "Rest assured, I take conflicts of interest very seriously. I'll look into the situation immediately and make sure proper protocols are being followed. Everyone deserves a fair chance at this contract. We will base our decision solely on the quality of their proposals."

"Thank you." Cassie's sweet voice was back again. "All I'm asking for is a level playing field. I've worked with the park system for years and have always respected the professionalism here. I just want to make sure that standard is maintained."

"Absolutely." The director sounded louder, like he was moving toward the door. "I'll be reviewing the situation thoroughly, and I'll ensure the remainder of the bidding process is conducted with complete impartiality. Would you be comfortable putting your observations in writing for our records?"

Kendall had heard enough of Cassie's lies. She burst into the room. "No need for that. I'm pulling my bid." She couldn't let this go on any longer.

"Are you sure you want to do that?" Director Martinez seemed surprised by her statement.

"Yes," Kendall said firmly. "I can't put Ivy's job in jeopardy."

The director glanced at Cassie. "Would you mind giving us some privacy?"

Cassie stood next to the desk with her mouth open. "What?"

"Would you excuse us? I need to talk to Kendall," Director Martinez repeated.

"Oh. Sure." Cassie moved toward the door. "What are you doing?" she whispered as she brushed Kendall's arm with her hand.

"Exactly what I need to do." Kendall pulled away, rushing past her as she entered the room farther.

Kendall took her seat and glanced around the spacious office, modest but professional, with large windows overlooking the park grounds. She was slightly nervous but still determined to make sure Ivy wouldn't be punished for being the wonderful person she was. "I'm sorry to barge in on you like this, Director Martinez. I appreciate you seeing me on such short notice."

"I'm glad you're here." After closing the door, he rounded the desk and took his seat. "I assume you overheard my conversation with Cassie."

She nodded. "I did, and just to be clear, Ivy hasn't given me any help with my bid."

"Cassie indicated that Ivy had introduced you to some of the board members. Is that true?"

"Well, yes. But that was only because we ran into them, and they spoke to her." Kendall shifted in her chair. "It would've been rude not to introduce anyone in that situation."

He nodded in agreement. "So, it was nothing more than a casual introduction."

"Yes." She lied. Ivy had told them how much she liked her designs, but the introductions had been unplanned. She couldn't tell the director that, though. And it didn't matter now.

"When Cassie came to my office, I was just reviewing the bids for the landscape renovation project. Your proposal is quite impressive. Are you sure you want to withdraw your bid?" He raised his eyebrows. "Your proposal is one of our top contenders. Your sustainable irrigation design is exactly what the park needs."

"I know, and I appreciate that. But I need to recuse myself from this process for other reasons as well."

The director frowned. "May I ask why? Is there a problem with your availability or resources?"

Kendall took in a deep breath. "It's about Ivy."

"Something other than what Cassie complained about?"

"Yes. We've been seeing each other for the past few months." It had been only a couple of weeks, but the story still had to match, or everyone would think they were lying about everything, which they were, but she wasn't being dishonest about her feelings. What a mess.

Director Martinez leaned back in his chair, seeming to begin to understand. "I see. And you're concerned about a conflict of interest."

"Exactly. Ivy hasn't shared any inside information with me. She's been completely professional. But I know how these situations can appear from the outside."

"Has she asked you to withdraw?" the director asked.

"No. She doesn't even know I'm here. She does know about Cassie, though. Cassie threatened both of us. Said she would cause Ivy to lose her job."

"Doesn't sound like this is just about the contract."

Kendall shook her head. "It isn't. Cassie and I used to be involved both personally and professionally."

"That changes the light around her complaint." He moved forward and jotted a note on the pad in front of him.

"I've seen how much Ivy loves working here, how passionate she is about the park's restoration. I don't want her integrity questioned because of me…because of our relationship." Even if there was nothing left of it.

"That's very considerate of you, Kendall. Though, I have to say, your withdrawal will disappoint the committee. We were excited about your vision for the space."

"I know, and I'm sorry about that." She was disappointed as well. "But there will be other projects. Ivy's reputation and position here are more important to me than any contract." That was absolutely true. The more she said it, the more she felt it in her heart.

Director Martinez studied Kendall for a moment before he nodded. "I appreciate your honesty and your integrity, Kendall. It speaks well of your character."

"Thank you for understanding. I want to do this right."

"Okay." He leaned forward and rested his elbows on the desk. "Would you like me to explain this to the committee, or would you prefer to submit a formal withdrawal letter?"

"I've prepared a letter." She handed him the folder she'd brought. "I've kept it simple, just stating that I need to withdraw for personal reasons."

Director Martinez took the folder from her and read the letter. "I'll make sure the committee understands that this isn't a reflection on the quality of your work." He slid the letter back into the folder. "And Kendall, for what it's worth, I think you're making an honorable choice."

"That means a lot." It was her only choice if she had any chance of making things right with Ivy. "Thank you."

Kendall stood, went to the door, and paused. "Director Martinez? When you see Ivy later, I'd appreciate it if you didn't mention my visit. I'd like to tell her myself." She had no idea when and where she would be able to do that.

The director dipped his chin. "Of course. This conversation stays between us."

CHAPTER SIXTY-THREE

Ivy sat nervously across the desk from her supervisor, Park Director Martinez. The office was small but tidy, with awards and conservation certificates lining the walls. Director Martinez's expression was blank as he reviewed some paperwork.

Finally, he looked up from the documents. "Ivy, thank you for coming in. I need to discuss a concerning matter that's been brought to my attention."

Ivy shifted in her seat. "Of course, Director. What's going on?"

We've received a formal complaint from Cassie Clark at Clark Solutions regarding the upcoming landscape redesign project. She claims you've been giving preferential treatment to another bidder, Kendall Jackson, from Horizon Designs."

Anger burned in Ivy's chest. "Preferential treatment? I'm not sure what you mean." She knew exactly what the director meant. Cassie had gotten to the him before she could explain the situation.

Director Martinez leaned forward and put his elbows on his desk. "According to Cassie, you personally introduced Kendall to several members of the selection committee during last week's park walk-through. She alleges you spent considerable time highlighting Kendall's previous work and credentials to these committee members."

"I was just being friendly." Ivy shrugged. "Kendall completed a beautiful restoration project at Children's Hospital in Oklahoma last year, and I thought it was relevant to mention it."

"Ivy, you know our procurement process requires absolute neutrality from staff. By speaking so highly of one bidder to committee members, you've created an unfair advantage. Cassie feels that her company wasn't given the same opportunity, and I agree."

Ivy briefly recalled the conversation she'd had with her dad. "I hadn't thought of it that way until recently, and I *had* planned to talk to you about it. I've known Kendall professionally for a few months." She lied. "I've seen her work, and I genuinely believe her work is exceptional. But you're right. I shouldn't have said anything to the committee members."

Director Martinez let out a sigh "I understand you didn't have malicious intent, but this is a serious breach of protocol. The state requires a fair and transparent bidding process. Your actions have jeopardized that and opened us up to potential legal issues."

Ivy looked at the ceiling and then back at the director. "I never meant to cause problems. What happens now?"

"First, you'll need to recuse yourself from any further involvement with the selection process. Although I don't think her proposal will be selected, Cassie Clark's company will be reviewed again before the final selections. I'm also requiring you to complete ethics training before the month ends. And unfortunately, I'll need to consider placing a formal note about this incident in your personnel file."

Ivy nodded as relief washed through her. She could deal with those consequences as long as she still had her job. "I understand. And I'm truly sorry. I should've been more careful about maintaining boundaries."

Director Martinez relaxed into his chair. "You're an excellent ranger, Ivy. Your passion for the parks is evident in everything you do. But we have procedures for a reason. Moving forward, I need you to be more mindful of these professional boundaries."

"It won't happen again, Director. I promise."

"I'm glad to hear that. I'll need to talk to the board to see whether we should contact all bidders to ensure transparency about what happened and potentially extend the submission deadline. You can help rebuild trust by maintaining complete neutrality from this point forward."

"Absolutely." Ivy sat forward in her chair. "Should I reach out to Cassie to apologize?" She didn't want to reach out to Cassie in any way, but she would do it if the director required her to.

Director Martinez appeared thoughtful. "Not yet. Let's handle the formal response first, and then we can discuss appropriate next steps. For now, focus on your regular duties and stay completely clear of the landscape project."

Ivy stood. "I will. Thank you for being direct with me about this situation."

Director Martinez nodded. "That's all for now. I'll send you an email confirming what we've discussed today. You'll need to respond that you understand."

"I will, and thank you again for considering my passion and service, Director."

"You're welcome," the director said with a nod. "You're good at your job, Ivy, and good for this park."

Ivy shivered as she left the office. She'd never put herself in a position like this before, and now she'd done it for someone whom she wasn't sure actually cared for her. She needed a hike to clear her head, somewhere that she wouldn't run into Kendall. She headed to Eagle Point to see how the newly hatched chicks were doing.

Ivy was leaning against the railing of Eagle Point Lookout, binoculars hanging around her neck. The evening sun was casting long shadows across the valley below when she heard footsteps on the wooden platform behind her.

"Beautiful view tonight." Director Martinez's voice came from the distance.

Ivy didn't turn and kept her eyes on the horizon. "One of the reasons I took this job. Never gets old."

Director Martinez stepped up beside her. "How's the eagles' nest doing?"

"Two healthy chicks. Mom and Dad are doing a great job." She turned to face him. "But you didn't hike all the way up here to ask about the birds."

"No. I didn't. I need to talk to you more about the landscape restoration contract."

Ivy tensed. The fact that Kendall had used her still stung. "I'm steering clear of everyone."

"I appreciate that." Director Martinez shook his head and sighed "I'm not filing the reprimand. Cassie has withdrawn her complaint."

Ivy turned to watch the sunset. "She did?" Ivy was confused. Cassie didn't seem to be the kind of woman who would admit she was wrong. Maybe she wasn't.

"I wanted to tell you personally before you heard it from someone else." He turned to watch the sunset as well. "The competition has thinned as well. I'm sorry to say that Kendall withdrew her bid this morning."

Ivy spun to face him. "What? Why would she do that? Her proposal was brilliant. Everyone knows it was miles better than the other options."

"She said she found that she had a conflict of interest."

"What conflict?" *She* was the conflict. "But she has all the right certifications, the experience…

"The conflict was you, Ivy," Director Martinez said. "I told her I wouldn't say anything, but I thought you should know."

Ivy's stomach dropped. "Me?" She didn't understand. If Kendall was using her to get the contract, why would she pull her bid?

"She overheard Cassie voicing her complaint and didn't want to jeopardize your job."

"She withdrew to protect my job?" Ivy blew out a breath softly.

Director Martinez nodded. "She simply stated that she has feelings for you and couldn't in good conscience proceed with her bid if it might impact your position."

Ivy turned back toward the valley. "She never said a word to me."

Director Martinez put a hand on her shoulder. "People make hard choices for those they care about."

Ivy blew out a slow breath. "Seems that way." She'd treated Kendall so badly. Hadn't believed her when she said she hadn't been using her.

"I'll give you some space." Director Martinez began to walk away. "Oh, and Ivy? The Rockside Trail needs attention before the weekend rush. Don't forget the reports."

"Right. Reports. I'll handle it." She couldn't think about trails or reports right now. She had to apologize to Kendall. She took out her phone and stared at it for a moment before she put it back into her pocket. A phone call wouldn't do. She'd need to figure out what to say and how to say it. She lifted her binoculars and focused on the distant eagles' nest as the sun continued to lower.

CHAPTER SIXTY-FOUR

The knock on the bedroom door pulled Kendall out of her wine-induced hangover misery. "Do you have to knock so loud?"

The door pushed open. "It was barely a touch," Noah said. "How are you?"

"I'm a little hung over and a lot miserable" Kendall put her fingertips to her head and kneaded. Alone, last night, while Noah and Taylor had been out to dinner and the movies, she'd polished off the majority of a bottle of wine without eating anything. She'd been immediately buzzed, and then she'd passed out.

"So, what are you going to do?"

"I pulled my bid."

"What? After all the work you've put into it?"

"I had to. Cassie threatened Ivy's job, and I'm not going to let money get in the way of my happiness. I did that before, and look how it turned out."

"Well, you're not in a much better situation currently with Ivy."

"Don't you think I know that?" Still fully dressed from the night before, Kendall stood and paced the room. "It's so much worse with my ex sabotaging everything I do…every move I make." Her head swam, and her stomach threatened to purge as she flopped onto the bed. "Ivy thinks I've lied to her about everything."

"At least you don't have to lie about your relationship anymore."

"That's the thing. Everything was a lie at first, but now none of it is."

"Oh." He raised his eyebrows as his mouth dropped open in exaggerated surprise.

"I loved everything about our arrangement. The good, the bad, and the messy." Kendall's chest ached, the space that she'd made for Ivy now beginning to hollow, filling with sadness.

Noah sat down beside her. "Honestly, from what I saw, I think she might have loved it as well."

She shook her head. "She hates me now." Her throat clamped. "Plus, she didn't believe me."

"She probably doesn't hate you, but I'm sure she's confused, at the least, about your true motives." He wrapped his arm around her shoulder and pulled her against him. "I bet if you put your mind to it, you can make her see that your true feelings outweighed your original motives, and those had nothing to do with anything Cassie has told her."

Kendall glanced up at him. "You think?"

"I absolutely think." He kissed her forehead. "Now, get cleaned up, and we can make a plan." He stood. "You can't talk to anyone with the stench of alcohol oozing from your pores." He left the room, pulling the door closed behind him.

Kendall stared at her fingers…they'd been so many places since she'd arrived here. All over Ivy's stuff at her house creating horrible fingerprints…shoved through her hair…places on Ivy's body that she'd never dreamed of a month ago.

Exhausted, Kendall sat in one of the large leather chairs in the common area of the lodge. She and Noah had walked nearly every trail, checked every campground, and looked around all the surrounding areas of the lodge. She couldn't find Ivy anywhere.

She closed her eyes and enjoyed the silence as the sun streamed through the windows to warm her face.

"Morning, Kendall." Susan's voice broke through the silence. "I heard you've decided not to proceed with your bid for the park landscape project."

She smiled slightly at Susan. "That's correct. I don't want to cause any more trouble for Ivy."

"Listen." Susan hesitated. "I was wondering if you could do me a favor."

"What kind of favor?" Kendall wasn't sure she could do anything for anyone until she found Ivy.

Susan placed a folder on the table in front of her. "Since we haven't had any luck hiring a director of eco planning, the department approved hiring a landscape advisor for the restoration project, and I need to get this job description reviewed before I post it on the website for Director Martinez." She slid the folder closer to Kendall. "Would you take a quick look at it to make sure it's accurate. You're the first person I thought of when I read it. Could be right up your alley."

Kendall raised an eyebrow. "You think?"

"I do. From what Ivy's told me, you have a master's in environmental design and at least three years of experience with native plant restoration. It would be a waste not to at least let them know about it."

"I'm not sure Ivy wants me here anymore after what happened with Cassie."

"This isn't about that. The project needs someone with your expertise." Susan paused. "It would be nice to see Ivy happy, and I believe she would be if you were here."

Kendall sighed. "Let me take a look."

The job description read

POSITION: LANDSCAPE RESTORATION ADVISOR
Diamond Mountain State Park—Full Time.

PROJECT OVERVIEW:
Advise bid winner of landscape restoration contract. Develop and implement restoration plan for all areas damaged in last season's flooding. Focus on reintroducing native species and creating sustainable landscape resistant to future weather events.

REQUIREMENTS:

- *Degree in Environmental Design, Landscape Architecture, or related field*
- *Experience with native plant species of the region*
- *Knowledge of sustainable land-management practices*
- *Ability to work independently and as part of team*

COMPENSATION:
$4,800/month plus housing accommodation in park residence

CONTACT:
Daniel Martinez, Park Director
Application deadline: December 30

Kendall slid the job description back inside and closed the folder. "This actually sounds perfect for me."

Susan smiled. "I know. So, I'll just leave it right here, and you can talk to Director Martinez about it."

"Did he ask you to give it to me?"

"He might have mentioned that you'd be a good candidate."

Kendall smiled. "Are you trying to give me a reason to stay in the area?"

"I have no idea what you're talking about." Susan smiled. "Oh, and don't tell anyone I accidentally left it out where anyone could see it. Make it seem like you just happened to come across it on my desk."

CHAPTER SIXTY-FIVE

As the coffee shop bustled with afternoon activity, Ivy sat alone at a corner table absently stirring her latte, lost in thought. The door chimed as it opened, and she looked up to see Susan enter. Ivy had asked her to meet there because she needed advice on what to do about Kendall, and she didn't want to risk running into Kendall at the lodge. She held up her hand and waved at Susan as she glanced around the shop.

Susan came over and slid into the seat across from her. "Hey. I'm glad you finally replied. I've been texting you all morning. You okay?"

Ivy sighed. "Yeah. Sorry. I've been distracted."

"Kendall's been looking for you."

"I know." Ivy ran her finger through her hair. "She called last night. Wanted to talk."

"And did you talk to her?"

Ivy shook her head. "I panicked and didn't answer. She left a voicemail message. Then she sent a text, and I said I was busy."

Susan raised an eyebrow. "Were you?"

Ivy shrugged. "I was reorganizing my bookcase."

Susan laughed. "Alphabetically or by frequency of read?"

"Color-coded, actually." Ivy smiled.

They both laughed and then fell silent for a moment. "I'm not ready to talk to her. I just don't know what to say after everything that's happened." *After doubting her.*

Susan leaned forward. "Look. I saw how you were with her—and how she was with you. Don't doubt that any of it was real, Ivy. You have to talk to her."

"That doesn't erase what happened between us—how I felt when I thought she'd lied to me."

Susan frowned. "But she didn't lie to you. And from what I can tell, Kendall has sacrificed a lot to make sure you know that and your job wasn't impacted." She grabbed Ivy's hand. "She gave up a huge contract for you."

"She hadn't actually won it yet." Ivy had no doubt Kendall would've won the bid.

Susan flattened her lips. "You know she would've." She tilted her head. "Does that really matter now?"

"No." Ivy shook her head. "I'm sure she would've done a great job on the project." She stared out the window.

"And she's tried to apologize too, right?" Susan tapped her finger on the table to keep Ivy's attention.

Ivy nodded. "She has. Without excuses, just accountability."

"That's more than most people ever manage when they've actually done something wrong, and she hasn't done anything to apologize for."

Ivy stirred her latte again. "But what if it's all just temporary? What if we try again and end up right back where we started?"

Susan shrugged. "Then you'll have my shoulder to cry on, and my freezer is always stocked with ice cream." She leaned forward on her elbows and whispered, "But what if it's not temporary? What if Kendall really does care for you?"

"I don't know." Ivy leaned back in the booth. "Has it been long enough to develop real feelings?"

"You tell me," Susan said quickly.

Ivy smiled as she ran her fingers across the edge of the table. "I was smitten on day one."

"I knew it." Susan grinned and slapped the table. "Who says she wasn't smitten as well?"

Ivy looked down at her phone on the table as it lit up with a notification. "It's Kendall. Again."

"The way I see it, the question isn't whether Kendall deserves a second chance, Ivy." Susan smiled softly. "It's whether what you had—what you could still have—deserves one."

Ivy sighed. "I'm scared. My heart already hurts."

Susan reached across and squeezed Ivy's hand. "Of course you are. That's how you know it matters."

Ivy took in a deep breath. "What would I even say?"

"How about meet me for coffee at the diner in ten minutes." Susan shrugged. "Low stakes. Public place. Just talk."

Ivy picked up her phone. "Just talk." She wanted to do so much more than just talk but didn't know how to get there yet. She owed Kendall an apology for believing anything Cassie had said.

"If it goes south, text me the code word, and I'll call with a fake emergency."

Ivy typed on her phone. "What's the code word?"

"Books," Susan said quickly.

Ivy finished her text and set her phone down on the table. "Done."

Susan smiled widely. "Look at you, giving second chances like a grown-ass woman in an adult relationship."

Ivy rolled her eyes. "Don't get too excited. It's just coffee. She hasn't forgiven me yet." She hoped it turned into more, but with Kendall living over four hours away out of state, she didn't know if being with her would be enough for her to stay.

"Everything important starts with just something. Just a date. Just a kiss. Just a chance."

Ivy smiled as they clinked their coffee cups together, a mix of nervousness and hope swirling in her belly.

CHAPTER SIXTY-SIX

The afternoon light filtered through the half-drawn blinds at the coffee shop where Ivy had requested they meet. When Kendall arrived, she could see Ivy through the window, sitting in a booth drumming her fingers on the table. She seemed to be saying something as well. Kendall didn't see anyone sitting with her. Was she rehearsing what she was going to say?

When she walked in and saw Ivy, mahogany hair wind-tossed and cheeks sun-kissed, Kendall's resolve nearly crumbled. Ivy did things to her that no other woman ever had. She took in a deep breath to still herself before heading to the booth.

"Hey," Kendall said, sliding into the seat across from her. "Sorry I'm late. I was helping Noah with the horses. I headed this way as soon as I saw your message." She noticed the empty coffee cup in front of Ivy and felt the coldness of the full one in front of herself when she wrapped her fingers around it. "You've been her a while, huh?"

"It's fine," Ivy said, attempting to smile. "I needed the time to think anyway." Ivy's expression shifted. "I thought we should talk about what happened with Cassie."

"Yeah. About that." Kendall took a deep breath. "I've made a decision. I'm going back to Oklahoma for a while."

"Oklahoma?" Ivy's voice rose slightly. "But you said you liked it here and wanted to stay."

"I know what I said. That was if I got the contract, which is no longer an option." Kendall traced the rim of her mug. "I need to go home. Clear my head. Let you clear your head. A lot has happened over the past couple of weeks."

"Is this about what happened with Cassie? Because I believe everything you told me. I know what she said was all lies, and I'm sorry I made you doubt that."

"It's not just about her," Kendall said softly. "It's about us. Everything's been moving so fast, and I'm not sure either of us knows what we really want." Plus, Ivy had doubted her so readily.

Ivy looked somber. "I know what I want."

"Do you? Because I think maybe we just got caught up in the momentum of this thing between us." Kendall reached across the table but stopped short of touching Ivy's hand. "We'd been circling each other for days, and then it turned so intense so quickly. It's beautiful and wonderful, I know, but it's also—"

"Complicated."

"Yeah."

"So, you're running away," Ivy said, flippantly, her tone accusatory.

"I'm giving us space." Kendall met Ivy's gaze. "I'm giving you space. You've got so much going on here—your work, your friends, your family, the landscape renovation."

"And you don't think you fit into that picture anymore?"

"That's the point. I don't know if I do. And I don't think you know either. I do know that I can't be an obstacle in your career path. That's why I took myself out of the picture."

Ivy was quiet for a long moment as she rubbed the handle of her coffee mug between her fingers. "How long will you be gone?"

"A few weeks. Maybe a month." Kendall swallowed hard. She wasn't sure if she'd be coming back at all. "My mom could use the help anyway. My dad's had some health issues lately."

"You don't talk about them much."

"I have reasons for that, and you're aware of at least one." Kendall attempted a smile. "But maybe it's time I faced some things back there too."

The silence between them stretched, filled with everything unsaid.

"Is this good-bye?" Ivy asked, her voice barely audible.

"No," Kendall said firmly. "It's just…a pause. A chance for you to figure out if this—if *I'm* really what you want—who you want in your life. Without the pressure of me being right here, waiting for an answer."

Ivy wiped quickly at her eyes. "And what if I already know the answer?"

"Then it'll still be true when I get back." Kendall stood, gathering her courage to walk out the door without Ivy. "I'm leaving in the morning."

"Tomorrow?" Ivy looked stunned. "That's so soon."

"If I don't go now, I might never have the courage, and that might ruin any chance we have of making this work." Kendall finally allowed herself to reach out, brushing her fingers against Ivy's cheek. "Think about what you really want, Ivy. Not just what's easy or what feels good in the moment. After you've done that, we can talk—*really talk*—about where we go from here. Or whether we should just let whatever this is go."

As Kendall turned to leave, Ivy caught her wrist. "I'll miss you," she said softly.

Kendall nodded, her throat tight. "I'll miss you too." More than Ivy could possibly imagine.

The bell above the door jingled as Kendall stepped outside, leaving Ivy alone at the table. She didn't look back as she let the tears she'd been holding back flow. When she made it to her car, she tried not to sob, but the loss overwhelmed her, and she couldn't stop her chest from heaving in and out.

CHAPTER SIXTY-SEVEN

Kendall was lying in bed feeling sorry for herself when her phone buzzed on the nightstand. Who would be calling her this early on a Saturday? She picked it up and glanced at the screen to see that it was someone from Diamond Mountain Lodge. She closed her eyes and hesitated before hitting the green button to accept the call. "Hello?"

"Kendall? This is Daniel Martinez, Park Director at Diamond Mountain Lodge."

Kendall propped herself up against the headboard. "Oh, hi, Director Martinez. How are you?"

"I'm doing well, thank you. How are you?"

"I'm good. I saw on the news that you've received a bit of snow on the mountain." It was early December, and winter seemed to be moving at a slow pace.

"We have. It makes for a beautiful view. The crew is working to clear the road as we speak."

"I'm sorry I'm not there to see it." She'd been kicking herself for the past couple of weeks about her decision to leave. She hadn't heard from Ivy and wasn't at all sure she'd made the right decision.

"That can change, you know." He paused. "I'm calling with some good news. After reviewing all the applications and conducting our interviews, I'm pleased to offer you the position of landscape restoration advisor at Diamond Mountain Lodge."

"Oh, wow. I'm honored, truly." It had been a few weeks since she'd applied for the position and hadn't expected an offer at this point.

"Your expertise in native plant rehabilitation and your ideas for the restoration project really impressed the hiring committee."

"But I didn't even interview." She'd lost hope when she hadn't received a call to at least schedule a virtual interview.

"Sure, you did." The director's voice rose. "Even though you withdrew your bid from the landscape design contract, we all saw your proposal, which was quite well thought out."

"Right." She hadn't forgotten about the proposal, but she hadn't considered that they would use that instead of interviewing her.

"We believe you're exactly what we need to help revitalize some of our damaged ecosystems."

"Thank you. That means a lot coming from you, Director. The preserve is doing such important work."

"Please. Call me Daniel. I think we know each other well enough for that." She heard what she thought was him taking a drink of coffee. "You could start as early as Monday, December 22nd, with the salary listed on the job description, which I believe you received from Susan, plus the benefits package."

"You know about that, huh?" She wouldn't have seen the job if it hadn't been for Susan.

"She looks out for the needs here at the lodge."

"Yes. She does." And also the needs of her friends.

"You'll be overseeing our three major restoration zones that the company who won the bid will be completing and also working with our team of rangers and volunteers."

Kendall's excitement was mixed with trepidation. "That sounds like an incredible opportunity."

Daniel seemed to notice her hesitation. "You don't sound as excited as I expected. Is everything all right?"

"I am excited. It's just that I need to consider some personal factors before I can accept."

"I understand. These decisions impact our lives in many ways. Does something specific about the position concern you?"

"No. It's not the position itself. It's, well, I'm going to be upfront about this. As you know, I have a complicated history with Ivy Patterson."

"I'm aware, but I thought we cleared all that up when you withdrew from the project."

"I thought we did too, but I haven't been in touch with her much since I left. The breakup was difficult for me." It had been less than a month since she'd told Ivy they needed a break, and Ivy had taken every minute of it without attempting to communicate. "Working closely with her every day might be challenging for both of us."

"I appreciate your honesty, Kendall. Ivy is indeed one of our senior rangers and would be collaborating with the restoration team regularly."

"I don't want my personal situation to affect the important work at the lodge. That wouldn't be fair to anyone."

"These situations are always complex. For what it's worth, the hiring committee asked Ivy for her input, and she supported your application enthusiastically. She spoke very highly of your professional capabilities."

"She did?" A little swirl began to stir in Kendall's belly.

"Yes. While I can't speak to your personal relationship, it seems she respects you tremendously as a colleague."

"That's...good to know." She put her hand on her stomach to calm herself.

"Would it help if I arranged for the two of you to have a conversation before you make your decision? Sometimes clearing the air can make these situations more manageable."

"Maybe. Actually, no. I need to think about whether I can separate our situation from the work that needs to be done." She really wanted this opportunity. The restoration projects were exactly the kind of work she'd always wanted to do, especially in a place as ecologically significant as Diamond Mountain.

"I understand completely," Daniel said. "This is as much about your wellbeing as it is about the needs of the lodge. How about taking a few days to consider the offer? We don't need an immediate answer." He hesitated. "If you decide to accept, starting on the 22nd gives you only a little more than a week to take care of things there before you start. I'd like to have you here and settled before the Christmas holiday. With kids out of school, it's usually a busy week for us."

"I appreciate that. How long do I have to decide?"

"Can you let me know by Tuesday? That would give us time to make arrangements either way."

"Yes. That works. Thank you for understanding, Director Martinez. I mean Daniel."

"Of course." He sounded happy with the resolution. "And Kendall? For what it's worth, we all have situations in our professional lives where we have to work with people with whom we have complicated histories. Sometimes those end up being our most valuable professional relationships because of the depth of understanding that comes from that shared history."

"That's an interesting perspective. I hadn't thought about it that way." She had thought about how good it felt when Ivy held her in her arms and wondered if she'd be able to keep that out of their professional relationship.

"Just something to consider. I'll email the formal offer letter today. Feel free to call if you have any questions."

"Thank you. I'll be in touch soon."

"I look forward to hearing from you. Have a good day, Kendall."

"You too." She hit the end button on her phone and dropped it on the bed next to her. "Well, this changes everything," she said aloud. She threw back the covers, tugged on her hoodie and sweatpants, then headed into the kitchen. "Mom. Guess what? I just got a job offer from the director at Diamond Mountain Lodge."

Her mom turned from the counter with clear excitement. "That's wonderful news! The park position you applied for?"

Kendall took a seat in a plastic cushioned chair at the old Formica table that sat in the middle of the kitchen. "Yeah. Daniel Martinez, the park director, called personally. It's the landscape restoration advisor role I told you about."

"That's the dream job you've been talking about for weeks." Her mom brought two coffees to the table and sat down across from Kendall.

"Not exactly, but another one very similar to it."

"Why don't you seem happier?"

"It's complicated. You remember me mentioning Ivy?"

"The park ranger you worked with when you went to see the lodge last month?" Her mom sipped her coffee.

"Yes. That's her. We dated while I was there. It ended badly when I left."

"Oh, sweetheart." Her mom drew her eyebrows together. "You didn't mention that part."

Kendall looked down at her coffee. "I know. I wasn't ready to talk about it. But now I'd be working with her regularly on restoration projects. Our duties would overlap constantly."

"I see." Her mom nodded thoughtfully. "I'm sure you're worried about the awkwardness."

"It's more than that. When I left the mountain, I didn't think we were breaking up, just taking a break to figure things out. But we haven't talked since I left." She let out a heavy breath. "It was my choice to leave.

Ivy wanted me to stay. I just thought we should take some time to figure things out."

Her mom frowned. "That sounds like it's less about your work and more about you being hurt by Ivy's silence."

"Maybe." Kendall shrugged. "Now I'm second-guessing myself. What if she was right? What if I should've stayed? And even if she wasn't, do I really want to face her every day?"

Her mom relaxed into her chair. "Honey, you've worked toward being the best at what you do since you started on this career path. Your master's thesis on native plant restoration was published in that environmental journal. This job sounds like a big deal. I'm sure the director wouldn't have offered it to you if he didn't believe in your abilities."

"I know, but—"

"Let me ask you something. If Ivy wasn't working at the park, would you take this job?"

"Absolutely."

"Then there's your answer." Her mom grinned at her. "You can't let one relationship dictate your career path. I'm sure the park is big enough for both of you."

Kendall knew she was overthinking the situation. "But what if she makes it impossible to work together?" *Would Ivy really do that?*

"Then that's the park director's problem to manage, not yours." Her mom got up, went to the coffeemaker, brought the carafe to the table, and topped off their cups. "First and foremost, you'll be colleagues now, not exes. Most adults find a way to work together professionally, even with history."

"I don't know, Mom." Kendall was still unsure about the situation.

"When your father and I have issues, we still have to work together at the school."

"That's different." Kendall wasn't going to let her mom get away with that comparison. "You two are married and have been for a long time. There's a lot of history for you to fall back on." Plus, Kendall was there to help them through it.

"And we had you kids." Her mom laughed softly. "We worked through it, but it wasn't easy. We established boundaries, kept conversations work-focused while at work, and eventually found a new normal. It can be done."

Kendall muddled through her thoughts. "I suppose I could try to talk to her before I start, clear the air a bit."

"I highly recommend that. Especially if you still have feelings for her." Her mom tilted her head. "But sometimes it's enough to just be professional and let time do the rest. What matters is that you don't sacrifice this opportunity because of discomfort that might be temporary."

Kendall smiled at the thought of going back to Diamond Mountain. "The restoration project they're planning is exactly what I've wanted to be part of for a long time. Reintroducing native species, working with the park staff, helping provide a natural space to the public."

Her mom grinned. "I can see your eyes light up just talking about it." She reached across the table and patted her hand. "That's the Kendall I know."

Kendall took in a deep breath. "You're right, as always. I need to accept this offer. I can handle Ivy, or at least I can try." She didn't have the slightest idea how at this point. "I've worked too hard to walk away from this opportunity."

"There's my girl. And remember, you can always call me after a rough day. I've got a few years of experience navigating workplace relationships gone wrong."

Kendall laughed. "I'm counting on those pep talks." She paused thoughtfully. "Thanks, Mom. I think I needed someone to remind me why I wanted this job in the first place."

Her mom squeezed her hand. "That's what moms are for. Now, how about we celebrate with some breakfast?"

"That sounds perfect." Kendall smiled, genuinely feeling happiness for the first time in a while. "I'll be right back. I need to call the director and let him know my decision." She would try to remain optimistic about the situation, at least until she got back to the lodge.

CHAPTER SIXTY-EIGHT

Ivy was at one of her usual spots on the ridge-line trail, checking for icy areas after last night's new-fallen snow. The morning light filtered through the pines, casting dappled shadows across the billowy white landscape. It was a beautiful morning.

"There you are," Susan called, sounding slightly out of breath from the climb. "I've been looking all over for you."

Ivy turned, holding up the pickax she used to clear the ice. "Just checking for slippery spots. Don't want anyone who ventures out to get hurt. What's up? You look like you're about to burst with news."

Susan grinned, resting against a boulder. "You might want to sit down for this. I just came from the admin staff meeting with the director."

"Oh?" Ivy pulled her brows together. "Is this about the budget cuts? Because I've already trimmed the education program as much as I can without—"

"It's not about budget cuts," Susan said, her smile widening. "It's about the new landscape restoration advisor position."

Ivy nodded slowly. "Right. For the lodge renovation project. Did they hire someone?"

"They did." Susan paused dramatically. "It's Kendall."

The pickax nearly slipped from Ivy's fingers. "Kendall? As in my Kendall?" That was a stupid thing to say. Kendall wasn't hers. She hadn't seen or spoken to her in weeks.

"Unless you know another brilliant landscape ecologist with that name who specializes in native plant restoration," Susan replied.

Ivy sank onto the boulder and then popped back up as the cold snow seeped into her pants. "When does she start?" She turned to look out onto the valley, a mixture of emotions flooding her.

"A week from Monday. She's driving in the weekend before." Susan stood beside her. "You okay?"

Ivy stared out at the valley below, her voice quiet. "It's been almost a month, Susan. We haven't exactly spoken. I mean, things ended."

"Messily?" Susan asked.

"Unfinished," Ivy said. She hadn't gone into detail with Susan about how they'd left things. "We both made decisions without the other and ended up in different directions. We never reached closure. Just left a lot of things unsaid." Although Kendall's cabin key left on the table made her leaving seem more permanent.

Susan nudged Ivy's shoulder gently. "Well, now fate has conveniently dropped her right back into your park. Maybe this is your chance to say those things."

"I don't know." Ivy shook her head. "What if she's moved on? What if she's with someone else now?" It had been several weeks since Kendall had gone back to Oklahoma.

"She's not," Susan said quickly.

Ivy snapped her gaze back to Susan. "How do you know?"

"Because I may have done a little reconnaissance when I processed her employment paperwork," Susan admitted with a mischievous smile. "Relationship status is single."

"That doesn't mean she isn't dating anyone."

"Well, I had to call her to verify a couple of things, and we chatted for a minute or two."

"Susan." Ivy didn't want her getting in the middle of anything, but she couldn't suppress the swirl of excitement in her belly.

"What? I'm just being thorough in my duties." Susan's expression softened. "Do you really think she would get over you this soon? I remember how you were after she left. You've never looked at anyone else the same way. And now she's coming back as a permanent park employee to work on a multi-year project with *you*. If that's not the universe giving you a second chance, I don't know what is."

Ivy ran a hand through her hair. "But what if she doesn't want to reconcile?"

"Then at least you'll know," Susan said simply. "Isn't that better than wondering 'what if' for another year? Or the rest of your life?"

They sat in silence for a moment, watching an eagle circle lazily above the tree line.

"She loved this view," Ivy whispered finally.

Susan smiled. "That's not all she loved here."

Ivy took a deep breath and straightened her uniform. "Okay. When she gets here, I'll talk to her. Really talk to her this time."

"I expect nothing less," Susan said, wrapping an arm around her shoulder. "And hey, if things work out, I also expect to be matron of honor."

Ivy laughed, the sound echoing across the valley. "One step at a time, Susan. One step at a time."

As they headed back down the trail, Ivy felt a lightness she hadn't experienced in weeks. Next Monday couldn't come soon enough.

CHAPTER SIXTY-NINE

Cold, damp air seeped into Kendall's car as she ascended the mountain. She wasn't due at work until Monday, but she couldn't wait that long to see Ivy—to tell her what was truly in her heart. Whether Ivy accepted it as true or not, Kendall had to tell her.

Her knuckles were white against the steering wheel as she navigated the winding road up the mountain, still an hour away from Ivy's cabin. The pine trees created dappled shadows across the windshield, but she barely noticed the beauty around her. Her mind was too full, her heartbeat too loud.

She pulled over at a small turnout overlooking the lake, put the SUV in Park, and took a deep breath. Before she could second-guess herself, she scrolled through her contacts and tapped Susan's name. One of Ivy's oldest friends. The person who might understand what she was about to do. She'd thought about calling Shauna, the vet, but she'd be angry and probably wouldn't help her at all.

The phone rang three times before Susan answered, sounding cheerful. "Diamond Mountain Lodge. How can I help you?"

"Hi, Susan." Kendall's words came out steadier than she expected.

"Oh. Hi, Kendall. We're excited that you're joining the team."

"Thank you," she said. "Listen. I need a favor." Kendall watched an osprey circle over the lake as she gathered her thoughts. "I need you to let me into Ivy's cabin. I want to surprise her with dinner tonight." A pot of beans, one of Kendall's favorite winter recipes. It was easy and comforting. "I've got all the ingredients, but I need to get there before she finishes work. Can you help me?"

"What do you plan to accomplish by fixing Ivy this dinner?" There was a pause on the line. "You're finally going to tell her how you feel."

It wasn't a question, and Kendall wasn't surprised that Susan knew. She'd always been perceptive, had probably seen what was between them before either Kendall or Ivy had fully acknowledged it themselves.

"I'm in love with her, Susan. I think I have been since the second we admitted our attraction to each other. Before that, even. I don't know if she feels the same way, or if she'll even believe me after all this time, but I have to try. I can't keep pretending that all I was feeling was—is just infatuation."

Susan was quiet for a moment. "You know, she keeps that selfie of you two from Eagle Ridge on her phone. The one where you both have a glow about you."

Something warm unfurled in Kendall's chest. "She does?"

"Mm-hmm. And she turns down dates. A lot of requests from June since you left." She laughed softly. "Says she's too busy, but she's not busy at all. Sits at home alone a lot."

"June's no dummy." Kendall watched the sunlight dance across the water below. "So, you'll help me?"

"I've got the spare key. I'll have to sneak out when she's working outside the lodge. Text me when you're ten minutes out, and I'll meet you there." Susan's voice softened. "For what it's worth, I think you're doing the right thing. Life's too short for maybes."

"Thanks, Susan." Kendall felt tears prick her eyes and cleared them from her vision. "This means a lot."

"Just promise me one thing," Susan said. "When you tell her you love her, really tell her. No hedging, no leaving room for misinterpretation. Ivy needs clarity."

"I will," Kendall promised. "No more half-truths or wondering what might have been." She needed that just as much as Ivy did.

After they hung up, Kendall sat for a moment longer, watching the osprey dive into the lake and emerge with a silver fish flashing in its talons. Decisive. Committed. No hesitation.

She started the Ford Bronco and pulled back onto the road, the midday sun warm on her face. In a few hours, everything might change. The thought terrified and exhilarated her in equal measure.

As she rounded the bend that would take her past the lodge and then to Ivy's cabin, she realized she was smiling. Whatever happened tonight, at least she wouldn't be left wondering anymore. At least she would have tried.

❖

Kendall pulled up to Ivy's cabin, her car tires crunching on the gravel driveway. Susan's small, red Toyota RAV4 was already parked beneath the towering pines. For a moment, Kendall sat still, grocery bags rustling beside her as she gathered her courage.

Susan emerged onto the porch, waving with a wide smile. She wore a casual flannel shirt over jeans, her curly hair caught up in a messy bun. "Took you long enough! I was beginning to think you'd changed your mind."

"Not a chance," Kendall said, stepping out and reaching for her bags. The mountain air was crisp, carrying the scent of pine and distant woodsmoke. "Though I'd be lying if I said I wasn't nervous."

Susan hurried down the steps to help with the groceries and peered into one of the bags. "Canned pinto beans, stewed tomatoes, vegetables, cornbread. Save some for me."

"Should be plenty of leftovers," Kendall said as they walked up to the cabin, and Susan opened the door with a twist of her wrist. The interior welcomed them with the familiar rustic warmth of exposed beams, the stone fireplace, and large windows framing the lake view that Kendall had sorely missed.

Kendall set her bags on the kitchen counter, then turned suddenly to Susan. "You didn't tell anyone else, did you? About what I'm planning?"

Susan raised an eyebrow. "Who would I tell?"

"I don't know. Ivy's mother? Your husband? Anyone at the lodge?" Kendall began unpacking ingredients with nervous energy. "I need this to be between just Ivy and me. At least until I know where we stand."

Susan leaned against the counter, her expression softening. "Kendall. Stop." She waited until Kendall met her gaze. "I didn't tell a soul. This isn't gossip to me. This is my friend's happiness we're talking about."

Kendall's shoulders relaxed slightly. "Thank you."

"Besides," Susan said, pulling out a cutting board from a drawer, "I've been watching you two dance around each other for too long. It's about time someone made a move."

Kendall laughed despite her nerves. "Pretty clear, huh?"

"Only to anyone with eyes." Susan's teasing tone gave way to something more sincere. "Look. I've known Ivy since we were kids. She doesn't let people in easily. But you—you're different somehow."

Kendall busied herself with rinsing the beans, not trusting what she might say. She didn't want to give too much away to Susan.

"The way she talks about you…" Susan shook her head with a small smile. "Even when you two were out of touch, you were never really gone from her life. I think that means something."

"I hope so," Kendall whispered. She cleared her throat. "Because I'm all in, Susan. I've tried to talk myself out of it, tried convincing myself that what I felt for Ivy was just intense friendship, but—"

"But some people just get under your skin and into your heart like lightning and are burned into it forever," Susan said.

"Exactly." She couldn't have described it better. Kendall looked around the cabin at all the small touches that were so uniquely Ivy. The handwoven blanket over the couch, the collection of smooth lake stones on the windowsill, the watercolor landscapes she'd painted herself—but no Christmas tree. "I can't imagine my life without her in it. And I don't want to."

Susan squeezed Kendall's shoulder gently. "Then tell her exactly what you just said." She glanced at her watch. "Ivy will be home around six, as usual. That gives you about five hours to work your culinary magic." She headed toward the door.

"Does Ivy have a Christmas tree in a box somewhere?"

"I knew something was missing." Susan stopped, went to the closet, and tugged out a tall, rectangular box. "I'll set it up for you, but I don't have time to help decorate it." She took another box from the top shelf and set it on the couch.

"Thanks. I can handle the decorating." She opened the box to find a gold garland, several small boxes of ornaments, and an angel tree-topper.

Susan had the pre-lit tree assembled in a matter of minutes and then headed to the door again.

"Do you want to come for dinner?" Kendall asked.

Susan turned back with a grin. "And be the third wheel on the most important night of your life? Not a chance." She opened the door, then paused. "Just promise me one thing?"

"Anything."

"Whatever happens tonight, be gentle with her heart. It's stronger than she thinks, but still…"

Kendall nodded solemnly. "I promise. I have no intention of hurting her. In fact, I'm hoping this move makes us both very happy."

After Susan left, Kendall stood alone in the quiet cabin, the weight of possibility settling around her. Outside, the afternoon light played across the lake. Cooking first, then decorations. She rolled up her sleeves and reached for a pot. It was time to cook up some courage along with those beans.

CHAPTER SEVENTY

The day had dragged on longer than Ivy anticipated and had been filled with incidents. A fallen tree blocking one of the main trails, a lost hiker who turned out to be just around the bend taking photos, and an emergency call about irrigation issues had left her shoulders tense and her mind weary. It had been a long week, and this was only Wednesday. As she navigated the familiar curves leading to her cabin, the forest grew denser, creating a natural barrier between her and the world's demands. This was why she'd chosen this place. Her sanctuary where she could breathe.

The golden hour light filtered through the pine trees as Ivy rounded the final bend. She frowned slightly at the sight of a car in her driveway, not Susan's familiar red RAV4, but a Ford Bronco she recognized instantly. Kendall's SUV. Her heart performed a complicated maneuver somewhere between a leap and a stutter.

Ivy parked beside it and sat for a moment, gathering herself. She hadn't expected Kendall back this soon. The last she'd heard, Kendall was to start work on Monday, and as far as Ivy knew when she'd left work, Kendall was still at least a four-hour drive away and would be until the weekend. What was she doing here now?

Ivy's boots crunched on the gravel path as she made her way from her truck to her cabin. The scent hit her the moment she opened the cabin door—rich, earthy, spiced. A fragrance that transported her instantly to a night not so long ago that had preceded stars scattered above them in the night sky, laughter emanating from the back of Ivy's truck, and followed by a night of lovemaking she'd never forget. They hadn't shared nearly enough of those nights.

Ivy noticed the Christmas tree in the corner near the fireplace, set up and decorated beautifully, something, due to the circumstances, she'd chosen not to do this year.

"Hello?" Ivy said, dropping her bag by the door.

Kendall appeared from the kitchen, wooden spoon in hand, wearing an apron Ivy had forgotten she owned. Her blond hair was pulled back in a short ponytail, a few strands escaping to frame her face. Still beautiful. Ivy's anxiety completely disappeared, lost somewhere outside in the cold. It was as though they were meant to be a couple, and the universe had control of her heart, and she had none.

"You're early," Kendall said, her smile betraying a hint of nervousness.

"And you're cooking." Ivy moved closer, drawn by both the familiar aroma and the woman before her. "Are those—"

"The beans I made while I was here. Yes." Kendall's eyes crinkled at the corners. "I thought you might like a reminder of some of the good things that happened then."

"How did you even get in?" Ivy asked, taking in the transformed space, the set table, the candles not yet lit, a small vase of wildflowers.

"Susan." Kendall gestured vaguely. "I hope that's okay. I wanted to surprise you."

"It is." Ivy surprised herself with how much she meant it. She moved to the stove, peering into the pot where the beans simmered. "I can't believe you made these."

"I remember how much you liked them," Kendall said quietly. "I remember everything about the time we spent together."

Something in her tone made Ivy look up quickly and meet Kendall's gaze. It contained an intensity, a purpose that made Ivy's pulse quicken. She looked away first, focusing instead on removing her jacket.

"Rough day?" Kendall asked, returning to stir the pot.

"The usual challenges." Ivy moved to the sink to wash her hands. "Nothing that won't look better after a good meal and a glass of wine."

"Already ahead of you." Kendall nodded toward an open bottle breathing on the counter. "It should be ready to pour."

They moved around each other in the small kitchen with the ease of long familiarity, yet Ivy was acutely aware of each graze, each moment their paths crossed. It had always been this way with Kendall, a heightened awareness she couldn't explain, a silent current running beneath simple, ordinary moments.

As Kendall ladled beans into bowls and Ivy poured wine, a comfortable silence settled between them. But beneath it, Ivy sensed something waiting to be said. Kendall's surprise dinner wasn't just about beans and nostalgia.

They sat across from each other at the small table by the window. Outside, the lake reflected the sky's fading light.

"This is perfect," Ivy said after her first bite, the flavors exactly as she remembered. "Thank you for this and for putting up the tree."

"It's nothing, really." Kendall smiled, but her expression remained serious. "I needed to see you."

Ivy was suddenly certain that whatever Kendall had come to say would change things between them. And while part of her tingled at the possibility, another part, the cautious part that had built this solitary life in the woods, trembled. She took a bite and then set down her spoon. "Do you have a recipe for these?"

"Not really. It's just chunked ham and pinto beans with stewed tomatoes, celery, onion, and cabbage. I use more or fewer ingredients depending on how big of a batch I want to make. These will last another day, and as you know, they're always better on the second day. You're not eating. Do they taste all right?"

"They're delicious." Ivy blotted her lips with a napkin. "I just think there's more to discuss right now than your cooking." Ivy took in a deep breath. "We left a lot of things unsaid when you went back to Oklahoma, and I need to make something clear to you."

Kendall's expression was hard to read. "I need to do the same." She held up her hand. "I'm here because I need to be here." She shook her head. "This isn't coming out like I want it to." She stiffened and wiped her hands on her jeans nervously. "I mean, I want you to know that I looked forward to every minute of every day I spent with you. I'm here because I want to be here with you permanently." She shrugged. "If you'll have me."

Relief and happiness rushed through Ivy. She wasn't sure what she'd expected, but a declaration like that wasn't even close. She let a slow smile creep across her face. "I want you here too."

"You do?" Kendall's voice rose.

Ivy nodded. "I hated the way you left. I wanted you to come back the next day. I just didn't know how to tell you." She shook her head. "I wasn't sure why I hadn't believed you about Cassie."

"And now you do?" Kendall asked softly.

"I do. I think I did then, but I was an idiot, let my insecurities get in the way, and took too much time to tell you." She closed her eyes and shook her head slowly. "Which, in turn, pushed you away." There was silence between them again, and Ivy was afraid she shouldn't have brought it up and reminded Kendall of her doubts. "What are you thinking about?" Ivy asked, her voice steadier than she felt.

Kendall looked down at her bowl, then back up, determination settling over her features. "Us."

One simple word, heavy with implication. Ivy took a sip of wine, buying herself time. *Us*. Had there ever really been an *us*, or just a series of meaningful glances, moments that led to mind-blowing sex, conversations that skimmed the surface of deeper waters, and a friendship that had always felt like it was waiting to become something more?

"What about us?" Ivy finally asked, her heart racing beneath her calm exterior.

"Everything." Kendall stared into her bowl before she dropped her spoon into it. The chair scraped against the floor as she stood and moved toward Ivy.

The way Kendall looked at her then, openly, hopefully, fearfully, made Ivy realize that whatever came next would require a decision. The comfortable ambiguity they'd maintained was about to end. And despite her misgivings about disrupting the life she'd carefully constructed, despite her fear of risk and change and potential loss, Ivy found herself in Kendall's arms, holding her, ready to hear what Kendall had come all this way to say, and hoping she intended to stay right here.

EPILOGUE

The morning mist hung low over the lake as Kendall balanced the last box on her hip and nudged the cabin door closed with her foot. Inside, the warm glow of early sunlight filtered through the windows, casting long shadows across the wooden floor. She set the box down with a few others in what was now their shared living room.

"Is that everything?" Ivy appeared from the kitchen, two steaming mugs in hand. Her ranger uniform was pressed and ready for the day, the badge catching the light.

"Last one," Kendall said, accepting the offered coffee with a grateful smile. "Not that I had much to bring. Most of my stuff is still in storage in Oklahoma." She'd made a quick trip over the weekend to pick up a few more essentials and had left them in her Bronco when she'd arrived after dark last night.

Ivy leaned against the doorframe, watching Kendall over the rim of her mug. "Having second thoughts already?"

"Not a chance." Kendall stepped closer, lightly kissing Ivy's cheek. "Though I still can't believe how perfectly everything worked out."

Three weeks had passed since that night with the pot of beans—three weeks of holiday celebrations, long conversations, and many glorious nights of lovemaking. All that, ultimately, had led to the decision that had brought them here. It had seemed like fate when Director Martinez, who was having no luck finding a director, had created a new position for an on-site landscape restoration advisor instead, to oversee their expansion project.

Cassie had apparently applied for both positions and hadn't even been considered after Director Martinez had learned more about the circumstances surrounding her complaint. She'd eventually found a contract to renovate an alligator sanctuary somewhere in Florida, which kept her far away from the Arkansas mountains.

Ivy glanced at her watch. "I should head out. First day of fire-season training." She hesitated, then added, "You sure you're okay getting to the lodge on your own? I could swing back by and pick you up. You know, carpool to save gas."

"Would that really be saving gas if you had to come back to get me?" Kendall raised an eyebrow. "Besides, isn't it your day to train the new seasonal rangers?"

Ivy nodded, but she lingered, taking in the subtle changes to the cabin. Kendall's drafting table by the window, her collection of architectural and plant books now mingled with Ivy's field guides on the shelves, the potted succulents brightening the windowsills.

"It's strange," Ivy said softly. "Good, strange. I've lived alone for so long, I wasn't sure…"

"If you could share your space?" Kendall said.

"If I could share my life," Ivy said. "The cabin was the easy part."

Kendall set her mug down and took Ivy's hands. "We're figuring it out together, remember? One day at a time."

Outside, a chickadee's call punctuated the morning quiet. Ivy smiled and squeezed Kendall's hands before releasing them. "I left park maps on your drafting table. Thought they might help with your site planning."

"Always thinking ahead," Kendall said with a soft smile. "I'll see you tonight. I should be done by six."

"Perfect. I'll bring home dinner from the lodge restaurant. The chef promised me his special enchiladas."

As Ivy gathered her gear, Kendall moved to the porch to see her off with an earth-scorching kiss. They had established this routine during the time since Kendall had come back. Coffee together, no matter how early, and a proper good-bye at the door.

Ivy paused at her truck, ranger hat now firmly in place. "Have a great day today. The lodge is lucky to have you."

"I'm the lucky one," Kendall said. "Not many landscape architects get to work in a setting like this." She gestured to the sweeping vista of mountains and lake before them. "Or come home to a sizzling hot park ranger."

Ivy's laugh echoed across the clearing as she climbed into her truck. "Save the charm for when I get home. Then, after dinner, we can talk about which of us is the luckiest."

Kendall watched until the truck disappeared down the dirt road and turned back to the cabin—their cabin now. Sunlight had broken through the mist, illuminating the boxes waiting to be unpacked and the empty spaces that Ivy had created for her waiting to be filled.

She had two hours before her first meeting at the lodge. Just enough time to unpack more of her drafting supplies and begin sketching more ideas for the natural playground the director wanted to add. She'd promised designs that would blend seamlessly with the surrounding wilderness—a challenge she was eager to tackle.

As she worked, occasionally glancing out at the view that Ivy woke up to every morning, Kendall felt the rightness of her decision settle deep in her bones. The city had its appeal, but this wild beauty, this quiet purpose, this shared life with Ivy—this was home.

The End

About the Author

Dena Blake grew up in a small town just north of San Francisco and is still a NorCal girl at heart. Just can't beat that weather. She eventually moved with her family to the southwest where she began creating vivid characters in her mind and bringing them to life on paper.

Dena currently lives in the southwest with her partner where she attempts to grow vegetables each year and is rarely successful. She loves to cook and enjoys lazy road trips that lead to new adventures.

Books Available from Bold Strokes Books

Beautiful Things by Emma L. McGeown. A warmhearted romance of missed chances, undeniable chemistry, and a stubborn love that maybe, just maybe, can find its way back. (978-1-63679-934-6)

Love Takes a Village by Karis Walsh. As Lena Preiss struggles to manage a busy restaurant in the Bavarian Christmas village of Leavenworth, Washington, chocolatier Devin Meyer brings an unexpected richness into her life, along with her delicious desserts. (978-1-63679-902-5)

Secrets of the Heart by Jenny Frame. When a beautiful stranger starts asking questions about Nikki Sharkey, head of an infamous crime syndicate, Nikki will stop at nothing to protect her daughter Isla. (978-1-63679-653-6)

Talon and the Songbird by Julia Underwood. In a world where survival depends on strategic alliances, Makayla and Talon must navigate not only complex politics but also the dangerous territory of their hearts. (978-1-63679-970-4)

The Great Popcorn Romance by Georgia Beers. Opposites attract, and Riley Shaw stands no chance of resisting Hannah Kramer's magnetic pull. But opposites know just how to drive each other crazy… (978-1-63679-910-0)

Three Blissful Days by Dena Blake. Kendall Jackson attempts to make her ex regret dumping her by announcing she's dating beautiful park ranger Ivy Patterson. But there's nothing fake about how attracted Ivy is to Kendall. (978-1-63679-707-6)

Chasing Her Scent by MJ Williamz. When Sheridan Rousseau walks into Lisette Mouton's charming little bookstore in Quebec City, she unknowingly holds the key to a mysterious box hidden in a secret room. (978-1-63679-900-1)

Heart's Run by D. Jackson Leigh. Hoping to recover an escaped racing mare, stock transporter Tobie Mason locks horns with local wild horse advocate Maggie Wilkes. (978-1-63679-825-7)

Scandalous by Kris Bryant. When a Hollywood actress trades places with her twin sister, everyone's in an uproar about getting duped, but Lindsay's more concerned about finding out which twin she made out with. (978-1-63679-874-5)

The Art of Love by Ali Vali. When Mimi and Bianca both set their sights on Jolly, sparks fly, loyalties are tested, and hearts collide as they navigate the unpredictable nature of their hearts (978-1-63679-719-9)

The Other Side of Forever by Kel McCord. Will Kenzie and Rachel be able to make love work when Rachel's cozy suburban dream feels like Kenzie's worst nightmare? (978-1-63679-812-7)

The Secrets of Rhydian Hill by Ronica Black. A doctor in need of a new start. A woman running from a killer. A love story that could end in tragedy. (978-1-63679-880-6)

Feeling Lucky by Krystina Rivers. What happens when, despite suddenly having enough money to buy almost anything, Lucy and Tanner start to discover that maybe all they need is each other? (978-1-63679-876-9)

Iceberg by Gun Brooke. When Lady Arabella hires Zandra, she never expects to find love, especially not as a disaster looms on the horizon. (978-1-63679-908-7)

It Happened One Semester by Aurora Rey. After a Pride night hookup, can eager new Assistant Professor Hudson Greene and Dean of Advising Callie Shaw overcome the odds and ace falling in love? (978-1-63679-814-1)

It's Kind of a Bad Idea by Sarah G. Levine. What happens when an emotionally unavailable serial dater meets the one woman she can't help but fall for—who happens to be the one woman who told her not to? (978-1-63679-920-9)

Thankful for You by Tagan Shepard. Everyone deserves to find their person, maybe Karen has finally found hers? (978-1-63679-884-4)

What Happens on Location by Nan Campbell. How can Helen produce a successful movie when its director is the woman responsible for the demise of her marriage? (978-1-63679-904-9)

When Love Comes Around by Radclyffe and Ronica Black. Can Maya Sanchez and Nolan Wright trust each other enough to build something real, or will the past tear them apart? (978-1-63679-930-8)

Anywhere with You by Margo Glynn. On a road trip through the Great American Southwest, two friends discover nature, hope, and each other. (978-1-63679-907-0)

Burning Bridges by Lesley Davis. Can Clancy and Jude crack the case of eight missing women—and the secrets of their own hearts? (978-1-63679-872-1)

Dreams Entangled by Sophia Kell Hagin. Amid self-doubt, secrets, a pandemic, fear of attack and attempted murder, Pirin and Gracie's attraction turns to love and their lives will never be the same. (978-1-63679-892-9)

Echoes of Love by Catherine Lane. As Hazel's and Jo's paths intertwine, they're swept up in a whirlwind of long-buried secrets, sizzling chemistry, and memories that won't be denied. (978-1-63679-835-6)

Moonlight Obsession by Sheri Lewis Wohl. All it takes to stop a clever killer is moonlight, love, and a silver bullet. (978-1-63679-831-8)

My Boyfriend's Wife by Joy Argento. Amid betrayal and heartbreak, can two women discover a love that could heal their pasts and rewrite their futures? (978-1-63679-866-0)

Tapout by Nicole Disney. A struggling MMA fighter finds her edge in an underground ring, but as she falls for the magnetic and ambitious promoter behind the matches, their dangerous world threatens to destroy everything they've fought to rebuild. (978-1-63679-924-7)

The Fame Game by Ronica Black. Wild child Hollywood actress Luna Kirkman begins dating Hollywood's leading man, only to fall for his straitlaced sister instead. (978-1-63679-858-5)